FORGOTTEN PROPHECY
ORACLE SERIES, BOOK 3

Jaemi Lee

Bamboo
Publishing

Forgotten Prophecy
Oracle Series, Book 3

First Paperback Edition: 2025

Copyright © 2025 by Jaemi Lee
All rights reserved.

Hardback ISBN: 978-1-956501-06-3
Paperback ISBN: 978-1-956501-07-0
eBook ISBN: 978-1-956501-08-7

Cover art by Ben (@benvenutoiven)

The characters and events in this book are fictional. Any similarity to actual persons, living or dead, is purely coincidental.

To everyone who stayed with me on this journey.
To my younger self.

The adventure is finally over.

1
SILENCE

Elliot peered out the frosty inn window. The harsh reality of nature obstructed his vision, as if it were trying to hide its true identity and secrets from him. The relentless snowfall painted the world in shades of white and gray, creating a barrier between him and whatever lay beyond. And although the fire was crackling in the room, the elf could barely feel its warmth. The thick blanket draped over his lap did little to soothe the cold that rampaged throughout his body.

He placed his finger against the frosted glass, absentmindedly tracing random patterns on the window, leaving temporary marks that faded as quickly as his memories.

Elliot didn't remember how or when he and the others had set sail to the Snowy Hills, nor did he remember how he'd made his way to his room in the nameless inn. Days passed before him, yet he had no recollection of the events. The journey was a blur of faces and landscapes he could not recall, all melting together into nothingness.

Why was he here?

What was he doing here?

Did his existence even hold a purpose anymore?

The questions haunted him endlessly, refusing to let his mind rest without receiving answers. But what answers could Elliot even provide? He felt like nothing would change, nor did it matter.

Answers or not.

The role of the oracle was supposed to make him feel proud. Make him feel like he mattered. Make him feel like he had a purpose. But now, all it did was weigh him down, like chains wrapped around his freedom as if he were a prisoner. Even though he'd been able to expand his horizons after leaving Mistfall, the prejudice and the responsibilities expected of him tore at his heels.

Elliot had lost count of how many nights it had been since he'd last seen Minari. And no matter how many nights passed, he couldn't erase the numbing memory that washed over him whenever he thought of the other elf. It filled his very mind and core. He couldn't shake the image of Minari's lifeless body on the ground. Elliot's entire body had become paralyzed, yet at the same time, his muscles had been ablaze. He remembered screaming, but he didn't remember the sound he'd made. He remembered wanting to run to Minari but didn't remember his legs having the strength to move. It was surreal. And Elliot refused to believe any of it.

The memory played on repeat, like a cruel performance that he was forced to watch again and again, whether his eyes were open or closed. The scene was burned into his mind with such clarity that it felt more real to him than what was happening in the present.

He didn't want any of this to happen.

Elliot and Minari were at odds, and Elliot was painfully aware they'd never have the chance to settle the distrust growing between them. Elliot couldn't deny that deep down in his heart, he had no reason to distrust Minari. But whether or not Elliot wanted to admit it, the seed of doubt had already been planted and flourished. The seed of doubt had grown rapidly, blossoming with each day. Anything that could be used against Minari's innocence was used. Anything that could justify doubting him was believed.

The guilt ate at him with each passing moment, reminding him of his own pitiful self-worth. Every moment of doubt he harbored toward Minari haunted him. The way Elliot found any excuse to doubt Minari . . . He deeply wished he could take it all back, wished he could revert time and trust the other elf.

Elliot's breath shuddered as he forced himself to swallow the bitter taste of betrayal. What kind of person was he? What kind of person couldn't believe their best friend? He hadn't considered supporting Minari when everyone and everything seemed to be against him. Was it because of Elliot's role as the oracle? Was the role itself changing him? Was he losing himself on this journey to find the warriors? Had he betrayed the trust, friendship, and memories they'd shared because of this?

He reached into his shirt, pulling out the wooden pendant Lily had carved for him. His thumb traced the familiar grooves of the leaf design. It provided him warmth, made him feel something.

Maybe things would've played out differently if Minari had told Elliot what had happened in Mistfall. Maybe he would've been more inclined to defend Minari against Mimi's and Sage's accusations. Maybe he could have convinced the group that Minari wasn't guilty of the murders.

And maybe Minari wouldn't have died.

Elliot's breath caught in his throat as he bit down a sob. Everything leading up to Minari's . . . death had been his fault. When they'd entered the chimeran tribe, Minari had been left defenseless. He had agreed to have Hiro hold on to his daggers. If Minari hadn't been forced into taking Lily's single dagger from Elliot, he wouldn't have gotten hurt. He would've been able to defend himself.

Each decision and each moment of mistrust had led them down this path.

Elliot pressed his lips together, fist tightening around the pendant.

Lily.

Elliot couldn't deny just how much he missed the female elf. When she had appeared that night, he couldn't believe it. After leaving Mistfall, he'd somehow known he wouldn't see anyone until the prophecy was fulfilled. So seeing Lily so far away from home had relieved him. Another familiar face he could trust had soothed his frantic nerves.

But while Lily's presence had brought a wave of calmness and comfort, it had also created chaos and confusion. She had told him Mistfall had fallen and everyone he knew and loved was gone. The family he missed dearly was no more. There was nothing left for him. And in one swift movement, she had ended Minari's life. And only then did she confess everything that had happened was her doing: the massacre of the chimeran tribe and the slaughter of Amelia's family. She laughed as she described the ox's family final moments before she killed them.

Elliot blinked away the vision of Minari's lifeless body against the ground. He willed himself to erase the image of red spreading from Minari's chest. He pushed away the memory of the cold ground beneath his best friend drinking the life Minari once had.

There was nothing left.

No home.

No friends.

In an instant, almost everything Elliot held dear had been ripped away from him, leaving him nothing but a hollow shell of his former self. The elf barely recognized himself anymore.

The prophecy had taken everything from him.

Elliot wasn't sure if it deserved to be fulfilled.

Elliot wasn't sure if the world deserved saving.

2
MARK

It was late in the evening. The group huddled inside Luka and Owen's room, gathered around the round wooden table. The sun had already set, and the cool air had begun seeping through the walls. The sizzling fireplace crackled, trying to combat the winter air that threatened their warmth. Unlike Etheria's mainland, the northern islands, known as the Snowy Hills, had constantly low temperatures, and snow would fall year-round.

Even now, Luka could see fresh snowflakes falling gracefully through the frost-covered windows. This kind of weather rarely bothered him, but his joints ached from hours spent reading ancient scrolls and books, and his eyes were strained from reading using candlelight. The cold only seemed to add to his discomfort.

"I've researched all the scrolls and documents within

the library, and I only found this regarding the prophecy," Luka started as he placed a single large book upon the wooden table. Its faded yellow pages were wrinkled. The book did not have any indication of what it contained, besides a single tree illustration that was etched on its deep burgundy cover. "Unfortunately, though . . ." Luka paused as he opened the book. "Most of the pages are empty." He flipped through the book, the pages effortlessly cascading to the other side. "The bit of information I could gather resides entirely on this single page."

Luka's long fingers glided across the open spread, tracing the elegant curves of the letters. There were only a few words written, and the ethereal knew he was the only one who could read it. The writing was in Etherian script, a type of communication used to keep information within the Etherian community and Snowy Hills safe from any falsification. This ensured the utmost purity and accuracy of the recorded knowledge. If a record of any sort did not use the ancient language, any ethereal would know not to trust it.

"What does it say?" Sage asked, leaning over the table to look at the page. He raised a brow. "It doesn't look like much."

"Because there isn't much," Hiro said, crossing his arms. His tone was sharp, making it clear that his patience was growing thin. "I don't suspect we'll get any information out of here."

"What makes you say that?" Mimi asked. "Whatever is written in here could be vital to finding the last warrior."

"Trust thy chosen oracle, for she shall find the lost souls

who are destined to protect all the lands from destruction," Luka said, translating what was written.

"Isn't that what we've been doing?" Sage asked. "How is that helpful?"

Luka frowned, rereading the same verbiage over and over. It was odd for such a large book to include only a single sentence. He was certain the meaning behind it was straightforward: Rely on the oracle, for they shall know who the warriors are. And this sentence held true. Yet Luka could not hide his disappointment. He had hoped there would be more information regarding the warriors and where they might be located. Or information regarding the Necromancers.

Luka's gaze shifted to their own oracle, and his heart grew heavy. The young elf had not moved from his position. Elliot remained still on his seat. His expression was . . . vacant. He was there, yet his mind was not with them. The elf had been that way for weeks. Ever since Minari had been killed, it was as if Elliot's will and soul had followed the other elf into death's embrace.

Luka had hoped Elliot would emerge from his trance once they boarded the ship to sail to the Snowy Hills, an experience he had assumed the young elf had never had. While Mimi and Sage had seemed to enjoy the experience, taking in the salty sea air and pointing out their new discovery of ocean creatures, Elliot had never left his cabin.

It worried Luka.

The ethereal knew Elliot would need to free himself of his reverie if they were to have any hope of finding the last warrior. Given the state the elf was in now, the possibility seemed grim. But Luka did not want to lose faith. He knew Elliot was strong. The anguish he was feeling now would eventually subside. He had to believe that. They all did.

It was only a matter of time . . . but unfortunately, Luka knew they were running out of time.

Luka felt how the air in the Snowy Hills was changing. It was thicker, murkier. Every breath he took, his lungs filled with a heaviness he had never experienced before. The air was usually light and calm. Being surrounded by nature helped alleviate any negative emotion or stress he had, yet he could still feel dread. It licked at his fingertips ever so lightly, keeping him on edge. He wondered if the others felt it too.

Ethereals were typically more sensitive to the changes in nature. They could sense whenever storm clouds approached or when the ground groaned, shifting into an earthquake. It was both a gift and a burden. His instincts were screaming at him that something was amiss. An unknown darkness was gathering. And it was gathering fast.

Luka knew humans, nixen, and chimeras shouldn't be affected by the changes of nature, but he was not sure if elves were. He studied Elliot's expression to see if he sensed the shift in the air the same way Luka did, but Elliot's features remained unchanged. He was still lost in grief.

"If this is all you two could find, then we should leave as soon as possible," Hiro said as he looked at Elliot. A hint of concern laced his voice. "Elliot doesn't seem to enjoy this place too much."

At the sound of his name, Elliot blinked, his head

nudging slightly up, only to glance at Hiro before casting his gaze downward again. The brief moment of awareness vanished as quickly as it had appeared.

Hiro pressed his lips together. "The cold doesn't sit well with elves. His health will not improve the longer we stay."

"When's the earliest we can leave?" Mimi asked.

Not many ships came through the Snowy Hills. The isolation made the area safe but also made it difficult to leave. A cargo ship only came once a month at most, and Luka recalled having seen it earlier in the week. "Three weeks at the very least."

"Three weeks?" Hiro stood, his chair scraping loudly against the wooden floor. "Three weeks is too long. We've already been here longer than we need to."

Luka narrowed his eyes. "What are you implying, Hiro?"

"We've been waiting around for two weeks. We waited for you and Owen to find any information on the last warrior, only for you two to find nothing that's useful. Elliot's health is declining, and you're telling us we have to stay here for another three weeks?" Hiro scoffed. "The Necromancers are going to destroy Etheria at this rate!"

"I do not understand," Luka began. He looked at Elliot, trying to find any signs of wear. Other than his mental state, the elf did not seem to be suffering from any physical ailment. His complexion was not dull, nor did he seem frail. "He—"

"We need to go back," Hiro interrupted. "You may assume you're all-knowing because you've lived for so long, but I know Elliot. I know him the most out of everyone here."

Luka took a breath. He needed to remain levelheaded. He acknowledged that Hiro was irritated, but he shouldn't let that influence him. Responding to yells with screams would contribute nothing to the conversation. "I understand, but there is not much I can do. Ships do not venture to the Snowy Hills as often as other places. We were lucky to catch one when we did."

Hiro took ahold of Elliot's arm, pulling the elf to his feet. "C'mon, Elliot. There's nothing else to discuss here."

"You're leaving?" Sage asked.

"Luka isn't going to tell us anything that I don't already know," Hiro said, irritated.

"And what do you know?" Mimi asked. He stood from his seat, hands balled into fists. "Luka and Owen have both been searching tirelessly, yet you make it sound like you knew something all along."

Hiro spared a glance at Mimi before placing a hand against Elliot's lower back, nudging the elf to leave. "There isn't a warrior here, and the book he found doesn't have any information we need." With those final words, Hiro and Elliot left the room.

"What do you think, Mimi?" Sage asked.

"I am not sure." Mimi shook his head. "But if there isn't anything left to discuss, we will take our leave too." Both Mimi and Sage turned their attention to Luka and Owen.

The silence between the two ethereals and two chimeras answered Sage's suspicion: There was nothing Luka nor Owen could add.

"Goodnight then," Mimi said before he and Sage left.

Luka heaved a sigh, collapsing onto his chair and rubbing his temples. He and Owen had stayed up late into the night and awoken early in the morning searching for any clues, only to bring in meager results. He would be lying if he said he was satisfied with what they'd found during their search. He was disappointed by the lack of information.

A warm hand rested on Luka's shoulder, giving it a soft squeeze. "Luka, we should rest," Owen said.

"There's something we must be missing," Luka said. He ran through his memories, trying to find any library or archives he might have left unchecked.

"Searching restlessly will do us more harm than good," Owen said, his grip on Luka's shoulder tightening slightly. "We should begin searching again once we clear our minds and rest our bodies."

Luka leaned back in his chair, eyes staring at the open book. The single line of text seemed to blur before his tired eyes. Perhaps Owen was right. Searching tirelessly would only lead to negative results rather than positive ones.

"A consciousness shrouded by exhaustion leads only to darkness," Luka said. He closed his eyes, remembering the words Maxwell had once told him when he had caught Luka late at night studying. His brother had always scolded Luka, insisting on the importance of rest.

"But awaken your thoughts to clarity, and your vision transforms into a weapon of extraordinary precision," Owen finishes. "Come, let us retire for the night and begin again in the morning."

Luka wondered how Owen had known Maxwell's

exact words. Had Luka mentioned it before without realizing? He shook the thought away, too fatigued to recall. The comforts of sleep were alluring him and he could not resist them any longer.

3

CLUE

Luka slid his finger against the top of the book's spine before pulling it off the shelf. A tired sigh escaped his lips as he saw the cover. He rubbed his eyes before returning the book back into its original place.

Luka had been wandering around the library for so long that he had begun reaching for the same books and scrolls. Seven days had passed since the group had gathered together, and he was certain the morale had dropped with the lack of progress. The weight of failure pressed heavily against him, reminding him that he was the reason their mission was stalled.

The group had fractured as a result, their disappointment evident in their actions. Mimi and Sage did not bother conversing with anyone other than themselves. They spent their time sparring with each other or stayed within their rooms if they found the outside temperatures too unbearable.

Elliot never left his room. Hiro would bring him food and water, playing the role of his guardian, but whenever Luka attempted to start a conversation with the human, the other would ignore him, only sparing a single glance at Luka before turning away.

The rift grew wider with each passing day.

Luka and Owen agreed to split their efforts to satisfy Hiro's request. While Luka kept up the search within the libraries, Owen spent his time at port, searching for a captain who was willing to embark back to the mainland earlier than scheduled. The constant snowfall made it difficult, but Owen persisted, knowing they could not afford to wait. Luckily, money wasn't an issue for the two ethereals, and it did not take much to persuade a captain with a boat large enough for the six of them to return.

They were to leave the Snowy Hills in nine days, which meant Luka had a limited amount of time to find any sort of clue that could lead them to the last warrior. But it was as if the library were mocking him as he constantly reached for the same recordings.

Luka hoped Ragnar wouldn't get to the last warrior first.

The kingdom was not on their side—not when they all believed the elves were the cause of the war that had happened 340 years ago. The prejudice ran deep, like poison that was fed through multiple generations. Though Luka himself was not aware of the true reason behind the war, he was certain in his heart that the elves were not behind it.

"Excuse me."

Luka's thoughts were interrupted by the sound of a soft voice behind him.

"May I know what knowledge you seek?" the female asked. She wore a librarian robe; the delicate silver material was adorned in pale gold snowflakes. A sash similar in color to the snowflakes was tied around her small waist. She was holding a batch of scrolls in her arms with others tucked into the folds of her sash.

Luka remained silent, merely moving aside, allowing the female ethereal access to the shelves that he was blocking. Odd. Luka did not recognize her.

The librarian knelt down, tucking her long, platinum-blond hair behind her ear before returning the scrolls to their rightful cubbies. Her movements were precise, practiced. It was obvious she had been here for a long time, yet Luka had not seen her before even though he had been searching through the library for over two weeks.

The female ethereal stood up once her arms were empty and pushed her round bronze frames up her nose before facing Luka once again.

"I've seen you in here wandering the corridors. You've been here for a little past two weeks. If I can, I would like to assist you in finding the knowledge or records you seek."

Luka hesitated, weighing his options carefully. He did not want to confess to the librarian that he was a warrior, nor did he want to confess that he was looking for information on the prophecy. Though the kingdom typically allowed those who resided within the Snowy Hills to follow their own traditions and rules, Ragnar was still an ethereal. And a powerful one. There was a good chance Ragnar's own personal reach was here.

Luka was certain the innkeeper had no ties with Ragnar, and neither did the captain Owen had made a deal with. But this librarian . . . He was uncertain.

The female ethereal felt mysterious. He couldn't get a good read on her aura or intentions. It was as if she were a blank canvas. He had never met someone he was not able to read.

"This library has been around for many generations. Though I may seem young, we can pass down our knowledge through our successors. I am the 287th head librarian. You may call me Eina Shiikoe," Eina said, as if she were reading Luka's inner debate and concerns. She gave Luka a gentle smile. "There is nothing you need to fear, warrior."

Luka blinked, eyes widening at the realization. He could not believe the amount of sheer luck that stood in front of him. He had heard of the family of ethereals, who had the ability to pass their knowledge and memories down to their successors. The Shiikoe line was famous among their kind, and only a few would ever have the opportunity to meet one in their lifetime. And if what Eina had just said was true, he had no doubt she knew where he could find information regarding the missing warrior.

Legends spoke of the process of passing down the knowledge and memories typically led to the death of the predecessor. Because of this, it was believed that the Shiikoe clan was well protected, ensuring no misfortune befell them.

The library was not empty, as there were other ethereals besides Luka, and other librarians besides Eina wandering the halls. But he had not seen one guard. So, why was Eina here, unprotected despite her immense value?

Eina tilted her head. "If you are still wary of me, I can at least point you in the general direction of what I think you are looking for. Would you care to follow me?"

It was a gamble, and Luka knew it. He had two choices: either trust Eina's words and accept her help or ignore her and continue his search. He knew his days in the Snowy Hills were numbered, and he was certain he had exhausted all his efforts in the library. If there was a section he had not been to yet, Eina would be able to show him the way.

Luka gave her a single nod. There was no point continuing the search on his own.

Eina smiled, her gray eyes sparkling. "Follow me. Quickly."

Eina began walking down the halls, looping around the shelves with ease. Luka was surprised at how quickly Eina was walking, weaving through the library as if she were a free spirit. Her movements were graceful, reminiscent of a soft, gentle breeze. Luka had to quicken his pace in order to keep up with her.

The constant turning was beginning to make Luka dizzy. The surrounding scenery moved quickly, blurring around him. He could not make out where he was or see which paths he was taking. The library seemed to have shifted and changed around him.

Luka was about to call out to Eina when everything suddenly stopped. His vision snapped back, no longer made blurry by the rapid movements of following Eina.

Luka slowly blinked, looking around before returning his attention to Eina.

Only to find her gone.

As if she'd never existed at all.

Luka was alone in the corridor.

But Luka knew exactly where he was. He was back where they had started. How was that possible? He was certain he had not imagined the entire ordeal.

Luka scanned the shelf in front of him. There were the same books and scrolls, alongside the scrolls Eina had returned. Everything looked exactly as it had before the bizarre journey through the library had begun.

Wait.

Luka drew a quick breath, his heart suddenly racing.

He knelt down, reaching for a scroll he knew for certain hadn't been part of the batch Eina had returned. The color of the parchment differed from that of the others. In fact, the quality of the parchment differed from what the ethereals used. The texture was foreign, showing a type of craftsmanship that was not usual to ethereals.

And it was because the scroll had not been written by an ethereal.

It had been written by an elf.

4

RECORD

Luka swung open the door leading to the room he and Owen shared before quickly closing it and clicking the lock into place. His heart was still racing from his encounter in the library, his fingers trembling slightly as he held the scroll close to his chest.

Owen looked up from his seat. There were numerous scrolls and books scattered across the table, evidence of their tireless research. Ever since Owen had secured a captain, he had returned to his search, aiding Luka in any way he could. A book was open in his lap. "Luka, is something the matter?"

Without a word, Luka made his way to the seat across from Owen. He pushed the documents to the edge of the table before setting the scroll he'd taken from the library down. His hand remained clasped over it, not letting go.

He was almost afraid it would disappear if he did.

"Luka," Owen slowly began, "this is not from here."

Luka squeezed the scroll. "No. No, it is not." He sucked on his bottom lip. He wanted to unravel the scroll and look through its contents. He still had not had a chance to fully wrap his head around what had happened in the library a few moments ago.

The encounter with Eina still felt dreamlike, almost like a mirage. He was not sure if Eina was a mere illusion his mind had concocted because of his lack of rest or if Eina was truly an ethereal from the Shiikoe clan.

The possibility that his mind was playing tricks on him was unsettling.

"Owen," Luka said, his voice barely above a whisper.

"Yes?"

"You can see what is in my grasp, correct?"

Owen nodded slowly. "Yes."

"I am not imagining things, am I?"

Owen shook his head. "No, you are not. I can see that you are holding a scroll, and it is not from here. It is not Etherian written."

Owen's response brought comfort Luka had not known he needed. Perhaps his mind was sound and he had not imagined it after all.

Luka took in a shaky breath before slowly loosening his fingers.

It did not disappear.

The scroll remained.

Luka withdrew his hand and stared at the item that lay on the center of the table. It was tied together by twine, in contrast to the silks ethereals used to keep their scrolls closed. The color of the parchment was a pale yet rich shade of golden yellow compared to the pinkish beige Luka was used to seeing. The texture of the parchment was also rougher compared to the smooth surface known to him. And while ethereal scrolls used rods with rounded ball ends, this scroll lacked a rod entirely.

Neither Luka nor Owen spoke as they took in the potential this single scroll had. The air grew heavier with anticipation.

Even if the scroll did not end their search for the last warrior, it could very well give them the strong lead they needed.

Luka finally reached forward, untying the twine and unraveling it. His eyes scanned the lines of information, taking in everything. The way it was written made it seem like a diary rather than proper documentation. The writing style was personal. Intimate. It carried emotions that formal ethereal records lacked.

"Luka." Owen's voice broke through Luka's train of thought. "You can read this?"

Luka tore his eyes away from the document, furrowing his brow. "What do you mean?"

Owen reached forward, his fingertips gliding across the written script. "All that is on here are wavy lines. There are no words or letters that I can make out."

Luka's eyes tracked the space Owen was referring to, but he could clearly see what was written. The words were legible. Clear like anything he had read.

"Interesting . . ." Luka mused. He placed his finger

against the scroll delicately. A small tingle zapped through the tip and into his hand. "Whatever is written in here is protected," Luka said, pulling his hand away. The sensation was not painful but rather pleasant.

"Then whatever is in here . . ." Owen trailed off.

Luka nodded. "Perhaps only those related to the prophecy can read it. Only the oracle and warriors." He tried to make out what language the diary was written in, but he could not decipher if it was in common tongue or Etherian script. It was possible that it was written in Elvish, though Luka would not know for certain unless Elliot was willing to take a look at the scroll.

And given the elf's current state, that in itself might prove challenging.

Luka continued reading the contents. Owen remained silent, allowing him to focus, though Luka could sense his curiosity and anticipation.

From what Luka could see, the scroll was part of a series. It had been written by someone who was close to the past oracle. The writer had recorded the events that had happened throughout the days on their journey. Those who had been with Myru, the oracle at the time, had not been called warriors like they were now. They'd been referred to as scouts and were elves of the same village, ones who had devoted themselves to protecting the oracle and fulfilling their duty.

Yumie.

Allix.

Kana.

Noé.

Hiro.

Their names jumped out at him, and a hint of reminiscence filled Luka's heart.

The first four were Myru's elven companions, while Hiro was referred to as "a simple human they ran into." If the Hiro written in here was the same Hiro that was here with them, it made sense as to why he had the skills to read Etherian script.

Hiro had been alive for at least three hundred years.

But if Hiro had been alive for that long while retaining his memories and becoming a magic user, shouldn't he have had a way of finding the last warrior? Had Hiro been keeping secrets from them? And if so, what were his intentions? What was his true motivation?

5

CONFESSION

Day 147, Year 1030 EA

Noé pulled her blades from the giant, spiderlike shadow beast moments before it disappeared into black dust. Using her pant leg, she wiped the blood off her blade before sheathing it back into its scabbard. The metallic scent of blood lingered in the air even after the shadow beast had disappeared. Noé scrunched her nose. She still could not get used to the heavy copper aroma.

Noé blew her lavender hair out of her eyes, placing her hands on her hips as she kicked the pile of dust that surrounded her feet.

Noé didn't know how long it had been since they'd left Rainwell. After leaving the village, she'd been assigned as Myru's scribe. In the beginning, she'd made sure to write in the book her father had given her every day without fail. But as time went on, there were days and sometimes weeks when she didn't have the energy to write. And when she did have the energy to write what had happened to them, she wasn't sure if she wrote the correct date. Eventually, she gave up writing a date and simply wrote the number of days since they'd left Rainwell. But even that was a guess.

Noé was embarrassed that she had failed to accurately capture the dates. She just hoped whoever ended up reading her entries and recording them into the oracle scripts didn't think poorly of her. Surely they would understand the situation they were in. The constant fighting, the endless travels, the responsibility of the fate of the world—who could maintain perfect records under such conditions, anyway?

Leaving Rainwell was something Noé had never imagined she would do. Encountering humans was by far a situation she'd never thought she would experience. To be seen as something lesser than the dirt below one's feet . . . How could anyone treat others that way? The memory of their first village encounter still burned. Mothers pulled their curious children away, and the fathers threatened to kill them if they did not leave. As brave as they tried to be, Noé could see how frightened they were. They saw them as threats. Dangerous. As if they were face-to-face with a bear.

"That's the last of them," Yumie said, her voice cutting through Noé's thoughts. She ran her fingers through her muted-rose hair, heaving out a sigh. Stray dust from the dead shadow beast still lingered in her hair. "How long has it been since she saw the sun?"

"Way too long," Allix said. He tore a piece of fabric from his shirt and used it to wrap a gash on his leg. The wound was deep, dark blood seeping through the makeshift bandage.

"Shouldn't you let Myru take a look at that?" Yumie asked, cocking her brow. "You know these things are poisonous."

Allix shrugged, completely nonchalant over the fact he'd just been poisoned. "Ever since I got bit the first time, I stopped feeling the effects of the poison. I don't think I need to see her for this." Allix made one last knot before straightening up. "I don't want to worry her. She already has a lot on her mind."

"How is she doing?" Noé asked, though she already knew the answer.

They all did.

It had not been long since Myru and Hiro had had a falling out. The two of them had been inseparable at first, and Noé was starting to worry that Hiro may have had an ulterior motive. She always saw him writing and sending the letters via owl or hawk, and she never knew what they entailed. Whenever the curious elf had asked, he would shrug her off and tell her to mind her own business. He'd never failed to mention that Noé kept whatever she wrote in her book a secret, so it was only fair she didn't ask what Hiro wrote in his letters. But the reason why she wrote was different from why he wrote. It was obvious he was reporting their whereabouts to someone, while Noé was simply keeping a record of their journey.

However, through continuous actions, Hiro had proved himself as someone they could trust, regardless of the fact he was a secretive human. He always had a way to get them into an inn when they reached a village or city and provided them with clothes in order to blend in with everyone else. Hiro being skilled in swordsmanship was also a plus. He always joined their rotational scouting during the night and fought shadow beasts whenever they would appear, never hesitating to put himself between danger and the group.

Noé doubted that anyone could pull off a charade for this long, especially if it risked their life, so she had no reason not to trust him, but that didn't mean she wasn't displeased to see Myru and Hiro avoiding each other. The uncomfortable tension between them affected the group as a whole.

"She's been quiet to everyone . . . I think," Allix said, slowly adding the last bit.

"Kana is with her now, right?" Yumie asked, scanning the darkened forest path back to camp.

"You know she wouldn't leave Myru by herself. Not with Hiro acting like that," Noé said. "Let us head back to camp. They're probably worried about us."

Noé watched the fallen leaves tremble against the soft night breeze. The wind was strong enough to make them wobble but too weak to make them fly. She looked up, finally able to see the glow of the moon through the perpetually cloudy sky. The Necromancers' pull against the world was increasing. There was no longer day and night.

There was only never-ending darkness.

When the sun was supposed to be out, the clouded sky shrouded everything in shadows. It felt as if it were still the dead of the night. One could tell it was truly night when the clouds separated, gracing them with clear skies and a large moon.

Noé and Myru were the only two still awake, both basking in the warmth of the fire. Yumie, Allix, and Kana were fast asleep while Hiro was scouting the area, protecting them from any surprise attacks.

Noé was thankful he still kept his dutiful promise despite everything that had happened. It spoke of his character and added to the trust she had in him.

Noé unsheathed her dagger, the familiar weight comforting in her hand. "What do you think about him?" she asked, breaking the silence. She tilted the blade up, allowing the moonlight to reflect off the weapon's silver surface.

"What do you mean?" Myru asked. She played with the hem of her brown skirt, keeping her eyes cast down. Her sage hair covered her features, but Noé could still see the soft pink tinge on the other elf's cheeks. Even in the dim light provided by the moon, Myru's shy and embarrassed demeanor was evident.

"Hiro." Noé cleared her throat. "I mean, what do you think of Hiro?" she asked, her voice gentle. She did not want to embarrass the other elf even more.

"He saved me." Myru's voice was quiet but loud enough for Noe's trained ears to pick up.

"I know he saved you. I'm asking what you think about him." Noé narrowed her eyes. "I've seen the way you two look at each other." She recalled how at first it had been with uncertainty. Then admiration. Now it was confusion.

Myru didn't respond. The edges of her cheeks darkened, and she looked away.

Noé smiled. Perhaps the situation between Myru and Hiro was not as bad as they had all thought. "Aha! You do like him. I'm surprised you'd fall for someone like him." It was likely they were acting awkwardly with each other because Hiro had confessed his feelings and Myru was too shy to accept them. It was the simplest explanation for their behavior.

"What do you mean by that?" Myru puckered her lower lip.

"I'm not making fun of you. I'm just saying it's surprising. He's probably the last person I thought you'd have a crush on." Noé sheathed her dagger. She lifted her arms up in a stretch and let out a groan. She leaned her elbow against her knee and rested her chin against her palm. She tilted her head slightly, her lavender fringe swaying away from her eyes. "You're going to tell him?"

Myru blew out her cheeks. She stuck out her tongue and turned away. It was a childish gesture that reminded Noé of simpler days back home.

Myru pressed her fingers against her lips.

Noé gasped, eyes widening. She pointed her finger at Myru. "You! You kissed him already, didn't you?"

Myru buried her face in her hands, the tips of her ears turning bright red. A muffled wail escaped her lips.

Noé whistled. "Wait until I tell everyone about this." They had all been worried for nothing. Relief flooded through her knowing the awkwardness would eventually pass.

Myru gasped. "You wouldn't!"

"Are you still giving him the silent treatment?"

"I—" Myru cleared her throat before heaving a sigh. "It's not as easy as you may think."

"Tell me, then." Noé crossed her arms. "Did I get it wrong?"

Myru shook her head. "You're right. I . . . I do like him. I do like Hiro, but . . ." She chewed on her lower lip.

"Stop doing that. You'll make yourself bleed," Noé snapped. She hated seeing Myru harm herself. After leaving Rainwell, Myru had developed habits where she would pick her fingers or chew on her lip whenever she felt nervous or anxious.

Myru quickly released her lower lip. "Sorry."

Noé raised a hand. "No need to apologize. I know you aren't doing it intentionally, but it still hurts to see."

"He confessed he has feelings for me," Myru said slowly. "And I was happy."

Noé waited for Myru to continue, not wanting to make her feel as if she needed to rush her thoughts out.

"But I couldn't stop thinking about how we live in two different worlds. I'm an elf, the oracle. When we finish this journey, we're going back home. We aren't staying here." Myru's voice shook. She took a steady breath before continuing. "And he's a human. There's no reason for him to leave his people."

Noé's chest tightened. Myru's beautiful emerald eyes became clouded with tears. Myru was worried. Myru worried that Hiro's affection for her wouldn't last and that he was wasting his time and feelings on her. He was human, and she was an elf. She had believed it was for the best for them to end things now, before their feelings deepened. Before the pain would be too much to bear. Noé knew of Myru's self-sacrificing tendencies, so she was sure she must've told Hiro something he wasn't expecting in order to make it easier for him to let her go.

"You think he deserves to be with someone who could love him back?"

Myru nodded, her hands balling into fasts, her knuckles turning white.

"You think there is someone out there who deserves him more than you because she could grow old with him. She could give him a family. She could love him more than what you can offer."

Myru let out a sob, and the noise tore at Noé's heartstrings.

"What did you tell him?" Noé frowned. It took all she had not to rush over and hold her friend.

"I-I told him . . . I told him he was a j-joke for confessing." Myru let out another choked sob. "I told him there w-was no way I c-could like someone like him. H-he was just a human! I'm the oracle! I . . . I . . ."

Noé's resistance snapped, and she stood, making her way to Myru, and wrapped her arms around her trembling body. She stroked the back of Myru's head, allowing the other elf to let out her cries. Noé pressed her lips together as Myru's distress was released against her, soaking her shoulder. "Shh, it's okay. Everything will be okay."

Noé looked over at their other comrades. By the sounds of their breathing, she knew they had been awakened by the conversation. None of them had missed Myru's confession. They remained where they were, completely still, allowing Myru this moment of vulnerability with Noé.

Unfortunately, Hiro had also returned from his rounds. He stood far enough so Myru wouldn't hear him return, but Noé could sense him. She knew the human had heard everything.

Noé held Myru tighter, wishing she could shield her beloved friend from the consequences of her own self-sacrifices.

6

FAILURE

Luka leaned back in his chair, running his fingers through his long, silver hair. The elven scroll lay unfurled on the table, untouched since he had finished reading. He had spent the last few hours processing the information, and he was certain the scroll was a diary of sorts but was not sure if there was a hidden message or not.

Luka was reading it from an outsider's perspective, but he knew he needed Elliot to read the scroll, to at least look at it to see if anything popped out at him. Perhaps the elf would be able to notice finer details that Luka could not. Maybe there was something else hidden in it that Elliot may discover. And maybe this would be what Elliot needed to regain himself, to bring himself out of the drowning darkness.

"Owen," Luka said.

"Yes?" the other ethereal responded immediately.

"I will need Elliot to take a look at this before we can uncover the mystery behind the final warrior." Luka carefully rolled up the parchment, not wanting to damage the aged material.

"Are you able to share what you read?" Owen asked.

Luka nodded, gathering his thoughts. "It was as if I was reading a diary of someone who was with the past oracle. Myru was her name." He paused, remembering the vivid descriptions he had read moments ago. "She was the original oracle who protected the world from the Necromancers. There are some differences between then and now, namely the people around Myru."

"Were there still warriors with her?"

"Not quite, but something similar." Luka's words caught in his throat as a sudden thought raced through his mind. "They were all elves." Luka turned to Owen, eyes wide. "Owen, they were elves." The discovery sent Luka to his feet. He quickly tucked the scroll into his sash before rushing out of the room, not giving Owen a chance to respond.

The ethereal's footsteps echoed through the hallway as he glided down the hall toward Elliot's room, unable to keep his usual graceful and quiet footwork. He hoped the elf was alone. As much as Luka appreciated Hiro diligently watching over him, Luka wanted to speak with Elliot privately.

"Elliot?" Luka called out, knocking on the door. He waited to see if Hiro would respond, but there was only silence.

Perfect.

Luka took a deep breath before he reached for the door handle, pushing the door open.

The sight that greeted him made his heart ache.

Elliot was sitting at the edge of the bed, his gaze fixated on what lay beyond the frosted window. His hands were loosely clasped together, and his once-vibrant green hair was now dull, as if it reflected his spirit. His complexion was sallow, and dark shadows had found their way under his unfocused, soft blue eyes. Luka frowned at the sight of how loose Elliot's clothes were on him now. Time was slipping away from them—both for Elliot and the world.

"Elliot," Luka said softly, gently closing the door behind him and clicking the lock into place. He approached the quiet elf carefully, not wanting to startle him. "How are you feeling?" Luka knelt in front of Elliot, taking ahold of his frail hands. They were cold.

Elliot blinked, his eyes shifting from the window down to Luka.

Good. A response.

Luka smiled. He hadn't expected a reaction so soon. Elliot usually needed several attempts of coaxing before he responded to anything.

"How are you feeling?" he said again, keeping his voice gentle.

"I . . ." Elliot's bottom lip quivered, his voice cracking from lack of use. "I killed him."

Luka furrowed his brow, tightening his hold. "What do you mean?"

"Minari." Elliot paused. Muttering his name seemed to

cause him pain. "I killed him. I let him die."

Luka shook his head, squeezing the elf's hand. "No, Elliot. That was not within your power. It was not your fault."

"But—"

"No. Minari died at the hands of a Necromancer. You had nothing to do with it." Luka's voice was firm, but he still tried to keep it soft enough to not add any more stress to Elliot.

Something broke in Elliot's eyes as his breath quickened. "I let him die! I did this to him!" He yanked his hands from Luka's grasp with surprising strength. "I did it, Luka! I was the one who killed Minari!" His voice pitched in desperation as his breathing became erratic. He clutched the front of his loose shirt, shutting his eyes. Choked sobs escaped his lips.

Elliot's mind was tormenting him in an endless spiral as the elf sat by himself, repeating the same thoughts over and over. He was drowning in guilt and grief, which warped and skewed his perception of reality. Elliot was lost. He no longer knew what was true and what was false.

Luka pressed Elliot against his chest and rubbed circles on his back, hoping that the sound of his beating heart would help ground Elliot back to reality. His breathing was turning into quick gasps.

"Listen to my heartbeat," Luka murmured. "Focus on it. You are strong. I know you are."

The ethereal kept his own breathing steady and deep, hoping the distressed elf would mimic his actions. Luka decided to seep a gentle amount of his magic into Elliot. He was unsure if it would bring comfort, but at the very least, it could provide a feeling of something other than darkness.

Luka remained still, not letting go of Elliot. The silence chewed against his nerves, but he knew this was not something he could forcefully change or rush. He needed to be patient. Elliot was the only one who could truly overcome the monsters in his head.

Luka only hoped to help aid in the battle.

Elliot's breathing eventually steadied, ending with one last shuddering exhale. He pulled away from Luka, though not completely. Luka's arms still loosely draped over Elliot.

"Thank you," Elliot whispered. "I'm sorry."

"You do not need to apologize. I am glad to have helped."

Elliot fiddled with his fingers. "I didn't want you to see me like this. Or anyone, for that matter."

Luka moved to sit next to Elliot, their shoulders barely touching. He wanted to keep physical contact with Elliot, letting the other know he was still here. "Elliot, you do not need to fight this on your own. We are in this together." Luka hesitated, unsure if he should bring up Minari. He didn't want to trigger another descent into darkness in Elliot's mind.

"Thank you . . . I appreciate it. But I think I'll be all right."

"I trust you." Luka decided to let the topic go. "I wanted to show you this." He reached into his sash, pulling out the scroll. "I found this in the library. I was hoping you could read this."

Elliot eyed the scroll before accepting it.

"Do you recognize it?"

Elliot shook his head slowly. "No . . . I'm sure I've never seen this before, but . . . Why does the library here have an elvish scroll?"

"That I am unsure of. Perhaps ethereals and elves met long ago and this was kept here for safekeeping."

Elliot unrolled the parchment, letting it lie over his lap. He grazed his fingertips across the surface.

"Are you able to read this?" Luka asked, watching Elliot's reaction carefully.

Elliot nodded. "Yes, this is in Elvish."

"It seems only certain people are able to read this. Owen took a look at it earlier and could not decipher the words."

"This was what Minari was doing . . ." Elliot whispered, frowning. "Whoever wrote this was a scribe. And Minari was . . ." Fresh tears spilled from Elliot's eyes, silently falling down his cheeks. "Minari was my scribe."

Luka waited patiently for Elliot to finish reading. If his suspicions were correct regarding the last warrior, everything they had done thus far would have been in vain. And if he was right, he was not sure how they would proceed with the prophecy.

Was everything for naught?

Elliot finally raised his head. He inhaled deeply before letting it go through pursed lips.

"What are your thoughts?" Luka asked.

"The person who wrote this," Elliot began. "I've seen her in my dreams. I'm certain Noé was that girl." He leaned forward, resting his elbow against his knee and pressing a hand against his forehead.

"Are your dreams like visions?"

"I think so. The event that was written in here was the same exact one I had in my dream. And in my dream, I'm Myru." Elliot turned to look at Luka. "Do you think this holds a clue to the last warrior?"

"Yes, after reading this, I had a good idea of who the last warrior might be." Luka's voice was tight. He just hoped he was incorrect.

Elliot shook his head. "I don't think you're wrong."

"Then . . . ?" Luka's worries were turning into reality.

"We're too late." Elliot's lips curled into a sad smile, full of resignation. "Minari was the last warrior, and none of us had the slightest clue. We let our last warrior die right in front of us."

7

ADAPT

Chloé heaved, hunching over. Her legs felt weak, and they trembled as they struggled to support her weight. The sun's rays bore down on the back of her neck, causing a slow formation of sweat across her brow. She never would have imagined herself in a situation where she would be outside breaking a sweat. Physical labor was foreign to Chloé. She'd grown up in Blanc Grotto, where the temperature was usually pleasant. It was never too hot or too cold. The magic that enveloped the area kept it comfortable—a complete contrast to her current situation.

"Feeling tired already?" Deveran called out from behind Chloé. "At this rate, we're all going to surpass you!"

Chloé looked behind her, wiping the sweat from her forehead with the back of her hand. Sure enough, the rest of the recruits were quickly gaining on her. She was grateful to Bunnie and the rest of Nighthawk for welcoming her into the guild and agreeing to let her join the newest members. They were to undergo training with their weapon of choice, in stealth, in persuasion, and in stamina.

Unfortunately for Chloé, today was stamina, her weakest trait. She had always relied on her magic to fight and not so much on her physical abilities. But now, without her core, she had no choice in the matter.

Chloé tried to prevent herself from recalling Gerald destroying her core. It pained her, knowing it was her own father who'd taken away her powers and identity. But at the same time, she was thankful. If he had not done it, she would not have been given this opportunity.

Deveran was overseeing today's stamina training with the recruits, ensuring no one was severely left behind and offering words of encouragement. His guidance and supportive leadership were what Chloé needed, especially when she struggled with simple physical tasks that seemed second nature to most.

Outside of Lonin, there were trees marked with Nighthawk's emblem on the trunk, checkmark indicators for their grueling exercise. They were to sprint to the designated area as fast as they could, allowing themselves only one minute to catch their breath before the next sprint. Each sprint took Chloé roughly three minutes. Her lungs and legs burned each time. There were thirteen checkpoints in total, and Chloé was on point six.

"Point seven!" Scarlet yelled as she passed another marked tree. She was one of the newer recruits, having joined after Chloé. Scarlet pulled ahead of another group, her timid appearance a stark contrast to her athleticism.

Though the training wasn't a race, Chloé found herself in a competitive spirit. The other recruits may not have realized how much each step meant for her, as each step felt like a new beginning for Chloé.

"I let Scarlet beat me last time," she muttered to herself, a smirk playing across her lips. "I won't let her this time!"

Laughter and chatter filled the inn's dining hall. Evening had finally fallen, and everyone's training was finished for the day. They all deserved a moment of relaxation.

"How are you doing?" Bunnie asked, approaching the table Chloé was sitting at. She held two mugs in her hands, handing one of them to Chloé. "Chamomile with lemon."

Chloé smiled, grateful for the familiar routine they'd established. "Thank you." She held the mug against her nose, allowing the smoked aroma to seep through her senses.

"May I?"

"Of course! You don't need to ask, Bunnie."

Bunnie took the open seat next to Chloé, placing her mug down on the round, wooden table. "You've been here for three weeks now."

"You're right . . . Three weeks, huh?" Chloé looked around the inn, admiring the scene before her. Never in her wildest dreams had she thought she'd be part of something so empowering. The members all looked out for one another. They remained positive and always had teamwork as a priority.

Growing up as a young council member, Chloé always had to defend herself. Defend her cause. Defend her reason. There was no one who was on her side. It was always them versus her.

Chloé felt Bunnie's fingers against her hair, tucking a stray piece behind her ear.

"I never got to tell you how much I like this new haircut. It's refreshing, and it suits you."

Chloé's cheeks warmed into a blush. "You think so?"

Bunnie nodded. "Our uniform also suits you. Who knew black and pink could complement each other so well?"

Chloé sipped her tea, attempting to hold back a wide smile. The compliment made her embarrassed yet giddy at the same time. Growing up, she'd received numerous compliments regarding her beautiful, long, curly, pink hair. It was bouncy and lustrous. Her hair had been the majority of her identity. She'd been recognized immediately because of it.

Now her hair sat a little above her shoulders, cascading across her cheeks.

It had been an impulsive decision.

After joining Nighthawk, Chloé had wanted to start over. With her status and family name having been taken away from her, she wanted to recreate herself. To forge something new. Who she was now was her own person, built entirely by her own achievements.

The new clothes she wore were also a significant contrast to her usual attire. She no longer wore pink frills and a skirt. Now she was clad in a full attire of black. Her top and pants hugged her figure close. She wore boots that laced up to her knees and a black trench coat similar to what Bunnie wore. But the things that made her uniform different from the rest of the Nighthawk members were her pink bootlaces, her pink fingerless gloves, and the pink hardware on her coat.

Perhaps it was not entirely all bad she still wore some pink. It was her favorite color, after all.

"B-Boss," a familiar voice stuttered. "May I . . . May I sit here? With you and Chloé?"

Scarlet sucked in her bottom lip, her green eyes turning away. A slight tinge of pink spread across her freckled complexion. Her dinner tray shook slightly in her hands as she waited for a response.

"I have no issues with you joining us," Bunnie said. "How about you, Chloé?"

Chloé shook her head, gesturing to an empty chair at their table. "Of course not. You can join us, Scarlet."

Scarlet's face lit up, eyes finally meeting theirs. "Really? Thank you!" She placed her tray down before taking the empty seat across from Chloé. She took her bread and ripped it in half, then dipped it into her soup.

"I heard you beat Chloé today," Bunnie said, causing Scarlet to nearly choke on her bread.

"N-no!" Scarlet's mouth dropped. She stuttered, glancing between Bunnie and Chloé. "I'm sure Chloé just . . . let me win! There's no way I would have been able to otherwise!"

Chloé chuckled at the sight of Scarlet's blush spreading

all the way to her ears. "Did I? I think you won all on your own." She took another sip of her tea.

Scarlet gawked at Chloé. "Not only are you fast and strong, you also don't have a cat's tongue."

Chloé blinked. "What do you mean?"

"I can see the steam coming out of the mug, yet you drank it like it was at room temperature." Scarlet looked at her soup. "My soup is too hot for me to eat, so I'm using bread to dip into it."

"The tea isn't that hot," Bunnie said. She lifted her own cup and took a sip. "I think you're the one with the cat's tongue, Scarlet."

"Really? I've always thought my tolerance was normal."

Chloé tuned out the conversation. She pressed her hands against the surface of her mug, attempting to feel how warm it was. She could see the steam rising from the liquid, but she couldn't feel it. The mug felt as if it were indeed at room temperature.

Chloé pushed away the thought. She was probably tired.

Chloé leaned forward until the tip of her nose was merely inches away from the mirror. She studied her face closely, trying to find any abnormal changes.

Ever since the destruction of her magic core three weeks ago, she'd noticed the subtle shift in her sensory perception. There were times when she did not hear certain noises or see certain things. She would practice in the firing range with Deveran and Oliver, yet the sound of the firing guns would fall on deaf ears. Sometimes the target she was aiming for would disappear or blur briefly before reappearing again, causing her to miss her shot.

Chloé had brushed it off as fatigue. Perhaps she was overworking herself, trying to reach the same level of skill she'd had when she had her magic. Now that she had to relearn everything from the ground up, she felt behind. She admired the way Deveran and Oliver moved, as if their guns were an extension of their bodies. The way the twins fought looked graceful, like they were performing a dance together.

The two of them were part of Minerva, so it made sense.

It felt like just yesterday that Chloé had first seen Bunnie, Deveran, Oliver, and Vivian in Venin. The four of them composed the traveling band Minerva. But after being in Nighthawk for some time, she'd learned that Minerva was just a front in order to gather information, a guise they used for obtaining intel.

Chloé sighed, pulling away from the mirror and glancing at the slowly filling tub. Steam rose from the water, engulfing the bathroom with a thick fog that should have made the air feel humid and warm.

Yet she felt nothing.

Chloé turned the faucet off, watching the last few drops fall into the bath. The water should be hot. She held her breath before dipping her hand in.

"Ah!" Chloé quickly pulled away, holding her hand close. Her skin was swollen and red.

The water was hot.

Maybe it was just fatigue after all.

8

WAR

"Are you sure this information is correct?" Bunnie asked, her fingers drumming against the table of the meeting room.

Oliver nodded. "Yes, Boss. We went through our sources multiple times to ensure accuracy. It seems Ragnar has removed the bounty on Chloé since she is no longer a part of the council. The Hunters have been recalled."

Chloé's eyes widened. The Hunters had retreated? The mercenary guild was known for completing any request, whether or not it abided by the law. And they were hired usually due to their disregard for the legality of their actions. To hear of them having been ordered to retreat was unheard of.

"So, he no longer sees Chloé as a threat," Bunnie said, eyes narrowing.

"That's where he's wrong," Chloé said, standing tall and crossing her arms. "I am more of a threat now. Not only am I a warrior, but I am also a member of Nighthawk."

"You got that right." Bunnie smirked, a hint of pride in her voice. "Oliver, how long ago did Ragnar send the retreat signal to the Hunters? And do you know if he's still working with them?"

"Ragnar called for the return of the Hunters right around when Chloé joined us," Oliver said. "And . . ."

Bunnie raised a brow. "And?"

Oliver glanced at Chloé briefly before returning to Bunnie. "Ragnar has ordered the Hunters to find Elliot, along with everyone he was with. He doesn't care if they're dead or alive. He wants them back in Valquent."

The meeting room fell deathly silent, and Chloé could feel the eyes of the other members against her back. Her chest tightened, and her hands felt clammy.

Was Elliot all right?

Chloé knew they'd made it out of Valquent, but had they made it to the Snowy Hills? But even if they had made it to the Snowy Hills, the area was still under King Valentine VI's rule. Ragnar was the closest to the king, and as his advisor, his words were the extension of the king's order.

Changing the focus and going after the others only meant that Ragnar was determined to stop the prophecy at its source. It was a calculated move. Regardless of the remaining warriors, if Elliot was to disappear, the prophecy wouldn't be fulfilled.

"And there's something else," Oliver said, cutting through the tense silence. "King Valentine VI has issued a royal decree." He paused before clearing his throat. "He is recruiting both men and women to become knights in his army. The king is issuing a war with the elves."

Chloé's vision spun. She leaned forward, planting her palm against the table for support. This couldn't be happening. A decree like this was more than just a declaration of war. They wanted to massacre the elves. Those in the lower lands were believers of Mykronos. They would be more than happy to eliminate anyone who opposed their god.

This was not just about the elves or the prophecy anymore. This was about to become a religious crusade. With how much negativity and hate the lower lands had for the elves, it would give them the fuel they needed.

Down with Vylantra.

Chloé could imagine the chant in her mind. She shook her head, attempting to think about anything but.

"We won't let that happen," Bunnie said, voice stern. She stood from her seat, pushing her shoulders back, commanding attention from everyone in the room. "If they're declaring war, then we are too."

What was Bunnie saying?

Chloé studied Bunnie's face for any sign of hesitation, but there was none. Their leader's expression was set. She was determined, her piercing golden gaze firm on her decision.

"This guild is not officially recognized by the kingdom. We can use this to our advantage. They don't have eyes on us, but we have eyes on them. We're going to do whatever we can to stop them from finding Elliot," Bunnie said. "Do we have any information about where they are?"

"Some of our members who were stationed in Solime said they saw Luka and Owen but not the others. It's safe to say they were probably under the ethereals' spell," Vivian said.

"So, they left for the Snowy Hills, then," Bunnie said. "How long ago?"

"Roughly two weeks."

"Do you know if they returned?"

Vivian shook her head. "There haven't been reports of any ship or boat returning to Solime with them."

"So, it's safe to assume they're still there. Deveran, the map, please."

"Yes, Boss." Deveran reached into his coat and pulled out a folded piece of parchment. He opened it quickly before laying it across the table, the corners curling slightly from frequent use.

There were already multiple red marks labeling each city Nighthawk had a base in. Not counting the capital and the coves, there were four cities, six towns, and nine small villages, and Nighthawk had a base in two cities, three towns, and six small villages. This was Chloé's first time seeing the map, and she was impressed by the network Bunnie and the team had created.

During Chloé's time in the council, she'd never once noticed them. Their ability to blend in with everyday people and still collect reports and data and maintain communication was remarkable. It made her wonder what else she had missed during her time as a council member.

"Before I continue, does anyone object?" Bunnie asked, her gaze sweeping across the gathered officers. "We will be against the kingdom, and there's a good chance the rest of Etheria will turn its back on us. I trust everyone here with my life, as you are my faithful officers. But I know there will be others who might disagree or might not wish to be a part of this war." Bunnie paused, looking around the room once again, waiting to see if anyone objected. "Not everyone will share this conviction, and I anticipate there may be those who will oppose us. This decision should not be taken lightly."

The silence that filled the room was different than that prior. Before, grave news had been thrust onto them, making the air shift uncomfortably. But now there was a plan. A goal. And with a determined leader, there was no way they would back down. Their shoulders squared, and they stood a little taller.

They waited for their leader to continue, the flames of determination evident in their eyes.

"It's decided, then." Bunnie nodded. "It's war."

Chloé straightened her posture, taking in a deep breath.

This was it.

A turning point.

For the first time since losing her core, she felt certain of this path. Whatever came next, she would face it as a member of Nighthawk and a warrior.

Chloé would be fighting for a future worth protecting.

9

FRACTURE

War. Chloé was going to be a part of war.

The nix lay on her back, arms stretched out as she stared at the ceiling. Moonlight filtered through her window, bleeding through the curtains, which were ajar. The wooden beams above her blurred as her mind drifted to the events that had occurred during the meeting.

Chloé had grown up believing peace would thrive in Etheria forever with the efforts of the king and the council; world conflict had never crossed her mind. The past few months should have made it obvious that that was not going to be true. And just hours before, Bunnie had announced Nighthawk was going to declare war against the kingdom. They were siding with the elves and the oracle.

All the officers were in agreement and had sided with

Bunnie, though the more Chloé thought about it, the more she was amazed at Bunnie's leadership. The unity Bunnie commanded was not just about following orders. It represented something deeper—something Chloé admired.

Growing up, everyone in the lower lands was taught the elves were the ones in the wrong. They were fed lies day after day, year after year, and Chloé's experience traveling through Etheria with Elliot and Minari had proved just how much the elves were despised. Parents taught their children to hate, and when those children turned into parents, continued the teachings of hate. It was an endless cycle and anyone would have rejoiced at the thought of eradicating the elves.

For Nighthawk, none of that mattered. Those in the guild had devoted themselves to Bunnie, and that meant they trusted her over the kingdom's teachings. They trusted her and believed Bunnie was in the right and would not lead them astray. They agreed Etheria needed a change.

They were choosing to reject generations of ingrained prejudice and loathing, and Bunnie was a beacon, shedding light and leading the way toward a brighter future of love and understanding.

A knock on the door startled Chloé from her thoughts.

"Chloé? Are you still awake?"

Bunnie.

"I'm awake. You can come in," Chloé said, pushing herself up into a sitting position.

Bunnie peeked into the room. "You still haven't changed?" she asked before entering and closing the door quietly behind her.

Chloé shook her head. "Just thinking."

"May I?" Bunnie gestured next to Chloé.

"Of course. You don't need to ask."

Bunnie took a seat before letting out a heavy sigh, the mattress dipping slightly from the added weight. "I hope I'm doing the right thing."

"Is there something worrying you?" Chloé internally flinched at her own question. Of course Bunnie would be worried. Anyone would. They were about to take on a massive ordeal. "That was a dumb question. Ignore it."

"It's okay." Bunnie smiled. "Just like how there's a lot going on in your mind, there's a lot going on in mine."

"I just never thought this would happen to me . . . Not just war, but . . . everything." Chloé didn't know how to explain how she felt.

"Do you want to talk about it? After everything that's happened these past few months, it does feel like we haven't had the chance to slow down and really digest everything."

"It just felt like there wasn't any time to." Chloé lifted her feet from the floor, crossing her legs. "Even now, I feel like the clock is ticking faster than ever."

"I understand, and I completely agree. It's important to keep moving forward, but it's equally as important to take care of yourself. Both physically and mentally." Bunnie took ahold of Chloé's hand, her touch warm and reassuring. "I never got to ask you how you were doing and feeling. I want to apologize to you."

Chloé blinked, surprised. "What do you mean?"

"As the captain of Nighthawk, I always check in with my officers to make sure everything is going well with them and their team."

"I'm not an officer though . . ."

Bunnie squeezed Chloé's hand. "You're not an officer, no, but you are still important to me, Nighthawk member or not. I hope you trust me enough to let me know if anything is bothering you."

Warmth spread across Chloé's chest. "I do trust you."

Bunnie smiled. "So, is anything bothering you?"

Chloé pondered if she should let Bunnie know about the random occurrences where her senses would become dull momentarily. She had chalked it up to fatigue, but it had happened again earlier in the day. They hadn't had training, and she'd had enough sleep the night before. Her sense of smell had disappeared for a few seconds while she was eating lunch, and then it came back full force. The onslaught of aromas had made her sick to her stomach, so she couldn't finish her meal. Luckily, it hadn't happened during dinner.

The episodes were becoming so frequent that it was difficult for Chloé to ignore. She was not sure why this was happening in the first place. It could be because her body was transitioning into not having a magic core.

Bunnie already had a lot to worry about, so surely this was not something she needed to hear. The other members probably had more important matters.

Chloé shook her head, deciding against it. "Just worried about the war is all. I mean, who would have thought they would be going to war in their lifetime? It's something you always read about. And I hope Elliot and the others are okay."

"Right. There's a lot of uncertainty about what happens from here on out. Our mission was to keep you safe, and now it's to keep the world safe." Bunnie gazed out the window, her grasp on Chloé's hand loosening. The stray bit of moonlight cast against Bunnie's features barely highlighted how exhausted she truly was. "Elliot was tasked with fulfilling the prophecy as the oracle. The prophecy to save the world."

"What about you, Bunnie? Do you trust me?"

Bunnie snapped back to look at the nix. "Of course. With my life."

"I mean . . ." Chloé tightened her hold on Bunnie's hand. "Do you trust me enough to tell me what you're thinking? What you're going through?"

Bunnie chuckled. "Of course. Other than the fact that I'm worried we're all going to die, I know we're going to do our best and do whatever we can to stop this. I already had Deveran send notices to the officers stationed at our other bases and to let me know if our numbers decrease based on our decision today."

"And if they do?"

"We'll just have to adapt. I don't think it would be a smart move to continue recruiting—not with a decree like this. I don't want the potential risk of a double agent joining our guild."

"How long will it take for us to know our final numbers?"

"I gave the order to give me their final answer within five days. I know it's not a lot of time to think things through, but time is not on our side." Bunnie stood. "It's getting late, and I think I've kept you up long enough. I'll take my leave here. Goodnight, Chloé."

"Bunnie, wait," Chloé called out.

"Hmm?"

"Thank you. For everything."

Bunnie smiled, and for a moment, Chloé could see the invisible weight on Bunnie's shoulders lift. "If I could, I would do it all over again. Have a good night."

The door clicked shut behind her.

10
SAIL

Errol leaned against the edge of the ship. The cloudless sky revealed a vast sea of stars, each one like a ray of hope. The full moon shone brightly as they made their way across the dark ocean, aiding in guiding them through the unknown.

A month had passed since the elves had left Mistfall. It had been difficult to leave behind everything they knew, but Errol knew it was for the best, that this was the right choice. When he, Silas, and Stella had announced their plan to seek new lands in the hope of living without fear, the villagers had all been in agreement. They trusted him and his judgement and would follow him with whatever he had decided. In fact, everyone was excited. The prospect of freedom from oppression had ignited a spark he had never seen before. Errol must not have truly understood how everyone felt.

Errol's inability to see and understand how the villagers were feeling made his chest ache. While Errol and the other scouts had dedicated themselves to protecting their village, they'd failed to defend them from the root of everything.

Lily had planted the seed of fear.

Their isolated location had been revealed. Their secret was no longer a secret.

Their safety had been jeopardized.

Finding new lands was the only hope they had left.

The weeklong journey to the coast had not been difficult for them, but the three weeks that followed had truly tested their resolve. They'd spent each day from sunrise to sunset collecting materials and had built boats big and sturdy enough to send them across the sea.

"Can't sleep?" Ara asked, her voice resonating within Errol's mind.

Errol looked down, meeting the water demigod's gaze. Her body disappeared underwater, except for her features above her nose. If she hadn't spoken to Errol, he wouldn't have noticed she was there. The way she flowed through the water was delicate and graceful. There wasn't a single ripple from her movements.

Errol shook his head and glanced back to his sleeping companions. Both Stella and Silas were huddled near the boat's edge, using their arms as makeshift pillows. The vessel was cramped with the three of them and their supplies, but they'd quickly adapted, knowing nothing would come out of complaining.

Around them were twenty-one boats. They carried the other villagers, as well as their precious ovis. Their numbers had dwindled after the attack, but survival itself was worth celebrating.

"We will reach shore soon. You should do whatever you can to conserve your energy," Ara advised.

"How much longer?"

"We should arrive by nightfall in six days. Once we dock, it will take about three weeks on foot to arrive at our destination."

Six days? Errol's stomach dropped. That was still a lot of time, especially considering their remaining food supply. Three weeks of travel afterward was manageable since they could replenish their supplies during the journey, but the six days before reaching land was worrisome. "Six days is plenty enough for me to rest," he said, unsure if the water demigod believed him.

"Ah. I have forgotten how time flows for mortals. Nevertheless, it is still wise for you to conserve your energy. Your provisions are low, are they not?"

Errol wasn't sure why he'd thought he could fool Ara.

The destruction of Mistfall had left them scrambling to gather what provisions they could. They hadn't had much while seeking refuge in the shrine, and they had even less now. Errol had been limiting himself to a single bite of food each day, ensuring the others—especially the younger elves—had enough to maintain their strength.

"The most I can do is purify the seawater so it is drinkable," Ara started. "I cannot provide any other sustenance."

"We'll manage." Errol attempted to sound confident, but he knew Ara saw through him. It was more so in case anyone else heard him.

"If you say so . . ."

Ara's form slipped beneath the calm waves, leaving only ripples in her wake, and disappeared into the sea.

Errol released a heavy sigh, his chest tightening with anxiety and uncertainty. His stomach twisted uncomfortably as he thought of the future.

There were so many unknown factors in the new lands. He didn't know what the area was going to be like or what kind of people lived there. Were they going to welcome them to their lands? Or were they going to be struck down and persecuted like when they were in Etheria?

As Errol laid his head down using his arms as pillows, a soft otherworldly melody drifted in the air. The song seemed to come from everywhere and nowhere at once, the gentle notes soothing his worries.

Errol closed his eyes, letting the voice carry him away from consciousness.

Errol's brows twitched as he stirred awake from sudden chatter.

"Look!"

"Over there! There's land!"

"We finally made it!"

Errol opened his eyes, blinking a few times to get rid of the lingering drowsiness.

The night sky still loomed over them.

How was that possible? Just how long had he been

asleep for?

Then he saw it.

First came the tiny dots of light.

Then land.

As Errol looked upon the horizon, its silhouette grew clearer with each passing moment. The mountains and the trees were reminiscent of their previous home. It was comforting yet bittersweet.

"We finally made it," Silas said, his hand landing firmly on Errol's shoulder. "Our new home. I was getting sick of this boat."

Stella covered her mouth as she yawned. "I felt like I was sleeping for a long time."

Errol could not agree more with that statement. His body felt completely refreshed, like he had finally gotten a full night's rest. He glanced at their food supply, surprised to find it exactly how it had been when he'd spoken to Ara. Except this time, the fruits and berries appeared fresher than when they had departed.

Had Ara's song done more than lull them to sleep? The elf wanted to ask, but the water demigod was nowhere to be seen.

Alder stood at the coast, as if guiding the boats. They glided onto shore one by one, their hulls digging into the sand and pebbles. As the last vessel made landfall, Ara finally emerged from the ocean, taking steps toward the shore.

The scales on Ara's body gradually faded, leaving only a scattered few across her skin, making it appear as if there were diamonds on her body.

"Welcome, everyone," Ara started, her voice carrying

across the shore, "to the kingdom of Astaria."

11
RAINWELL

The three-week travel to the new village was quiet. Errol was grateful that their journey was peaceful and uneventful. The atmosphere was bright, cheerful, and light as they followed Alder throughout the morning and evening, the chatter and excitement never dying down. Their smiles and laughter were contagious, and Errol found himself enjoying the mood.

Errol joined in on the conversations more than he'd expected. His usual stoic demeanor softened as he conversed about what their future would be like in the new lands.

Would the new place offer larger fields for their crops to grow?

Would there be more land for the children to play and the ovis to roam?

What kind of people lived in the cities and towns nearby?

What kind of clothes did everyone wear?

When they finally reached the last hill, the sight before everyone left them awestruck.

The elven village stretched across the valley below and was certainly at least twice the size of Mistfall. The buildings had been built with a mixture of stone and wood, perhaps proving to be more durable than the ones they were familiar with. The roads were paved, providing a clear walkway for travel. Unlike in Mistfall, a river ran through the middle, meaning they would no longer need to travel to the lakes for fresh water. Trees with luscious green leaves and flowers in vibrant colors were spread across the entirety of the area.

"This place is beautiful," Stella breathed, her voice barely above a whisper, her mouth ajar.

"I never would have imagined a place larger than Mistfall," Silas added.

Errol frowned. Alder had told him the elven village was abandoned.

This was the complete opposite.

The village was pulsating with life—a life Errol never would have imagined was possible for elves.

It wasn't long before their group was noticed. Curious eyes turned to them. There were hushed whispers amongst them, but none moved toward them or seemed threatened by their presence.

One of the elves stepped forward. His figure was tall and slim, and his long, pale, golden hair was styled in a loose braid and rested on his right shoulder. His clothing wasn't too different from what they wore: a simple cream tunic and dark brown slacks paired with brown boots. "Welcome, everyone, to Rainwell," he started. His emerald eyes twinkled as he smiled. "I'm Azriel Elmwood, the leader of Rainwell."

"Azriel," Alder said. "I am pleased to see you are doing well."

Azriel smiled. "Of course. Luckily, it has been peaceful here. With the help of the villagers, we have homes and stables ready for you. I'm sure everyone here must be famished and tired."

"You knew we were coming?" Errol asked.

"Yes. Alder contacted me a while back. I understand you escaped your previous home because of the Necromancers, correct?"

Errol's eyes widened. He'd been certain information regarding the prophecy had been kept in secrecy in Mistfall. How was it that Azriel knew?

"You seem surprised," Azriel observed. "Do not worry, you're safe here. I can answer any questions you may have, but first, I think it's best if everyone settles into their new homes."

"We just harvested a fresh batch of carrots and potatoes. I hope you find my cooking palatable," Azriel said as he began scooping soup from a large pot into wooden bowls.

A young female elf took the bowls and set them on the rectangular table. Her hair was a similar color to Azriel's, styled in a loose braid.

"Do you need help?" Stella asked, standing from her seat.

"I can do it myself!" the younger elf said, a grin spreading across her cheeks. "It's nice we're having guests over. Daddy's cooking is delicious, and it's always exciting to share it with others."

Azriel chuckled. "Rayna, you're making me blush. You say that every time you bring your friends over."

Rayna puffed her cheeks. "It's true! Everyone thinks so too!"

Errol adored the scene before him. It triggered memories of earlier times when Elliot was younger and would always be excited whenever it was Errol's turn to cook. He'd never thought of himself as a good cook, but Elliot had insisted his cooking was delicious. Thinking back on it now, how many nights had he left Elliot and Estelle alone while he tended to his scout duties? How many precious moments of Elliot's childhood had he missed?

Errol's chest tightened painfully as he balled his hands into fists across his lap. Those nights were now a distant memory, never to be repeated again.

Estelle . . .

Would Elliot forgive him? Would Elliot forgive him for failing to protect his mother? For failing to protect Lyla, his grandmother? For failing to protect Mistfall?

"Now that everyone has their meal, I'm open to answer any questions," Azriel said, snapping Errol back to reality.

Azriel's deep green eyes met Errol's, and he gave the elf

a smile. Azriel seemed to sense Errol's preoccupied attention. Errol was glad Azriel had interrupted his thoughts before he spiraled further into them.

"How did you know we were coming?" Silas asked, offering the first question.

"Alder notified me of your planned arrival via telepathy." Azriel took a spoonful of his soup, blowing on it carefully before putting the contents into his mouth. "I'm the leader of Rainwell, thus giving me certain powers. One of them is having the ability to communicate with Alder. Although our communication has limitations. He can speak to me whenever he pleases, but I cannot speak to him unless he opens the line of communication first."

"Is it normal for elven leaders to be able to communicate with Alder?" Stella asked, tilting her head slightly. "My mother was our late leader, but I do not recall her mentioning being able to communicate with Alder."

"Family members can as well. Does anyone in your family have the ability to speak to Alder?"

Stella's brows rose. "Ah, yes! My younger brother. He was able to communicate with Redd, Alder's familiar."

"Perhaps before your younger brother was born, your mother was able to speak to Alder."

"I see . . . That makes sense," Stella said.

"Melvin might've been able to," Silas added. "He was our leader before Lady Mayleen, but he passed away in an accident."

"I might have been too young to remember, but I think you may be right," Stella said.

"How do you know of the Necromancers?" Errol

asked. He needed to know why they knew of the prophecy.

"We know of the prophecy. Everyone in Rainwell knows the prophecy."

"Information regarding the oracle and the prophecy was kept in secrecy within Mistfall. How is it possible that you know?" Errol's throat tightened.

Azriel set his spoon into his bowl. He clasped his hands together, resting them against the table. "Myru was the original oracle. Her story was passed down through many generations." He paused, allowing the information to settle. "And Rainwell is where Myru was from. This place is her home."

12
PURPOSE

"Luka, we can't stay here," Elliot said. "We need to leave." His stern voice was in contrast to how he'd sounded earlier.

"Our departure from the Snowy Hills is set for nine days from now," Luka said. "We cannot leave any sooner."

"Nine days is too long. We need to leave. Now." Elliot knew they weren't safe here. It was a mystery as to why they hadn't been found yet.

"Elliot, what is wrong?" Luka asked.

Elliot couldn't find the words to explain why he suddenly felt the need to act. The need to do something.

Before Luka brought him the scroll, Elliot had been consumed with thoughts of returning home. He was willing to do whatever it took, prophecy be damned. But reading the records from Myru's scribe, Noé, had awakened something within him, as if reminding him what he'd been sent out to do in the first place. And although Elliot's regrets stilled gnawed at his heart, he wanted to fulfill the prophecy. He was sure of it.

He had to. For Minari's sake.

The thought of his friend brought an all-too-familiar ache to his chest. Minari wouldn't have wanted Elliot to wallow in despair, blaming himself for everything and carrying the full weight of shame on his shoulders. He would've wanted Elliot to press forward, to chase his dreams and fulfill his goals. After everything they'd been through, Elliot couldn't let Minari down.

"They'll find us here if we stay," Elliot said. "The Necromancers."

Luka's eyes widened. "Do you sense them?"

Elliot shook his head. "I don't." He pressed his hand against his chest, feeling his beating heart. "But something tells me they'll find us eventually. Our journey doesn't stop here, Luka. We can still fulfill the prophecy."

Luka's brows rose, and his eyes softened as his lips curled into a smile. "Welcome back, Elliot. We were waiting for your return. Your determination is quite contagious." He chuckled.

Luka's words lifted the invisible weight on Elliot's shoulders. His true self began to resurface. The darkness in his heart was finally disappearing.

Luka placed a hand on Elliot's shoulder. "Whatever comes next, you have all of us by your side."

Elliot smiled. For the first time since Minari's death, he felt like he could finally breathe. His body was no longer heavy and burdened by the regrets of the past, like a prison of sorrow. He had to keep moving forward, had to fight for the future that Minari had died believing in.

"It's good to be back," Elliot said. "Let's gather everyone and discuss what we found."

"I will notify everyone," Luka said. "They'll be relieved to hear from you."

"Thank you," Elliot responded.

He would not fail the prophecy.

He would not fail those who believed in him.

The familiar faces of his warriors and comrades gathered in his room. They waited patiently for Elliot to start, their expressions a mix of curiosity and excitement. Elliot had not realized just how much he'd made everyone worry and the negative impact he had caused. He made sure he wouldn't repeat the same mistake.

This was the turning point in their journey. And Elliot had to be the one to lead them. He would no longer sit on the sidelines.

"How are you feeling?" Mimi asked, breaking the silence. "We were all worried about you."

"I'm all right now," Elliot said. He cleared his throat. "No. Actually, I'm feeling a lot better. I'm sorry to have worried you all."

Hiro smirked. "By the look on your face, you probably have something to tell us."

Elliot nodded. He took a deep breath before starting. "Luka found a clue to the last warrior. There was a scroll in the library that was a transcription by someone who traveled with the previous oracle. As my scribe, Minari carried a book with him, but this is a scroll. So, this must be a copy."

"Who is it?" Sage asked. "The last warrior."

Minari's name caught in Elliot's throat, and his lifeless body flashed before Elliot's eyes. The memory of him lying on the ground, dagger in his heart, ground stained in crimson plagued Elliot's mind, haunting him day and night. Sometimes in his nightmares, Minari's eyes would open, filled with accusation and anger.

Minari hadn't even been given a proper burial.

They'd just left him there. Alone.

No matter how much Elliot tried to remember, he couldn't recall what had happened afterward. The memory remained a dark void in his mind.

Elliot felt a firm hand on his shoulder. He looked up, meeting Hiro's calm expression.

"Don't rush it," Hiro said quietly, loud enough for only Elliot to hear. "Take all the time you need."

Elliot closed his eyes, urging his nerves to calm and his racing heart to slow. He could do this. He would move past this. He pushed the image of Minari's bloody figure from his mind, replacing it with the Minari he had always known: his closest friend with messy purple hair. Confident. Trusting. Always rooting for him.

Even now, Elliot was positive Minari was here with him, lending him strength.

Elliot took a deep breath. "The last warrior . . . was Minari."

"What?" Sage's disbelief echoed through the room.

"You can't be serious."

"That cannot be true," Mimi said, frowning. "I didn't sense him at all. None of us did."

"I do wonder that as well," Luka said. "Why I wasn't able to sense his presence as a warrior."

"You grew up with him, right?" Confusion laced through Sage's voice. "How was it you didn't know either?"

Elliot shook his head. "I'm not sure . . . but I do know for a fact that Minari was a warrior." He understood why Sage was frustrated. The answer was within their reach, but they had all been blind to it.

"I believe you," Hiro said. "Maybe the Necromancers cast something on him so none of you could sense him."

"That seems like a plausible reason," Luka agreed.

"Lily . . ." Elliot whispered. Maybe Lily was the one who'd done something to Minari. It made the most sense. The three of them had grown up together, and Lily was a Necromancer. It was likely she was the one who'd hidden Minari's identity from them.

Elliot's chest tightened at the thought. The Lily he had known and loved seemed like a stranger now. Deep down, he wished this were all a dream. He wished he would eventually wake up from this nightmare and the three of them would still be in Mistfall, preparing for the Bloom Festival.

Unfortunately, that wasn't the case. Elliot had to accept that the Lily he knew was gone, that perhaps she was just a stranger who'd deceived them. He didn't know why Lily had waited as long as she had to make her move when she knew who they were, but he was grateful to have shared fond memories together.

Whether they were real or part of her deception, Elliot would cherish them for as long as he lived.

"If we take into account that Lily knew who we were, then she might've done something to Minari," Elliot said, echoing his thoughts. "And with his death, she must've been hoping to put a stop to the prophecy."

"Can it?" Mimi asked. "You need all of us, don't you?"

Elliot shook his head. He had come to the realization moments ago, finally understanding Vylantra's words. "No. This journey was to bring all of us together. While I possess Myru's—the original oracle's—soul, you all possess her past companions' souls." Elliot reached over, taking ahold of Mimi's hands. "Allix."

Mimi looked at Elliot confusingly. "Wha—" His golden eyes suddenly glossed over, shoulders relaxing. "Myru . . ."

Elliot smiled. He let go of Mimi's hands. The chimera blinked rapidly, eyes refocusing.

"Mimi, what happened?" Sage asked. "Why did you call Elliot that?"

"Call him what?" Mimi asked.

"You called him Myru," Sage said.

Mimi furrowed his brow. "No, I didn't say anything."

Elliot took ahold of Luka's hands. "Kana."

Luka's breath hitched before he closed his eyes. When he opened them, his lavender eyes were glossed over, unfocused, similar to Mimi's. "Myru . . ."

Elliot released Luka's hands, and the ethereal's eyes

refocused.

"What did you do?" Sage asked.

"It appears Elliot has the ability to call for the souls of Myru's companions," Hiro said.

"I'm positive the prophecy's purpose was to reunite us because they stopped the Necromancers before. But even without Minari, I think we can do it." Elliot paused. "No. We can do it." He was surprised at his own tone, steady with determination and conviction. Nothing would stand in their way.

"What do we do now?" Mimi asked. "We know who the last warrior is, so where do we go when we return to the mainland?"

"We aren't going to back to the mainland," Elliot said. "Not there."

"Where else would we go?" Mimi asked.

"Home," Elliot said. "To Rainwell."

13
STEP

"Rainwell? The village you said you were from?" Sage asked.

Elliot shook his head. "Minari and I are from Mistfall. Rainwell was actually a place I made up when we first met, since I wasn't sure if it was safe to tell you where we originally were from," Elliot confessed. "I didn't know it was an actual place."

"Myru's memories are probably mixing into your own," Hiro said. "Otherwise you wouldn't have known of Rainwell."

"What about Chloé?" Mimi asked, wanting to remind everyone about their missing companion. They had been separated for so long, he hoped the nix was all right. "We should reunite with her at least."

"As much as I want to, I think we're running out of

time," Elliot said. "With Minari's death, I'm positive they're making their move."

"You believe they are heading to Rainwell?" Luka asked.

"I know for sure they're heading to Rainwell. I can't say why, but I can feel it. Something is there, and we need to stop them from reaching it."

"In that case, we need to leave as soon as possible," Hiro said, turning his attention to Owen. "Is there a way we can get the captain you were in contact with to sail to Oxing?"

"Oxing?" Owen asked.

"It's the kingdom of Astaria's port city. We're going to need to go there before we can reach Rainwell."

"How do you know how to get to Rainwell?" Mimi asked, raising his brow. The way Hiro had quickly decided their next plan of motion was suspicious.

"I've been there." Hiro's tone was clipped.

Mimi frowned, not appreciating Hiro's dismissive response. Hiro's role in the prophecy explained his knowledge, but the constant secrecy made Mimi uncomfortable. It was like he did not trust them, but what reason would he have to keep secrets? Were they not on the same team, working toward the same goal? Mimi knew Hiro cared for Elliot the same way everyone else did. The chimera felt frustrated by the human's aloof behavior, unable to understand what was driving his increasingly distant demeanor.

"Astaria, huh?" Sage mused. He and Mimi shared a single glance, both nodding in agreement.

Mimi had originally thought Etheria was the only place

he and Sage could live in. But learning of another continent opened the doors to new possibilities. Perhaps living freely without persecution was closer than Mimi had originally thought.

Just how big was the world?

The two of them had initially hoped Chloé's influence within the council would aid them in their search for a home, but because Chloé had been exiled, they'd had to scrap that hope. Now Rainwell, or anywhere in Astaria, represented their last chance at a true home.

"I will need to inquire with the captain to see if it is possible for us to venture to Oxing instead of returning to Solime," Owen said, breaking Mimi from his thoughts. "I will do my best to get us where we need to be."

"As long as it gets done," Hiro said.

"Thank you, Owen," Elliot said. He looked downward, clasped his hands together, and bowed. "I want to apologize for how sudden this was and for my recent behavior."

"No worries, Elliot," Hiro said. "It's good to have you back. I'll notify Boss of our decision. Hopefully Nighthawk can find a way to get Chloé to Rainwell. We need all the help we can get," he added, not giving anyone a chance to respond.

"How long will it take to reach Bunnie?" Elliot asked.

"Hard to say. I hear Ragnar and the king are making moves. No concrete details yet, but communication between us and them has been delayed by a few days. If I were to send something now, it might take anywhere from five days to a week."

"Wouldn't that cause problems?" Mimi asked. A delay of several days seemed excessive, especially given the urgency of their situation. Letting Chloé know where they were heading was crucial.

"Best-case scenario, it doesn't. But the rumors I've been hearing don't seem to be in our favor either," Hiro said.

"What are the rumors?" Elliot asked.

"I don't want to say until I know for sure the rumors have concrete evidence," Hiro started. "I don't want to cause unnecessary stress for us. We already have a lot on our hands."

Mimi's earlier suspicions resurfaced. He had set aside his doubts when they'd learned Hiro was a member of Nighthawk and his role as the hero, but the secretive behavior unnerved the chimera. It was as if Hiro only trusted Elliot and disregarded the rest of the group.

Perhaps Hiro felt the need to console Elliot, especially because of what had happened to Minari. But everyone was working toward fulfilling the prophecy, and it seemed like as long as you were not Elliot, Hiro did not care to converse with you.

Warrior or not, the human believed he didn't need to explain himself.

"But the rumor is the cause for the delay in messages," Mimi pressed. "Shouldn't we at least know?"

Hiro clicked his tongue, placing his hands on his hips. "If the rumors are true—"

"Let us say they are," Mimi interrupted. "We should prepare for what's to come. And if they aren't true, then it will be better for us. I would much rather prepare for something that doesn't happen rather than not be prepared for something that is going to happen." Mimi couldn't help but raise his voice.

"What is it, Hiro?" Elliot asked.

Mimi let out a soft huff, grateful Elliot interjected. Maybe Hiro would finally give an answer.

Hiro glanced at Elliot before letting out a sigh. "Okay. All right. Let's plan for this, then." He reached into his coat, pulling out a small piece of paper folded into a square. Hiro handed it to Elliot.

Elliot opened it, his eyes scanning the contents. His shoulders slouched, and he took a deep breath.

"What does it say?" Mimi asked.

"Thank you for showing me this," Elliot said, returning the paper to Hiro. "Chloé is part of the Nighthawks now," Elliot started. "She . . . no longer has the ability to use magic, but she is receiving training to fight without the use of her core." Elliot paused, his face draining of color. "The kingdom has declared war on the elves."

Mimi's eyes widened. He had not expected something so drastic.

"War?" Luka asked, his expression mimicking Mimi's. "King Valentine VI would not have made this decision himself. This is Ragnar's doing."

"They're going to find them . . ." Elliot whispered. "There's already nothing left of Mistfall. We have nothing. So why . . . ?"

Hiro placed his hands on Elliot's shoulders. "Let's not focus on this right now. Like I said, this is just a rumor. We don't know if it's true."

"But there's a possibility it is . . ." Elliot's balance began to sway, and Hiro helped him onto the bed. Elliot hunched over, hands pressing against his face. "This can't be happening."

"It's unlikely the kingdom will send troops to your village as soon as you may think," Luka said. "I am sure the king is recruiting knights, and they will need time to train. Remember, they believe the elves are skilled in combat. I'm certain he will want to prepare his men for the battle."

"Luka is right," Hiro said, rubbing Elliot's back. "It probably won't happen for another few months. By then, maybe the prophecy will be fulfilled and the kingdom will see the elves as heroes."

Mimi knelt in front of Elliot, placing a gentle hand on Elliot's knee. "We're in this together," he said. "No matter what happens."

Elliot leaned into Mimi, his forehead resting on Mimi's shoulder. Mimi wrapped his arms around the trembling elf.

"Thank you," Elliot said, his voice wavering.

Mimi felt warm tears soaking into his shoulder, and his heart clenched painfully. He desperately wished that he could do more, but he knew that sometimes simply being by someone's side was enough. Elliot's determination to continue the journey and fulfill his role as the oracle was ablaze, and Mimi would be there every step of the way.

Mimi stroked Elliot's hair, hoping it would help soothe the elf's worries, even for a brief moment.

14
GUILD

Chloé hesitated outside of Bunnie's office. Her hand hovered over the wooden door. She had received a summons request earlier from Oliver, and while it didn't seem like it was anything dire, Chloé couldn't stop herself from being nervous.

With a final deep breath, Chloé knocked on the door. "You wanted to see me?" she said, entering Bunnie's office.

Bunnie looked up from a letter she was reading. "Oh, Chloé! Yes, come in."

The office was smaller than most of the bedrooms in the inn, yet it held everything Bunnie would need. There was a small bookshelf with a few scrolls and books occupying the shelves and a desk for Bunnie to work at. A fireplace crackled in the corner, its flames providing warmth to the cozy room. Though it was still summer, the nights had become considerably colder.

It was unusual.

"I thought your office would be bigger," Chloé said. Her eyes swept across the room, stopping right in front of Bunnie's desk.

Bunnie chuckled. "Well, I never kept anything, just in case we ever got raided. Didn't want to leave any evidence behind." She nodded toward the bookshelf. "See those? They're just random books Oliver picked up during our trips. They don't really mean anything, and I haven't read them myself."

"That makes sense." Chloé felt silly for making that comment. The logic was obvious, making the nix feel naive for thinking otherwise.

"I wanted to show you this." Bunnie reached into one of the desk drawers and retrieved a scroll. She unraveled the ribbon and laid it across the dark walnut surface. "This is from the council. It looks like we received the approval to become an official guild of Etheria," Bunnie said.

The parchment was of high quality, as expected for a document from the kingdom. Each signature was clearly visible at the bottom, all eight remaining members having inked the declaration.

Chloé's eyes fixated on the royal family's wax seal. Even after spending years as a council member, this was the first time she'd laid eyes on it. All previous declarations had been approved and moved on without needing her signature.

The royal seal depicted a shield with a sword that lay diagonally across it, crowned with an ornate headpiece that was decorated in jewels. On each side of the shield were wings made out of flames.

"You changed the name," Chloé said, her fingers delicately grazing over the word. "Stryx."

"Technically, this is our name with the kingdom. I didn't want to give the kingdom our actual name. With how things are now, they don't deserve it." Bunnie rolled the scroll back up.

"Is there a reason you wanted to show this to me and not the others?" Chloé asked.

"I wanted you to be the first to see it." Bunnie placed the scroll back into the drawer before reaching in for something else.

"Any reason why?"

Bunnie shook her head. "I guess I just wanted to know your thoughts. We'll be swindling the kingdom right under their noses. I also had to submit the list of names of our officers." She paused, placing a pin on her desk. The pin was a falcon, its wings spread apart as if it were midflight, getting ready to lunge for its prey. The gold caught the light of the nearby candle, giving it a beautiful warm reflection. "I want you to have this."

"Me?" Chloé's eyes widened. "This is the symbol of an officer. It being gold means whoever wears this is of high rank." She shook her head. "How did you even get one for me? They know my name. I can't take this."

Bunnie chuckled. "They needed your name, but you no longer have your family name, right?"

"N-no . . . I don't. Did you give them a fake name?"

"Kind of." Bunnie pushed the pin closer to Chloé.

"Take it."

"What name did you give them?"

"If I tell you, will you accept the pin?"

Chloé hesitated, her heart beating uncomfortably against her chest. "What do you . . . What do you expect from me?" Chloé cast her eyes down, chewing the inside of her cheek. She was afraid to take on a role of such responsibility when her last one hadn't ended well. She'd been dismissed from her council duties and thrown into confinement because of the unlawful things she had done. She'd neglected her duties because she thought her beliefs were more important than the peace and well-being of the civilians of Etheria.

The cost had been steep.

The thought of disappointing Bunnie was unbearable. The nix had so much respect for the older human female. She had already shown Bunnie a side of her she didn't want anyone to see. She had been defeated and stripped of everything that defined her. She was left feeling vulnerable and powerless. To have been accepted as someone and welcomed into Nighthawk was something she would be forever grateful for. The idea of failing again and of showing weakness to someone she respected so deeply made her chest tighten with anxiety.

Bunnie leaned forward, her fingers intertwining beneath her chin. A gentle smile spread across her lips. "Whether you're aware of it or not, you inspire people. Some of our new recruits look up to you."

The words hit Chloé unexpectedly. Her jaw dropped, words stuttering from her mouth. Inspired? Her? She couldn't believe what Bunnie had just said. Surely, she must've said that just to persuade the nix to agree to become an officer.

Bunnie smirked. "I had a feeling that would be your reaction." She leaned back in her chair and crossed her legs. "The recruits know who you are, Chloé. You were once a council member who defied the laws and took things into your own hands. Even with the repercussions and consequences, you refused to stay down. You continue to rise and continue to believe what was right."

"I . . . But, how . . . ?"

"If you still don't believe me, Scarlet can fill you in."

"Scarlet hasn't been part of Nighthawk for that long—"

"Exactly. It doesn't matter how long someone has been part of this guild. They can see your dedication. The twins are difficult to impress, and even they noticed a positive change with the recruits. That's what I need in an officer, Chloé. Someone who can motivate and give energy to those around them. Someone like you. Even in the midst of despair, I know I can trust you to thrive."

Warmth blossomed in Chloé's chest. She didn't know what to think. Her mind swirled as she thought of how much of an impact she was making within the guild.

Chloé didn't need to be part of the council to make a change.

Sometimes the most significant transformations happened from unexpected places and through unexpected means.

With steady fingers, Chloé reached for the golden pin. She felt the cool metal against her palm. She pierced the metal piece through the front of her coat, securing it in its place.

There was no turning back now.

"I accept."

15
AWAKE

Lily sat cross-legged against the cool grass. She leaned back, gazing up at the cloudless sky. The stars glowed brightly, as if their eyes were bearing down on her, judging her for every decision she had made, every life she had taken.

But she did not regret a single one. Everything she had done was for a purpose. For a reason. In her heart, she knew this way was the only way she could free the world from cruelty.

Lily could recall the memory of Mykronos's first words to her as if it had happened yesterday. In actuality, it had been 320 years ago, but nothing could cloud the clarity of his voice.

Mykronos's powerful words had comforted her in the midst of her darkest times, soothing her of all her worries and woes. She lived in a small village south of Valquent. She couldn't recall the name or the people who'd lived there, but she could recall the countless soulless eyes that had bored against her very being. The plague had devastated the villagers. The doctors, those who were supposed to heal and protect, had fled in search of uninfected lands, leaving the sick to their fate.

Lily believed she was alone in the world. She locked her parents in their bedroom once she realized they had fallen to the plague. Days and nights were spent listening to their painful cries. Their fists would bang against the door, and their nails scratched against the walls. No matter what Lily did—humming, singing, covering her ears—she couldn't drown the harrowing noise out. They wanted her to know of their suffering. Each attempt to block out their cries only emphasized how utterly alone she was.

Lily had an older brother who had left the village prior to the breakout, promising to return with his closest friend, who had studied under a renowned doctor in Valquent. Lily had clung to that promise, believing he would be her salvation.

Reality could not have been crueller.

A mere two days after the noise from her parents' bedroom had ceased, a knock echoed through their quiet home.

Lily rushed to the door, knowing it had to be her brother and his friend.

But there was only one figure.

And the person on the opposite side was someone Lily didn't recognize.

The gentle and charming friend had been replaced with a grotesque figure. His once-shining blond hair was now matted, blotches of mud stuck in the strands. His clean, tidy clothes were now covered with holes and mud. His eyes were bloodshot. Drool dripped from the corner of his crooked lips, and dried blood stained his fingertips. He let out an eerie, inhuman groan when their eyes met. Lily knew her brother was lost to the plague. To Death's Kiss. The only reason his friend had returned here must've been because this was the only memory he could muster up in the midst of his delirium.

Lily had to end his life. That was the only way to save him. To save herself. Maybe that was what he wanted. He hoped his friend's little sister would relieve him of his suffering. But in doing so, he had also admitted that her older brother had failed. He had broken his last promise to her.

Lily took a deep breath and released it through her lips. She chuckled to herself. Why had she decided to bring up those memories? They weren't pleasant in the slightest and served absolutely no purpose.

Lily glanced over at Minari. He lay next to her, one hand resting against his stomach and the other against his side. His chest rose and fell in gentle motions. He had been peacefully asleep for eight days now. And those eight days felt gruesomely long. Ragnar had ordered her to stay by his side to ensure no one else found him. But who was going to go out of their way to look for him? The oracle and the others had watched her kill him. They had no reason to seek out a corpse.

She was getting restless as her patience was growing thin.

"Just how long are you planning on keeping me waiting?" Lily muttered, scoffing at Minari's still form. "You made me wait before, and you're still making me wait now. Do I need to kill you again? Or do you find this slumber enjoyable?"

As if hearing Lily's words, Minari twitched, and a shudder left his lips. His chest expanded as he took a deep breath, and his eyes fluttered open. His once-purple right eye was now gray, matching his left eye. He blinked a few times before turning his gaze to Lily.

They stayed in silence, taking in each other's presence.

"Rhea?" Minari—no, Valor—was the first to break the silence. She hadn't heard that name in such a long time. It unleashed waves of memories and emotions she found difficult to contain.

Rhea's chest tightened as she bit back the tears that were severely threatening to fall, struggling to maintain her composure. "Valor." Her suspicion had been correct. The Necromancer spirit that dwelled in Minari was her older brother's closest friend.

Valor leaned up and looked at his hands. He clenched and unclenched his fists a few times, experimenting with his mobility. "I can tell this body is agile and went through physical training. Though I'm a little stiff at the moment."

"You have been sleeping for eight days now," Rhea said. "Lying on the ground there probably didn't do you any good."

"What year is it?"

"Year 1350."

"Three hundred and twenty years," Valor mused. "How many of us have awoken already?"

"You're the last one."

A familiar smirk crossed his features. "I'm always late to the party."

"You died, and that still didn't change," Rhea joked.

"What's the plan now? Since I'm the final one, I'm guessing we should head to where it all ended."

"Hypothetically, we should, but Ragnar probably has a plan he wants us to follow."

Valor furrowed his brow. "Ragnar . . ." He pressed his lips together. "Ah, is he Father's host?"

Rhea nodded. What was that expression?

"I should apologize the next time I see him. I was quite rude to him before. Well, this body was rude to him before. Though I should be thankful I ended up in this one and not in a useless body." Valor paused, examining himself. "This one is definitely better than the first one I had."

"You lucked out. I was surprised you were still able to control your powers, even though you were asleep in that body."

"Even though I was asleep, I was able to see what was happening as if I were dreaming," Valor said. "I saw everything that occurred while I was in this body." Valor's lips curled into a small smile. "It's unfortunate for those three. I almost feel sorry for them."

"Who?"

"Elliot, Minari, and . . ." Valor turned to look at Rhea. "Lily."

16
ROYALTY

Arielle moved quickly down the familiar hallways of the castle, her footsteps muffled by the plush, crimson carpet beneath her feet. The walls were painted a cream color with golden accents meeting the crystal chandeliers that hung off the ceilings, illuminating her path.

Arielle's father had just released a royal decree. Throughout her life, she had accepted both her father's and Ragnar's decisions without question, but this announcement of war against the elves was insane. Why would they announce war against the elves? Just because two had made it down into the lower lands hardly meant they posed a threat to the kingdom.

When humans ventured into elven territory, the elves never announced they demanded to go to war. They remained silent, letting the kingdom do as they pleased.

And even though none had returned since venturing into the mountains, the kingdom had never ceased their curiosity. They continued to send men through unknown territory, not realizing the risk it could've posed to the kingdom. At any point, the elves could have raided or declared war, yet they were quiet.

Despite being a princess, she had been deliberately kept away from matters of politics, history, and military strategy. Her skills were focused solely on the superficial aspects of royal life: musical performance, needlework, and the art of polite conversation. That was all her family wanted for her. She was a princess. A delicate figure of royalty.

They wanted to keep it that way.

And she was tired of it all.

For seventeen years, she had submitted to her family's wishes. Seventeen years of being treated as something so delicate that she could easily break. Perhaps they babied her due to what had happened to the late queen. But regardless, why treat her like she was in some sort of prison? She had no freedom to be herself.

Arielle paused in front of the family's painted portrait. She looked up, admiring the genuine blissful expressions everyone wore. She was about four years old when the royal painter had created the piece.

King Valentine VI stood proudly next to Queen Ainna on the left, who sat upon the throne. Arielle's older brothers, Elias and Alexander, stood to the right of Queen Ainna. Elias was on the left with Alexander on the right. Arielle stood in front of her brothers in the center. The five of them wore their traditional royal attire, dressed in full crimson silks adorned with golden trim.

Arielle's father had deep brown hair while her mother had bright blond hair. Arielle and Elias had inherited their mother's locks, while Alexander had inherited their father's. Queen Ainna had bright olive eyes. King Valentine's eyes were a brilliant purple shade in the painting, which was in contrast to the dull ones he had now. They were never the same after Queen Ainna passed away. And Arielle was the only sibling who'd inherited Queen Ainna's eyes.

To say the least, Arielle was a spitting image of the late queen.

"Princess Arielle!" The sharp voice of her personal assistant blared behind her.

Arielle suppressed a sigh. Eve had been trailing after her all morning and would not leave her alone, no matter how much she requested Eve to leave her to her thoughts.

"Princess Arielle! I finally found you," Eve started as she caught her breath. "Please do not abruptly leave like that again. You instructed me to brew black tea, and when I returned, you were gone! You know you have a piano lesson today. The king would be furious if you arrived late or missed this lesson."

Arielle tuned out Eve's lecture. She didn't want to hear how much her father expected her to do this or to do that. She needed to find her brothers and ask them what was going on. She wanted to understand the reason for this decree.

"Princess, are you listening?" Eve asked, cutting through Arielle's thoughts.

"Yes," Arielle huffed. "Now, will you please leave me alone?"

"I cannot do that, Your Highness. Your tea is waiting for you back in the study room, and your presence is needed in the piano room shortly. Instructor Iris will be here any moment."

"Eve, it is barely past noon. Iris is scheduled to arrive at two. I have time." Arielle struggled to keep her voice level. She had to remain poised.

"That may be true, but I cannot let you wander on your own."

"And why is that?" Arielle placed her hands on her hips. "My two brothers wander this place alone all the time. Why do I get treated so differently?" she snapped.

"That is because the king wants to ensure your safety." Eve frowned. "Princess, you are aware of this."

Arielle wanted to fight back. But she knew even within the walls of the castle, she was not safe. No one was.

Queen Ainna had been murdered within these walls.

Arielle's memories from when she'd found her mother's lifeless body were fuzzy. She could not recall who had found her or where they'd taken her after she found Queen Ainna dead in her parents' chambers. But she did remember seeing the culprit.

Arielle recalled seeing someone jump from the large window into the storm. From his size, he must have been someone young. He wore a feathered black cloak, hiding his face, so Arielle couldn't make out who it was. But the one who'd been executed for treason was not the same person Arielle had seen escape through the window. A chimeran servant had been sentenced to death. A servant Arielle had been close to.

Zane.

He was a chimeran dog.

Zane's sole purpose within the castle had been to prevent any passing of poisoned food or water. He'd been tasked with protecting the royal family at all costs.

Unfortunately, the doctors believed Queen Ainna's cause of death was poison. And the one person who was to prevent that from ever happening was Zane. They'd ignored Arielle's words, claiming she had been experiencing shock and her memory had been fabricated as a result.

The following morning, they'd executed Zane and the entire kitchen staff working that night.

Life within the castle walls had never been the same.

"Arielle? What are you doing here?" Elias asked, rising from the stairs. "Shouldn't you be in the study?"

Arielle clenched her fists. Those few words were enough to make her blood boil. Why did everyone think she needed to be somewhere? Why couldn't she just be where she was because she wanted to be? It was as if she did not have any free will. She was like a marionette being strangled by her marionettist.

It was suffocating.

She hated it.

Elias was the middle child between the three of them. His appearance was clean; not a single strand of hair was ever out of place. His belt was never crooked, and his boots were always pristine. Arielle knew Elias put a good amount of effort into his appearance. And she knew Elias had his own struggles. No matter what he did, their father never gave him recognition. He always favored Alexander's words, even if Elias spoke of the idea first.

But Arielle was still envious of Elias's opportunity to learn the ways of the kingdom. If illness was to strike King Valentine VI, either Alexander or Elias could take over the crown. Arielle wouldn't even be taken into consideration.

"Arielle?" Elias called out. "Why are you spacing out?"

"I was not," Arielle said, gritting her teeth. "I was taking a walk. The study room can be suffocating sometimes."

"Is the room too small? You never complained before."

Never complained? Arielle scoffed internally. It was not that she never complained. Her complaints had never been heard because no one truly listened. Her feelings, her thoughts, and her desires were all dismissed or overlooked in favor of maintaining the perfect image of a proper princess.

"Anyhow, you know you are not allowed to be unaccompanied. I heard Eve calling for you from below the stairs. Even if she's here now, you know you are not to be separated from her."

"I know that." Arielle's voice was sharp, breaking her poised demeanor. "I know Eve is to be with me at all times. But sometimes, dear brother, I would like to be alone with my own thoughts. Now, if you will excuse me, I will be returning to the study room since that is where I am to be expected," she spat, full of spite.

Arielle turned on her heel, ignoring Eve's frantic calls

for her to slow down as she strode back toward the study room.

17
HOPE

"I thought the original oracle was from Mistfall," Errol started. "That was what we were all told." He bit back the bitterness in his voice. Another lie.

Azriel blinked. "Interesting."

"The scrolls and books from that time did not mention anything of a place called Rainwell," Stella said. "At least, none that I can recall. There are no records of any other elven village other than Mistfall, so we all believed that was where she was from."

"I assume Alder has never mentioned Rainwell or Astaria," Azriel said.

"No, he has not," Errol said. "We only thought the world was as big as the kingdom of Etheria."

"I can only assume it was to protect us," Azriel said. "It makes the most sense to keep this place a secret, but desperate times call for desperate measures. And now is as desperate a time as I have seen."

"We lost our home," Silas said. "We were displaced."

"But why?" Stella asked. "Why keep this place a secret? If our ancestors knew of this place during the war, we would not have had to hide deep in the mountains. We could have escaped here."

Though Errol hadn't lived through the civil war or the early days of their people's displacement, the weight of past events and decisions pressed down on him now. His mind wandered to how different their lives would have been if they had known about Rainwell, the peaceful existence they could have had. He wouldn't have needed to recruit scouts, to send them on endless patrols, to train their people for combat.

They wouldn't have lost so many lives during the last attack.

Mayleen would still be alive.

Errol pressed his fists against his lap. He suddenly did not have much of an appetite. The food before him lost its appeal.

"It seems the mood has soured," Azriel said as if sensing Errol's discomfort. "I apologize if I said something to offend you."

Errol shook his head, forcing himself to relax. "It isn't your fault. It isn't your fault that your home was kept a secret from us."

Azriel frowned. "I am positive Alder has his reasons as to why he kept this place a secret."

"Not just Alder," Stella said quietly. "Vylantra as

well . . ."

"We could have saved so many lives," Errol said. The faces of fallen comrades flashed through his mind. "So many sacrifices were made because this place was hidden from us."

"Nothing can bring them back," Silas said. "But what we do from here on out can change the fate of future generations. We won't need to live in fear."

"No, nothing can bring them back . . . but this could have all been prevented."

"Errol, we shouldn't be focusing on things we can't change. We need to focus on the things we can do," Silas said. "We need to focus on rebuilding what we've lost."

Errol knew Silas spoke reason. But the more reason Silas spoke, the more the anger inside him grew. He didn't want to acknowledge that things were simply the way they were. To accept things because it was just beyond their control.

Errol slammed his hands against the table, rattling the bowls and cups. "You're telling me to just ignore everything? To forget what we've been through? To move forward while everyone we lost will forever remain in place?"

"Errol, you know that's not what—"

"Enough!" Errol seethed. He squeezed his eyes shut, biting back frustrated tears that threatened to fall. "This place was kept a secret from us. And not only that. Alder lied to us. He said this place would be vacant, yet here we are, intruding on someone else's home." He took a shuddering breath. "A man can only take so much betrayal before he breaks."

The air was heavy, and no one uttered a single word. Errol could feel everyone's gaze on him, waiting to see if he would say anything else. But what could they say? Silas was right. Nothing they said or did would bring back the dead.

When Errol finally opened his eyes, the initial heat of his anger had cooled, leaving behind exhaustion in its wake.

"I apologize," Silas said softly. "I spoke out of line. I didn't realize how much this weighed on you."

"Out of all of us, you are the one who suffered the most," Stella said. "I am positive Alder and Vylantra kept this place a secret from us for a good reason."

Errol bit the inside of his cheek, tasting blood. What reason could be good enough? What justification could possibly balance against the weight of their losses?

Errol stared down at the table. He shouldn't have lost control like that. He shouldn't have let his emotions get the better of him. Mayleen had entrusted him with her role. He was supposed to be their leader. He was supposed to be strong, stoic, the pillar of support. Yet here he was, crumbling and breaking down over the revelations of Rainwell's secrecy. It was pathetic of him.

It was not Azriel's fault the divine beings had kept Rainwell a secret from them. It was not fair to blame him. The other elf was probably just as bewildered as they were regarding the secrecy. Perhaps Alder and Vylantra had kept this place hidden as a final sanctuary, a last resort should their people face extinction.

Errol pressed his face into his hands, elbows resting on

the table. He let out a deep sigh. "You do not need to apologize, Silas. You did nothing wrong. I shouldn't have behaved like that. It was uncalled for." He lowered his hands, meeting the gaze of his comrades. "You're right. We should move forward and not dwell on the past. We have to do what we can for our future. To honor those we lost and to keep hope for those who are still here."

Errol turned his attention to Azriel. "Azriel, please let me thank you properly for allowing us into Rainwell." He rose from his seat, slightly unsteady from his outburst earlier, but he pushed past it. He made his way, standing before Azriel. Errol paused, gathering his courage. "But first . . ." The elf took a deep breath before offering a deep bow before Azriel. "Please accept my apology for my outburst just now. It was out of line, and as the leader of Mistfall, I should not have lashed out. You have shown us nothing but kindness and hospitality. And for that, you have my deepest gratitude." Errol rose before giving Azriel another small bow. "Thank you. From us and from all of Mistfall. Thank you for giving us a new place to call home."

"Please, there is no need to be so formal," Azriel said, placing his hands on Errol's shoulders, urging him to lift his gaze. "After everything you've been through, this is the least we could offer."

Errol opened his mouth to speak, but Azriel raised a dismissive hand. "Errol, the elves of Mistfall are my kin. We may not have known of each other's existence until recently, but I assure you, the bond we share runs deeper than what you may think."

Azriel placed a hand against his chest. "When Alder contacted me regarding Mistfall's demise and your plan of escape, it struck me deeply. Straight to my very soul. I couldn't even attempt to fathom the emotions you all had to go through. You are elves, just as we are. Our home is your home."

Errol was speechless as Azriel's words washed over him.

For centuries, the elves had needed to live in fear and on high guard when it came to meeting anyone outside of Mistfall. Anyone they met had always been hostile, wanting to cause them harm. When he had made the decision to leave Etheria, he feared they would experience the same hatred and disgust as they once had.

But here, there was none of that.

Instead, they'd found kindness. Hospitality. Hope.

Errol choked as tears welled up in his eyes. They spilled, cascading down his cheeks before he could stop them. All the fear, the doubt, and the grief he had been holding back came rushing out at once.

Azriel's, Silas's, and Stella's eyes widened. Their voices jumbled together as they called his name.

"Captain, are you all right?" Silas's voice was frantic.

"What happened?" Stella's concerned voice called out.

"Errol?" Azriel questioned.

A smile tugged at Errol's lips, and warmth swelled in his chest. Their worried voices only made his tears fall harder.

They would be all right. Everything would be okay.

Tomorrow brought a new day, a new dawn for the elves of Mistfall.

And this time, they wouldn't be facing it alone.

18
SHOULDER

Several days had passed since the Mistfall elves' arrival in Rainwell. Each day blurred into the next as Errol watched his people and their ovis settle into their new haven. The Rainwell villagers did their best to aid their new neighbors in any way possible, ensuring they felt comfortable and at ease.

But now that the initial rush of activity had subsided, Errol felt the familiar bitterness of betrayal creeping back into his thoughts.

The elf wandered across the fields, each step taking him farther and farther away from the bustling village. A soft breeze carried the sweet aroma of flowers through his senses. It reminded him of home, yet home had never truly been this beautiful. Rainwell possessed a vibrancy that Mistfall never had. Their village was more open, homes spread comfortably across abundant land. What they had in Mistfall was enough. Just enough. They couldn't afford to be picky when they'd been forced to leave the lower lands and start anew in the mountains.

They'd not had the privilege to spread out.

Move too far north and the winters would be too harsh. Move too far south and they'd run the risk of being discovered by the humans or anyone else who opposed them. Mistfall's location was precise and calculated. Small enough to be under Alder's protection and large enough for them to survive.

Errol would be lying to himself if he said he wasn't jealous. The constant twisting of his gut as he surveyed Rainwell's prosperity was unbearable. Why had Mistfall been the one to suffer? Why had his people been the ones to face such hardships? Why had they been excluded from knowledge that could have saved them?

Errol's feet carried him to the edge of the river that cut through the fields, finally bringing him to a stop. The water was crystal clear, and the riverbed's stones' vibrant colors danced under the ripples of the water. He knelt down, his solemn expression reflecting back at him. He hadn't noticed how much his features had changed throughout the ordeal, how much his eyes had dulled, and how gaunt his face had grown.

Errol scoffed at the reflection that looked back at him. What right did he have to look this terrible? To look so defeated? He had the luxury of being alive. To be breathing. He should be happy. Grateful.

Errol cupped his hands, darting them into the water,

and sent the water across the grass, distorting his reflection.

"Errol!"

The sudden voice startled him, causing his heart to race against his chest. He hadn't sensed anyone approaching him, a mistake that would have been detrimental in Mistfall.

Luckily, he recognized the caller.

But when had he become so lax?

Azriel gave Errol a gentle smile. "I apologize if I interrupted anything. It looked like you were meditating, so I didn't want to come closer until I got your attention." He lifted the two wooden buckets in his hands. "I came to fetch some fresh water. It's nearly dinner, and little Rayna was nagging at me to get more water for tonight's meal."

Errol shook his head, shame creeping up the back of his neck. The leader of Rainwell had once again seen him lash out like a child, had seen him during his moment of weakness. "No . . . no, you didn't interrupt anything." He kept his gaze cast down to the river, unable to meet Azriel's eyes.

Azriel closed the distance between them. He knelt down and dipped an empty bucket into the water, allowing it to fill the container. "Sometimes when my emotions get the better of me, I like to come here to calm down." Azriel lifted the full bucket, placing it against the ground before filling the second one. "I come here to empty my mind as I take in the sound of the running river and breathe in the fresh perfume of the flowers."

Azriel set the second bucket down on the ground next to him, then settled himself onto the grass. "When Alder contacted me regarding your arrival, I was pretty shocked, to say the least." He let out a small chuckle. "You can imagine how I felt when I had to somehow inform everyone that they'd need to start sharing their homes with complete strangers."

Errol's eyes widened slightly at Azriel's confession. His tone of voice was more casual, completely different from when they first met.

"I was frustrated when Alder left." Azriel shifted, crossing his legs and relaxing his posture as his gaze became fixed on the horizon. "It was my first time hearing of elves other than those who lived in Astaria. Of course, I knew there were other continents and kingdoms, but I didn't know there were other elves. Alder didn't give me a choice in the matter." He chortled. "Imagine having an entire village forced out of their homes and needing to provide room and board for them. Without warning, the pressure of ensuring their safety and comfort was suddenly in my hands."

Azriel paused, his expression softening. "As the leader of Rainwell, it was my duty. I couldn't simply shut my doors when my kin was in danger. Luckily, everyone here felt the same way." A gentle smile crept across his lips. "Perhaps I was just lucky. Lucky to have the opportunity to lead elves with such kind hearts."

Errol's earlier frustrations disappeared. His chest warmed as his heart reached out to the other leader.

Azriel was someone who truly understood the weight of leadership.

The constant responsibility, the isolation, the need to

appear strong even when doubt gnawed at your resolve. He was someone who knew what it meant to make sacrifices for their people, to carry the burden of every life under their protection.

Errol knew Azriel's words were meant to comfort him and distract him from his worries, but they were doing more than that.

Errol felt like he finally had someone he could lean on.

As a leader, Errol was responsible for every elven life that was left in Mistfall. Just like how Azriel was responsible for every elven life in Rainwell. When the decision had been made to abandon Mistfall and venture to new and unknown lands, there hadn't been a single objection. Perhaps Errol was just as lucky as Azriel. To lead a group that believed in him. Even through the hardships of losing their village, they still remained hopeful and believed in his judgement.

Errol's vision started to blur as tears began to well in his eyes. He blinked, attempting to push them back, but it only succeeded in making them fall. He turned away from Azriel, hoping the other elf hadn't noticed his abrupt display of emotion.

A hand pressed against Errol's shoulder. He stiffened momentarily, then quickly relaxed. The simple gesture comforted him.

Errol breathed, closing his eyes. He let the feelings cascade down his cheeks as they sat together in silence, bathing in the warmth of the setting sun.

The clatter of dishes and the splash of water filled Azriel's small kitchen. Errol was currently staying with Rainwell's leader for the time being. At first, he was supposed to live with Silas and Stella, but the home they were staying in was already surpassing its comfortable capacity, a result of a small miscalculation. It was obvious fitting in another person would make the living conditions less than ideal. The villagers had been insistent about maintaining adequate space for everyone's well-being, refusing to crowd their new housemates into cramped quarters.

Errol had been taken aback at first with the modesty of Azriel's home. It was smaller than the one Silas and Stella were residing in. He had expected the leader to have at least one of the larger cabins, remembering how Mayleen and Minari's place had been double the size of this one.

"Thank you for helping me clean," Azriel said as Errol wiped down the last corner of the dining table. "You know you didn't have to. You're a guest here."

"As a guest, I should at least do my part to help," Errol said, making his way to the kitchen sink. "Rayna looked like she was coming down with something."

Azriel chuckled, extending a hand to take the rag that Errol was holding. "I appreciate it. Truly. Little Rayna probably got overly excited and overexerted herself with all that happened this past week. A good night's rest will perk her back up." Azriel wrung the rag before draping it over the faucet to dry. "You know, Errol, I've been meaning to ask you something."

"What is it?" Errol asked.

"Do you want to know the true origins of the oracle?

How the prophecy came to be?"

"I . . ." Errol was caught off guard by the question.

"I ask you this because I believe you have the right to know. And it might help you prepare for what is to come."

"What do you mean?" Errol furrowed his brow. Were they not safe here? He didn't want to bring any misfortune to Rainwell—not after everything they'd done for them.

"Your child is the oracle, is he not?"

Errol's eyes widened, his stomach dropping. "How did you know that?"

"You seemed to be the most sensitive whenever there was a mention of the prophecy, specifically how it was common knowledge here and how the facts differed slightly. It led me to assume someone you knew was the oracle. And the way you behaved around Rayna reminded me of how a father would be around their child. It only made sense that the oracle was your child. If not yours, I would have guessed it was Stella's brother, or someone else who was possibly close to you."

Errol merely blinked, completely lost for words. Ever since he'd stepped foot into Rainwell, it was like his ability to conceal his thoughts and emotions had disappeared, abandoning him and leaving him out on display.

Or was it because being around Azriel made Errol this way?

Melvin had been Errol's closest friend, and when he passed, Errol only had his late wife, Estelle, and Elliot to keep him company. He'd drowned himself in scout duties to avoid forming new attachments, keeping his worries locked tightly inside. He'd kept all his thoughts to himself, never letting anyone else know what tormented him. They had not needed to know his burdens.

Azriel smiled. "I'll make us some tea. Why don't you go ahead and take a seat?"

Errol nodded.

Perhaps it was time to stop carrying everything alone.

19
PROPHECY

There was a comfortable silence between Azriel and Errol. Neither of them spoke as Azriel finished boiling water and poured it into the teapot. The room immediately filled with the sweet aroma of rose petals and chamomile, reminding Errol of countless evenings spent in Mistfall. Azriel placed the kettle down before picking up the tray and making his way over to the dining table. Azriel waited a few minutes before pouring the tea into the small teacups and taking a seat across from Errol.

"Thank you," Errol said. He wrapped his hand around the cylindrical cup, the warmth seeping into his fingers. "The aroma reminds me of home."

Estelle appeared in his mind. She would always have a cup of rose-and-chamomile tea before going to bed. It had soothed her, helped her sleep.

"I hope it brings fond memories," Azriel said, his voice gentle.

The corners of Errol's lips curled into a small smile, his chest filling with a wave of nostalgia. His thoughts swirled back to the quiet days they used to share. To the cozy dinners they used to have. The image of her smiling at him with her soft blue eyes flashed before him, as vivid as if she were here, sitting beside him now. She always had a habit of tucking her emerald hair behind her ear before drinking her tea.

All of it had ended when Errol learned Elliot was the oracle. It had shattered their peaceful existence. Nothing he said or did could've changed that. Elliot's path was predetermined and had already begun unfolding, leaving Errol little to no time to prepare.

Errol would never forget the day Elliot had left Mistfall. The memory was etched deeply into his mind. How tormented Estelle was to see him go. The way she wailed day and night, scratching at the door and attempting to pull the door handle. Errol hadn't had a proper chance to bid his son farewell, too preoccupied with Estelle.

In the deepest depths of Errol's heart, he hoped Elliot could forgive him. Forgive him for his inability to protect his mother when she was unjustly murdered. Forgive him for allowing his grandmother to meet the same fate. Forgive him for letting the village down and allowing its demise, leaving behind only memories of what it had once been.

"I apologize." Azriel's voice broke through Errol's thoughts. He reached into his pocket, pulling out a soft, tan handkerchief.

Errol touched his cheek, surprised to find it wet. When had he started crying?

"I didn't mean to bring back hard memories. Here," Azriel said, offering the soft cloth.

Errol accepted the handkerchief, dabbing it against his cheek. "I . . . I did not realize I was crying." His voice came out rougher than he'd expected.

"You seemed lost in thought for a moment. I wasn't going to interrupt, but when I saw you tear up, I wanted to make sure you were all right."

"Thank you. I'm all right."

Azriel smiled. Errol was grateful the other elf didn't try to push the topic further.

"If that's the case, then let us begin. Though I want to warn you, what I'm about to tell you I don't want you to take negatively. Do not think about our differences, but try to understand why our stories may differ from each other," Azriel said.

Errol nodded. "That seems fair. Go on." His tone was neutral but attentive.

"As you know, the original oracle was Myru. She had the task of protecting the world from the uprising Necromancers. She had four companions with her, known to us now as warriors. She also had her most trusted keeper. The keeper was known as the hero."

"Why was the keeper known as the hero and not the oracle herself?" Errol frowned. Having someone else claiming Elliot's burdens and struggles as their own did not sit well with him.

"Essentially, it's because he was the only one who survived. And he should still be alive today."

"Alive?" Errol's eyes widened. "How could he be alive? That was over three hundred years ago."

"He was cursed with immortality. I wouldn't wish immortality on anyone—not even my most hated enemies." Azriel paused. "At the time, Myru couldn't bear killing the Necromancers, no matter how dreadful their actions were. She had a pure heart. She saw them for what they were at their core: hurt souls. They were in pain. Constantly mourning. They had lost their loved ones and had been led astray. Myru did not want to kill them—not without giving them a chance."

"But they did so much damage. Killed innocents. They were the reason all of this happened."

Azriel nodded. "It's not that I disagree with what you're saying, Errol. I'm simply stating she couldn't bring herself to stop the Necromancers."

"So, what then? Vylantra tasked her with stopping the Necromancers, and because she was not able to, Elliot has to continue where she left off?" Errol bit his lip, taking in a deep breath. He needed to calm down. He was beginning to overreact again.

"To say it plainly . . . yes. Because Myru was not able to fulfill her duties, the prophecy, as you know it, came about. Though I want to believe that this time, our oracle will be successful."

At first, Errol was hopeful Elliot would fulfill the prophecy. Something in him wanted to believe it was a simple task. But he came to the cold realization that thinking that way was foolish. There was nothing simple about the prophecy.

Errol knew how soft and gentle Elliot was, and his son had never liked causing or bringing about any kind of trouble.

Errol couldn't imagine Elliot taking the lives of others.

Would Elliot find the courage to stop the Necromancers from wreaking havoc upon the world? Or would he succumb to his gentle nature just as Myru had before him?

Errol took a sip of his tea, attempting to distract himself from the creeping endless thoughts.

"This village was the final resting place for Myru and the Necromancers. Underneath Rainwell lie the bodies of the Necromancers."

Errol's eyes widened as he nearly spilled his drink from his mouth. He promptly placed the cup back on the table. "Underneath?"

Azriel nodded solemnly. "During the final confrontation, Myru cast a binding spell on the Necromancers and placed a banishing spell on their souls, but it was only temporary. It would only be a matter of time before they were drawn back to their original bodies. Without them, their souls would have remained lost in the ether forever. She hoped that whenever the time came, she would have the strength and dedication to fulfill the task as she was set out to do."

Errol clenched his fists. If what Azriel was saying was true, it was apparent Myru had used all of her strength in order to seal the Necromancers and, in doing so, prevent the rise of Mykronos. But at what cost? She'd sacrificed herself because she could not bring herself to kill them. Errol hoped Elliot wouldn't do something so foolish. "What about those who were with her?"

"They sacrificed themselves in order to gain enough time for Myru to seal the Necromancers' souls. With their borrowed strength, they were lost during the battle."

"And how did the keeper fall into the curse of immortality?"

Azriel shook his head. "That is unknown to us. We just know that he has been alive all this time and cannot die. He has tried to take his own life numerous times to no avail."

Errol's hands shook as he clenched and unclenched his fists, his body filling with dread. There had to be something he could do to stop history from repeating itself. If Elliot failed the prophecy, the others' lives would be in danger. He couldn't let Mayleen down—not when she'd entrusted Minari to him. And Stella would have no family left. It would be a devastating blow.

Errol let out a heavy sigh. "What can I do? What can I do with this information you've given me? What can I do so this doesn't happen again? How do I stop this cycle?"

Azriel placed a hand over Errol's, giving him a light squeeze. "I can only imagine what you must feel, Errol, but do not let this responsibility crush you. What your son needs right now is for you to believe in him. To trust he will make the right decision. The rest is up to fate."

Errol's shoulder slouched. "You're right . . . I have to trust Elliot. I know he will make the right choice." He paused, his throat tightening. "I just cannot help but feel like Myru and Elliot are similar to each other simply based on what you've told me. I'm afraid history may repeat itself."

Azriel listened quietly. His hand still hadn't left its firm position over Errol's.

"What do you think will happen, Azriel, if Elliot were to follow in Myru's footsteps?"

"We must be prepared, no matter what the outcome may be. That is our responsibility as leaders." Azriel gave Errol's hand another squeeze. "But as a father, there is nothing that can prepare you for the pain and anguish of losing a child."

20
MUSIC

Arielle couldn't feel the keys beneath her fingers or hear the tones the grand piano was emitting. Her body moved automatically, playing purely by muscle memory. Iris, her instructor, had taught her this song a few weeks ago. It was not like any classical songs she'd practiced before; rather, it was something Iris claimed he'd written himself.

When Iris had first presented the song to her, he hadn't provided a name, insisting there wasn't a name fitting for it quite yet. The piece was like a disoriented waltz, yet it somehow conveyed a sense of desperation and longing. It was the complete opposite of what Arielle was used to playing. The classical pieces were elegant and refined, designed to showcase technical prowess and proper form. Iris's piece was raw and emotional, as if demanding vulnerability from its performer.

Arielle had been hesitant to learn it at first because she knew if her father learned about this deviation from her usual curriculum, he would fire Iris immediately. Her father had always insisted on pure classical training, viewing anything modern or experimental as beneath them. Normally, Arielle wouldn't mind having another piano instructor, since she'd had plenty over the years, but there was something that drew Arielle to the piece. Iris was not afraid to express his feelings to the princess. He was not afraid to express his vulnerability to her, showing her that even he, an instructor, could be human with his own passion and wishes.

Arielle felt that connection.

Arielle had wanted to learn the piece from Iris, regardless of what the king might think. She wanted to create music that evoked how she truly felt, not just the perfectly polished performance expected of her. The classical pieces felt like a cage. This piece felt like freedom.

Iris had agreed to teach her the unnamed piece, but she must also practice the usual curriculum King Leonard VI had instructed him to teach Arielle. Eve had promised to keep Iris's piece and Arielle's practice of it a secret, and Arielle was surprised that she'd actually kept her word. She had always thought Eve would report anything to her father—every detail, no matter how small.

As excited as Arielle had been at the beginning, today her heart and mind were elsewhere.

And Iris could see through her lackluster performance.

"Princess." Iris's voice cut through the dull music notes. It was sharp but not unkind. "What do you think you are doing right now?"

Arielle removed her hands from the piano. "Apologies. My mind is filled with nonsense right now." She looked up at her instructor. "Please allow me to start from the beginning again."

Iris merely looked at her, his lips pressed together. His sharp, deep amethyst eyes scanned Arielle up and down, as if analyzing how capable she was at this very moment. His long, platinum hair was tied into a high ponytail and styled in soft, wavy curls, letting a few pieces loose to frame his face. His cream blouse and dark brown slacks hugged his body, complementing his slight curves. His bright red heels were a trademark of his. Though he was an ethereal, he chose to keep the feathered wings on his head hidden.

"Your brothers again?" Iris tilted his head, his expression softening.

"Is it that obvious?" Arielle frowned.

"Princess, I have known you for two and a half years. Though it may seem I am only just your piano instructor, I am good at reading people as well. I pay close attention to my students. If something is troubling them, it is my duty to try to calm their worries." Iris knelt, placing a hand on Arielle's knee. "Were they being overprotective again? You've mentioned it to me before."

Arielle heaved a heavy sigh. Even though Iris had known Arielle for two and a half years, it felt like he'd known her all her life. The way he understood her and comforted her was something she longed for in her family. Yet they were only good at ignoring her and insisting her worries were minuscule and unimportant in comparison to what they normally dealt with.

Iris was the first person after Zane who listened to her without any judgement. He would allow her to speak fully, without any filter, taking in every detail and only offering his thoughts if Arielle was willing to listen to them. Arielle felt like she could finally breathe.

"You know me too well, Iris," Arielle confessed.

Iris chuckled. "Only what you are willing to share. I'm positive Eve would've reported me to the king by now if you said something to me that I shouldn't be hearing."

Arielle glanced behind Iris to look at Eve. Her personal assistant stood with her back straight, hands clasped together in front of her. Eve's brown hair was straight, cut slightly above her shoulders. She wore a white blouse and a red vest with gold trim and buttons. Her matching knee-length red skirt hugged her feminine body, and she stood on black heels. There was a gold brooch right below the collar of her blouse, the royal crest marking her as a loyal and trusted servant of the crown.

Eve's hazel eyes met hers. She smiled, giving Arielle a slight nod.

Even though Arielle found it unnerving at times when Eve would hound her to fulfill her so-called princess duties, she would be forever grateful for the times Eve allowed Arielle to be free. Those small moments of rebellion, carefully hidden from the watchful eyes of the royal court, had become precious to her.

And right now, she was giving Arielle free rein of her choices.

"My father recently issued a royal decree. I'm sure

you've heard . . ."

Iris nodded. "Yes, he is recruiting anyone who is willing to join the knights in their efforts to defend our land from the ever-threatening elves." Iris chortled. "I can hardly contain my fear," he mocked, clearly disagreeing with the king's decision.

Arielle smiled, appreciating the mood-lifting gesture. "Unfortunately, I don't agree with that decision, and I can see you do not as well. But no matter what I say, my father and two brothers will not listen. I am fully disregarded. Sometimes I don't even know what I'm supposed to do. I'm getting tired of not being able to contribute to any of the decisions." Arielle sighed, her shoulders slumping. "I feel like a decorative piece."

Iris shook his head. "Do not say that about yourself, Princess. You are so much more than that. I can see how brave you are in your eyes, the devotion and love you would give to something that was truly important to you."

Arielle's cheeks warmed. "I'm not so sure. I've never had the opportunity to try, so how could you know for sure?"

"Simply put, I can tell by your music. The strong desire in wanting to learn a personal piece I created rather than a classical one. The way you learned and put your heart into the song. Though it's a piece I created, you turned it into your own. It's different from mine." Iris turned to look at Eve, pausing before returning his attention to Arielle. "Princess, what I am about to offer you may come as a surprise, but I want you to know you have complete control of your answer. I will not think of you any differently, and our relationship will not change. Do I have your permission to proceed?"

Arielle was taken aback by the statement, her heart beginning to race. She blinked, glancing between Iris and Eve. Did Eve know something about what Iris wanted to tell her? What was the relationship between the two of them? "Iris, I trust what you're about to say will be in my best interest. So you may continue."

Iris bowed his head, placing his right hand over his chest. "Princess, please do not feel betrayed by what I will now tell you. I am loyal to you as your piano instructor, though this is not the only role I play."

Arielle held her breath, her mind racing with possibilities. Was Iris actually one of her father's advisors? Were Iris and Eve working together to keep tabs on her and report her activities to the king? It made sense if it was true. It was a valid reason as to why they continued to remain silent as she and Iris grew close. Had she been a fool for trusting him?

Arielle bit the inside of her cheek, biting back the tightness in her chest.

"Eve and I are actually part of a guild. Unofficial, though officially undercover," Iris said, his voice barely above a whisper.

Arielle blinked. What?

"We are members of Nighthawk, though registered under the kingdom as Stryx due to the royal decree King Valentine VI issued," Iris continued.

Arielle was at a loss for words. She had so many questions swirling in her mind. Had he and Eve infiltrated the kingdom? What did they want with her? Were they disappointed that they'd been assigned to the useless princess instead of one of her brothers? Were they confessing who they were before killing her out of pity?

Arielle's eyes darted between Iris and Eve, waiting for their first move, her body tensing.

"Princess, I can sense your distress. You need not worry," Eve said, smiling from her position. "Iris and I mean no harm to you. In fact, we are here to offer you an escape."

"An . . . escape? What do you mean?"

Iris stood, taking ahold of Arielle's hand, leading her up to her feet. "Princess, we would like to offer you a position as a member of Nighthawk. Joining us would mean you will be able to finally breath. To freely express yourself without the pressure of your royal status. But this offer is not without its requirements. Joining us would also mean turning your back on the kingdom."

"You want me to betray my family?" Arielle pulled her hand away, shaking her head. "You know I can't do that."

"At first glance, it may seem so, but with the current state of the kingdom, it's the only way to save the kingdom." He closed the distance between them, his lips resting close to her ear. "King Valentine VI announced war against the elves. It's a mistake that could cost not only the kingdom, but the entire world. We should be allying ourselves with the latter. We need them if we are to fight the true enemy." Iris paused. "The end is near, Princess Arielle. We must be hasty with our decisions."

Arielle opened her mouth before closing it again, her

mind reeling. Everything Iris had said could make him be tried for treason. Siding with the elves? Turning her back on her father's decision and the royal decree? If she was caught discussing this with Iris and Eve, not only would their lives end, but perhaps her own as well. She did not have the slightest idea what her father would do to her if he found out what they were alluding to.

Yet she couldn't stop herself from wanting to take the risk. She would be free from the suffocating grasp of her family. She wanted to do something with her life. She wanted to make an impact. A change. A difference. She didn't want to be the little princess who did whatever her father and brothers wanted her to do. What they expected her to do. Arielle was her own person.

And perhaps it was time to prove it.

Arielle straightened her shoulders. "What would you have me do?"

21
ECHOES

Valor and Rhea had left the chimeran village and teleported right outside the gates of Valquent. They walked across the bridge, feathered black cloaks draped over their shoulders. The guards paid no mind to them, allowing them through the gates without batting a single eye.

They made their way through the busy chatter of the night scene. The city had changed drastically since he last remembered being here. Vibrant, colorful lights hung off the edges of the rooftops, illuminating the city. They made it appear as though it were day rather than night. The streets buzzed with vendors and city folk who were eager to see what was new and what they could spend their coin on. Children ran through without a care in the world, their laugher echoing through the streets.

Valor's memories of Valquent were filled with

desolation and ruin. The plague that ravaged the city had torn through it, stripping it of any life it had. Doors barely hung on their frames, creaking in the wind. Claw marks etched deeply into the wood from those desperate to escape or enter. Shattered glass had littered the sidewalks and alleyways, crunching beneath the feet of the infected. Abandoned buildings and bodies were left to rot, their decay permeating the air. Bloodstains had painted the walls and ground, illustrating stories of the city's final moments.

Valor's chest swelled as he observed the incredible transformation. The survivors poured their heart and soul into reviving the city. He'd never imaged it could return to its former glory. It was perhaps even better than how it had been before. It was amazing what devotion could do. It was as if the harrowing site had never existed.

Valor's eyes briefly caught a performance in the city square. A singer stood in the center, and three violinists stood behind the star performer. The singer's flowing white robes seemed to shimmer from the city lanterns. His powerful voice commanded the audience to heed him, to listen to his fighting spirit. His hands danced through the air with elegance and grace, weaving a tale of resilience and hope.

Valor had not seen the singer before, yet the violinists all seemed familiar. He was certain he had seen them before—or rather, the host of his body had seen them before.

Something small suddenly collided with Valor, hitting him at his waist. He looked down to see a child quickly rushing away to catch up with her friend.

"Come on, Minerva already started! We need to find a good spot so we can see them!" the child's friend called out behind her.

Valor blinked. That was why the performers looked familiar. His host had seen them back in Venin.

"Valor." Rhea's voice tore Valor's attention away from Minerva. "Keep your eyes ahead. We're already running late. Father won't be happy."

Valor nodded, suppressing his urge to linger and watch the performance. "Apologies. Let us hurry."

Valor and Rhea finally made it to the gates leading to the castle. Rhea looked at the guard, flashing him something in her hand. The guard nodded once before opening the large metal gate, letting the two of them through.

"What was that?" Valor asked.

"The royal crest," Rhea responded. "No more questions. We need to move."

Valor didn't push the topic further, despite being curious as to why Rhea had an item from the royal family in the first place.

Valor followed Rhea through the courtyard, rushing down the stone path, their steps silent, proof that the two of them were merely borrowers of their bodies. They would always remember their original owners and the training they had gone through, the muscle memory persisting even after death.

They entered through the castle doors and made their way through the halls. Valor's skin prickled as he felt the familiar dark thread pull at his senses. The others were here with Father. As Rhea led him through the cream walls, the feeling grew with each step.

Rhea stopped in front of a door. Before she could knock, Ragnar's voice rang on the other side.

"Come in. Rhea. Valor."

Valor's heart skipped a beat, and he caught his breath as soon as Ragnar's voice reached his ears.

Was he going to be upset with how his host, Minari, had treated him?

Was he going to punish him for not having a better hold on Minari or taking control of this body sooner?

Rhea must've sensed his distress, as she took ahold of his hand, giving it a slight squeeze before releasing it. She opened the door, the hinges squeaking quietly at the movement. Valor flinched at the noise, not used to his sensitive hearing.

Valor's gaze didn't wander as the two of them entered what appeared to be Ragnar's study. Through his peripheral vision, he saw two others, one of them being another familiar face. Searching through his memories, he recalled the human male as Aiden.

The other was a human.

The human had curly, deep red hair that stopped at his chin, framing his face. His stature was on the smaller side. Perhaps the body had been killed before it went through its growth spurt, forever frozen in adolescence.

But for some reason, Valor could not sense which spirit lay in which host. His senses felt muddled, cloudy. He was able to see what they were but not who they were. It was not as clear as when he first saw Lily as Rhea.

"The two of you took long enough," Aiden said. "Who knew you were the last Necromancer?"

"Shut it, Aiden," Rhea said, her voice sharp.

Aiden shrugged, casting a mocking smirk at Valor.

Valor clenched his hands, flexing them open and closed. Going through Minari's memories, he could see the elf had numerous years of training. But that did not come without death. The young elf had killed more than he could count. He'd devoted himself to protecting their little elven village. If he met with anyone who posed even the slightest threat, they were greeted by his blades, their life ending abruptly.

"This body is an assassin," Valor said. "I can let you taste death once more if you want to mock me again."

"Valor, stop," Rhea said. "He's just obnoxious."

"Valor?" Aiden raised his brow, scoffing. "You call him by his true name but don't call me by mine? I'm hurt, Rhea."

"Do. Not. Call. Me. That." Rhea's white eyes narrowed as she glared at Aiden. "No one is allowed to call me that except for him."

Aiden clicked his tongue. He nodded toward Valor, crossing his arms. "You're nothing special. Why does she even favor you?"

"I see nothing has changed between you three," the human said. "And you know how it feels to be called by our true name, Aiden—or shall I call you Mason instead?"

Aiden shivered, holding himself. "Gross."

"I rest my case," he said. "For some reason, our bodies do not appreciate being referred to as someone other than the host's name unless you are Father." He paused, turning to Valor. "I am Hazel, but you may call me Raven."

Valor could now feel the Necromancers' spirits more accurately, as if hearing their voices cleared his senses. Aiden was Mason. And Raven was Hazel.

But where was Rurik?

There were only four of them here.

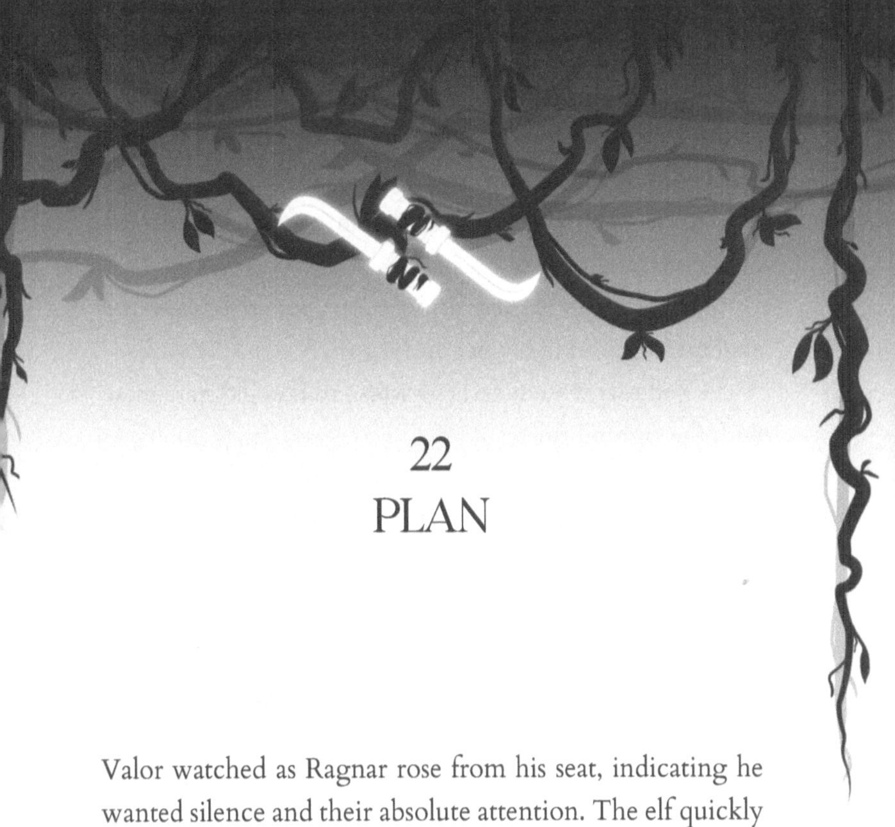

22
PLAN

Valor watched as Ragnar rose from his seat, indicating he wanted silence and their absolute attention. The elf quickly knelt down, bowing his head, the others following suit, their movements swift.

"As you all know, I did not summon you here to listen to your childish banter." Ragnar's voice was stern and strong, each word resonating through the office.

Valor closed his eyes, his head throbbing painfully with each syllable Ragnar spoke. The pain only intensified.

"To show me such behavior at such a crucial time . . . I ought to punish you all." A pause. "But I have no time for that. I summoned you here to issue out your final mission."

Valor couldn't breathe. Every word Ragnar spoke was as if a thousand knives were piercing his body, each word driving deeper into his flesh. He clenched his eyes tighter, trying to focus his attention on anything else but Ragnar. But he knew the attempt was futile. Valor's very existence was to serve Ragnar, as he would eventually become Mykronos.

The god that would bring ruin upon the lands and eradicate misfortunate once and for all.

A god that would reset the world so it could start anew with the rightful ruler.

There was no place for the two gods.

Vylantra and everything she'd created had to perish.

Failure was not an option.

"Valor."

Valor choked out a breath. He forced himself to look up at Ragnar. His breathing came out in ragged puffs, his entire body running cold as his vision blurred. He slowly realized the office only contained him and Ragnar. The others had already left, leaving the two of them alone.

But when had everyone left?

How long had he been kneeling here by himself?

Was Ragnar going to punish him for how Minari had tried to attack him?

"I have a special mission for you, Valor."

A small yelp escaped Valor's lips. Every time Ragnar said his name, it felt like a blade was being driven into his heart, twisting into the organ. The pain was unlike anything he had experienced before.

"You are to become Princess Arielle's new royal guard and knight. I will see her old one dismissed. I want you to monitor her."

Valor didn't have time to contemplate who Princess

Arielle was. He merely nodded, gritting his teeth against the overwhelming agony coursing through his body.

"Follow her wherever she goes. Inform me of her activities and who she talks to. I want everything in detail."

Valor broke his gaze and clenched his chest. He couldn't feel anything, yet his nerves felt like they were on fire. Every small breath he took intensified the burning sensation throughout his body.

"If you believe she may plot against me or the kingdom, I want you to kill her. Do not even hesitate."

Valor swallowed, struggling to find his voice. When he tried to respond, a viselike grip encircled his throat, preventing him from speaking. He choked and clawed at his neck, desperate for air.

"Do not betray me."

In an instant, the torture vanished. Valor collapsed forward, his arms barely supporting his weight. He took in deep gulps of air, sweat dripping down his brow. The pain was gone, but his body trembled, tingling in the torment's wake.

"The others have already gone on their mission. You are dismissed."

"Y-yes, Father," Valor managed to say, his voice low and rough. He stood slowly, his legs threatening to give out beneath him. He left the study, closing the door behind him.

Valor's vision returned slowly. He blinked, looking down the hallway he and Rhea had come from. He was certain what he'd felt was Ragnar's way of punishing him. For letting his host get out of hand and for not making his host perish sooner. He must have ordered Rhea to kill him.

Ragnar did not trust him to perform the simplest of tasks.

It made sense. The political implications were clear. Ragnar couldn't leave the castle, at least not until all preparations were complete. What better way to keep an eye on Valor than within the castle walls?

Even after all these years, no one but Rhea truly trusted him.

Valor vowed not to make the same mistake twice.

A castle maid led him to his living quarters shortly after Valor was issued his assignment from Ragnar. The maid spared no pleasantries when she spoke to him. She kept her words short and curt. Valor was not sure if the woman was frightened because of his position or because his body was an elf. The prejudice against elves remained constant, regardless of the changing times. Humans were still fearful and skeptical.

The following day, Valor was introduced to Princess Arielle and, true to Ragnar's words, was appointed as her royal guard and knight. His duties required him to shadow her movements and remain stationed outside her living quarters throughout the night.

Being a Necromancer meant he didn't require sleep, making his duties possible. Unfortunately, the elven body he inhabited did need rest. After the first night of standing guard, he noticed his movements became sluggish. It was unnoticeable to the untrained eye, but Valor could feel the slight delay in his reactions.

Princess Arielle's days were precisely scheduled. Rather than attend political meetings like her elder brothers, she was subjected to activities that made her appear softer and more feminine. Something more befitting of a princess. Her days were filled with practicing her needlework, musical lessons, and social etiquette.

After a week of staying awake, Valor was not sure how much longer the elf's body could handle this. It was showing signs of severe strain. He found himself in a daze more often than he would like, and there were moments where sounds would fade entirely. He rubbed his hands over his face, attempting to resist an incoming wave of exhaustion. He was once again standing in front of Princess Arielle's quarters. The hallway was dim and quiet. If not for the moonlight that bled through the tall windows, Valor would have been in total darkness.

A quiet whisper caught Valor's attention. He froze, straining to locate where the noise was coming from.

The whisper was soft and gentle. Murmurs seemed to come from all directions, but Valor did his best to focus on the voice.

There.

The voice came from below.

But Valor was currently on the third floor of the castle. Below him would be the grand ballroom. The area should be vacant at this hour.

The voice grew slightly louder, but only for a moment, as if it was beckoning Valor to follow. The only presences he felt on the floor were those belonging to the royal family, who slumbered peacefully in their chambers, and their guards, who were stationed outside their doors.

Without a single thought, Valor left his post, confident he would return before the others could notice his absence. There was a pull in his chest, urging him to heed the whisper's call. Each step he took closer to the grand ballroom made the hair on the back of his neck stand.

Valor took a breath before pushing the grand doors open and slipping inside.

23
WONDER

Valor's eyes widened at the sight before him. He was certain he'd entered the grand ballroom, but where he'd ended up was certainly not the ballroom.

Valor was in a rose garden.

And behind Valor were not the same doors he'd walked through. They were gone, replaced by a long stone trail leading to a tall metal gate. The moon above him was unnaturally large and oppressive, looming dangerously over him as if it had eyes and were watching him closely, observing his every move. Its presence felt malevolent, as if it could perceive not just his presence but the very rhythm of how shallow his breaths had become. His instincts warned him, advising him to remain completely still and that the slightest movement could send warning signals to whoever ruled this realm.

The faint whisper from before suddenly echoed through the thorny branches, and the invisible force that demanded Valor remain still vanished. He drew in a careful breath through slightly parted lips, exhaling slowly through his nose. His body straightened, and he realized only then how tightly he had curled in on himself.

Valor walked through the garden, eyes scanning to see if anyone else was here. Darkness would've enveloped the sea of flowers if not for the moon and magic that wove throughout the air. The roses emitted a soft glow, as if illuminated from within, their petals ranging from pristine whites to delicate pinks to deep crimsons.

As Valor reached for one of the petals, a sharp stinging sensation sparked from his fingertip into his arm. He quickly jerked his hand back, the sudden pain and numbness leaving him gasping, body shuddering as his chest filled with frozen air. Despite the roses being in full bloom, there was no life force emanating from them. The entire garden was as dead as it was beautiful.

Then again, there was no life in him either.

"What are you doing here?"

Valor froze, the whispers from earlier now a clear, distinct voice.

"You should not be here."

Valor's eyes narrowed. The voice was familiar. A memory deep within knew who the voice belonged to, but he could not form a face. The figure behind the mysterious words was just barely out of reach.

"You need to leave. Now."

Valor opened his mouth to question the mysterious

speaker, but the moment his lips parted, a violent wind tore through his body, stealing his breath. The ground beneath his feet vanished, and he found himself hurtling through the air.

Valor grunted as his feet landed on solid ground. He staggered backward, colliding against a door with a loud thud that echoed throughout the hallway. He placed his hand against his chest, attempting to ease his racing heart. His breaths came out as ragged gasps, and cold sweat clung to his back. Though his senses screamed with alertness, they felt frayed and scattered. He glanced around, attempting to calm his confusion.

Valor was back in the royal wing in the castle.

The door behind him cracked open.

"Valor?" Princess Arielle's soft, tired voice came from within. "What was that noise?"

"Nothing," Valor managed to say, forcing himself to steady his breathing. He cursed at himself, hearing his voice crack. He cleared his throat. "It was nothing. Please return to your chambers."

There was a slight pause. "If you are tired, then I can permit you to rest. I can let Father know to switch out your night duties with another knight. Everyone else does that."

Valor shook his head. "That will not be needed."

Arielle sighed. "I appreciate what you have done for me, Valor. You have been the most diligent guard for me, but at the same time, I am aware of how much it drains you. Do you sleep?" she asked, clearly concerned.

"My duty is to protect you, Princess Arielle. Please return to your chambers." Despite Valor's burning curiosity about the rose garden and what had just transpired, his primary task was to report the princess's activities and whereabouts. He would not let his curiosity betray Ragnar's trust.

Valor let out a breath he hadn't known he was holding when he heard the door behind him click closed. He listened to Arielle's footsteps treading back to her bed before she returned to her covers, settling herself underneath the warmth.

The Necromancer's mind wandered back to the mysterious voice. He replayed their message over and over, attempting to find who the voice belonged to. Though the more he tried to visualize it, the more he realized his memories were beginning to blur and overlap.

Valor attempted to weave between his various existences. His original life, when he first became a Necromancer, all the hosts before, and his current one. The timeline between them grew increasingly muddled. Though he could recall specific events and locations, their chronological order eluded him. He knew what events had happened and where they'd occurred, but he could not determine when they had happened.

Which memory was he trying to reach for? The deeper he delved into his mind, the more confused he became.

It was as if there was someone else. Someone else he hadn't accounted for. Past memories that weren't his own.

A female silhouette formed in his thoughts, her features obscured but familiar. He could make out her outline, but her form remained shrouded in gray. Valor attempted to grasp any detail that might bring her image into focus. He concentrated on her eyes, imagining different colors until something resonated.

Sharp pain shot through Valor's skull. He winced and pressed his hand against his head. It felt as if someone had driven a blade into his brain, twisting it in every possible direction before impaling his skull with another. The corners of his eyes watered as he tried to ride out the agony.

Crimson.

Crimson was what Valor had last seen before the piercing pain exploded in his head. The owner of the voice had red eyes—he was sure of it. But that was all he could manage to remember. Everything else remained locked away.

Valor took deep breaths through clenched teeth, the pain slowly subsiding. His head still throbbed, though he would take it over the excruciating pain he'd felt prior.

Valor sighed in relief as the sensations ended, yet what was left in their wake was pure emptiness. His mind went completely still, devoid of thought, while his body grew increasingly heavy. He shifted position, leaning against the cold stone wall and sliding down to the floor. Feeling fled from his arms and legs as the strength to keep his eyes open rapidly diminished.

As the last bit of consciousness slipped away, the darkness around Valor enveloped him, pulling him down into the pit of the abyss.

24
ALWAYS

"What makes you think you can protect her?"

"What do you mean by that? I've been training my whole life for this." Noé tried to hide the annoyance in her tone, but she couldn't stop herself from frowning. The question struck deeper than she wanted to admit, echoing doubts she'd pushed aside since leaving Rainwell.

Yumie shook her head. "Sorry, Noé, that came out wrong." She tucked her knees underneath her chin. Her shoulders tensed as an icy breeze passed.

Autumn was ending, and they weren't ready for the rapidly changing season, especially since the sun never came out. When it was day, the temperatures rose just enough to keep them barely comfortable. But when night fell, they wished for another layer of warmth covering their bodies. The darkness seemed to seep into their bones, making even the simplest tasks feel heavier.

"We've trained our whole lives to protect Myru," Yumie began, "but sometimes I wonder, what makes us think we can do anything against the hands of destiny? What makes us special? Why were we chosen?"

"Why were we chosen, huh?" Noé agreed with Yumie, her gaze drifting to the starless sky. Why had they been chosen? What about them made them different from the others back home?

A familiar knot twisted in Noé's stomach, the same one she'd constantly feel when she doubted herself. The nervousness and the unknown gnawed at her, threatening to overwhelm her carefully maintained composure.

"Hey." Yumie's voice broke through Noé's endless internal questioning. "I . . . I didn't mean anything by it. Sorry."

Noé shook her head. "No, you're right. It's something we've both been wondering since we began training."

"And we both agreed not to question it." Yumie reach over and held Noé's hand. The other elf's touch was warm against the night's chilly air. "Questioning why we were chosen isn't going to get us anywhere. What we know now is that we have to protect Myru and help her fulfill the task Vylantra gave her by defending the world against the Necromancers. That is our duty and the reason we are here now."

Noé sighed, softly gripping Yumie's hand in hers. "Right."

"Remember that you're not alone, Noé. You have all of us here with you. Myru. Allix. Kana. Me." Yumie paused.

"And Hiro."

"You still don't trust him?"

"And you do?" Yumie raised a brow.

Noé chuckled. "I trust Myru's judgement. And maybe that is what we need right now. We just need to trust one another; otherwise, the darkness will devour us and we'll lose our way."

Yumie leaned in, resting her head against Noé's shoulder. Yumie's soft curls tickled Noé's cheek, but she ignored it, leaning in against the warmth. The gesture reminded her of days back home when their biggest worries were wondering when they would see each other next.

"Thank you. I think I needed to hear that," Yumie whispered. "I was starting to doubt us."

Noé smiled. "We'll get through this together. All of us."

"I can't wait until we can go home . . ." Yumie mumbled. "My garden is probably all dried up by now."

Noé closed her eyes, calling back the memory of when Yumie had first showed her her garden.

Yumie had originally kept the garden her secret. It was a safe place, somewhere she could truly be herself. But then it had become their secret, a hidden sanctuary where the weight of their duties couldn't reach them. As Myru's protectors, they were trained to maintain constant vigilance, to strike swiftly and without hesitation. But in the garden, Yumie could embrace the colors of life, nurturing her flowers and watching them grow and blossom.

Yumie took great pride in the primroses in her garden. She had them in every color one could possibly imagine, ranging from pastel pinks to vibrant corals, deep blues and bright purples. They would brush against one another at the slightest breeze, swaying gently like a wave of colors.

Noé remembered the way Yumie's eyes would light up whenever she danced through her garden. Whenever her fingers gracefully caressed the petals. It was as though they responded to her, returning the love and affection she showed them.

It was there, among the blooms and gentle breezes, that Noé had first realized she had fallen in love.

Noé's training and scribe duties were her identity. She had never entertained the thought of finding love and had never believed she would ever experience it. She'd done her best to bury the undying feeling of affection she had for Yumie, but the more time they spent together, the more difficult Noé found it to deny her growing feelings.

The night before they left Rainwell changed everything. Noé's father had announced which protectors would be leaving the village with Myru to fulfill the divine task Vylantra had bestowed upon her as the oracle. Even through all the training and preparation she'd had her entire life, Noé must not have done a good job hiding her nervousness.

The next thing she knew, Noé found herself in the dead of the night, wandering through Yumie's garden. The petals glowed against the moonlight. Darkness did nothing to dim the colors of life of the flowers. The sweet scent distracted her, allowing her mind to slowly calm down from the whirlwind of worries. She let herself be embraced by the primroses, her eyes closing as she relaxed in the moonlight.

And that was when she felt soft lips press against hers.

The feeling left as soon as it came, and Noé's eyes slowly opened.

No words were said between them, but they both knew what the kiss meant.

Fear.

Worry.

Anxiety.

Nervousness.

Affection.

Noé wrapped her arms around Yumie, bringing her body close. The familiar comfort of her presence helped steady her racing thoughts, reminding her that whatever challenges lay ahead, they would face them together.

Yumie pulled away and plucked a pale red primrose from a nearby bush. With gentle fingers, she brushed Noe's hair aside and delicately placed the flower behind Noe's ear.

"I'll always be there for you," Yumie said, cupping her hand against Noé's cheek. Her eyes held the same determination Noé had fallen in love with. "No matter what. If you lose your way, I'll help you find it again. Together, we'll make it home."

Noé leaned into her touch, allowing herself this moment of vulnerability.

Tomorrow, they would embark on their new journey, facing whatever dangers and unknowns awaited them.

But for now, Noé gave Yumie her entirety.

25
SIX

"Chloé, can you hear me?" Concern laced Bunnie's voice as her gentle hands carefully brushed Chloé's hair away from her face. The touch felt distant, as though coming through layers of fog.

"Huh?" Chloé gasped, blinking rapidly. She felt like she was asleep in a dreamless slumber before waking up abruptly, unaware of what had happened before.

The nix glanced around, trying to orient herself. She was sitting in one of the meeting rooms. She squinted, attempting to clear her vision. The faces of her fellow officers blurred at the edges as she rubbed her eyes, fighting against the persistent sleepiness. Blinking again, she saw the worried looks the other Nighthawk officers gave her.

"Chloé?" Bunnie asked again. "How are you feeling?"

"What do you mean?" Chloé pushed back the slowly

returning fatigue, straightening in her chair. Had she not slept enough the night before? She hadn't felt this exhausted when she woke up that morning.

"We were in the middle of discussing the next steps of our plan when you suddenly zoned out," Deveran said. "You sat there staring blankly. We tried calling you, but you wouldn't respond."

"I even said I would kiss you, but you still sat there unresponsive," Oliver said.

"Oliver, that information didn't need to be shared," Lavender said, crossing her arms and leaning back against the wooden chair. "Matter of fact, Chloé, best you just forget about that."

Chloé's eyes darted between the voices. She recognized them, but the longer she kept her eyes open, the more her vision blurred. Their features were starting to mesh into a sea of colors. "I apologize. I must not have gotten enough sleep last night. I know this is an important meeting. The first we've had since declaring ourselves as Stryx." Chloé needed to pull herself together. The rest of the guild was here, focused on the task at hand. She couldn't waste everyone's effort just because she hadn't gotten enough sleep.

A quiet knock on the door interrupted her thoughts. "Excuse me," an unfamiliar voice said from the other side. The doorknob twisted before the door opened, revealing a figure Chloé had never seen before.

"Welcome, Asher," Bunnie said, smiling at the newcomer.

"Did I miss much?" The tall figure strode gracefully

across the room, taking an empty seat next to Lavender. Though he did not have wings on his head, Chloé knew he was an ethereal. No other race could manage the same elegance. "I was caught up with my duties in the castle."

"I take it that means you have good news for us?" Bunnie asked. "What you tell us will determine how we go from here. But first . . ." She paused, turning her attention to Chloé. "This is Asher, also known as Iris when he's performing. I don't believe you two have met."

Chloé opened her mouth to speak, but Asher spoke first.

"Everyone, I would like you to leave the room," Asher said, his voice stern and authoritative. "Bunnie, you may stay."

"Is something wrong?" Oliver asked.

"Nothing concerning you," Asher said, his tone clipped. "Please leave. I will notify you when we can resume the meeting."

Without another word, Deveran, Oliver, and Lavender stood and left the meeting room. The sound of the door closing behind them seemed unnaturally loud in the sudden silence.

"I suspect you sense something," Bunnie said. Reaching over, she held Chloé's hand, giving it a gentle squeeze.

Asher nodded. "Chloé, you are a nix, are you not? Ex-member of the council?"

"I am." Chloé frowned. What was Asher getting at? Did he know something of her past?

Asher extended his hand, his palm facing upright. "If I

may, Chloé, please place your hand on top of mine."

Bunnie released her hold, giving the nix a nod.

Chloé hesitated, uncertainty coursing through her. She was sure Asher was someone she could trust since he was another officer of Nighthawk, yet it did not sit well with her that she had never met him or heard of him. Why had he decided to make his appearance now?

"Chloé," Asher said, his tone void of the urgency and demand it'd had earlier. It was soft. Comforting. "You can trust me. Believe me, I do not wish any ill fortune to come your way."

Taking a breath, Chloé placed her hand atop Asher's. Almost immediately, a wave of warmth rushed into her body, rapidly flowing through her veins. It spread across her entirety, making even the tips of her toes tingle. The sensations were odd but also intoxicating. The feeling collected in her chest, and she felt as though she were floating. Her senses sharpened as she began to hear the ticking of the grandfather clock in the corner of the room and smell the calming aroma of the chamomile tea in front of her.

Chloé saw the definition in Asher's face and the silkiness of his platinum hair. His deep purple eyes sparkled as he looked at her, like a pair of perfectly cut amethysts.

Asher pulled away, and the sensation he brought quickly went with him. "How do you feel?" he asked.

Chloé placed a hand against her chest. Her fatigue was completely gone, and her mind was sharper than it had been in a while. It was as though she had been placed in an entirely different body. "I feel good."

"I'm glad. Unfortunately, this feeling will only be temporary."

"What do you mean?"

"Chloé, have you not sensed that something has changed within you? Rather, something is missing?" Asher frowned.

"I have been feeling tired lately, but I assumed it was just because of all the training I have been doing," she responded slowly, unsure how she should answer.

"You sense it, then?" Bunnie asked the ethereal. "What she's missing?"

"Yes." Asher nodded. "Her body lacks a magic core."

Chloé bit her lip. She hadn't wanted others to know that she no longer had her core. It made her feel weak. Defective. Like less than what she was supposed to be.

Asher's expression softened. "Chloé, how long have you been feeling this way?"

"I . . . I am not too sure," Chloé said quietly, shaking her head.

"How long has it been since you lost your core?"

Chloé racked her brain, trying to remember when she'd last seen her father. The memory felt both recent and impossibly distant. "I'm not too sure. Perhaps two months?"

"I see. Then it would be safe to assume you have been feeling the effects of your missing magic core for about two to three weeks now."

"Fatigue?" Chloé asked.

"Not just fatigue. Your senses will start to disappear as well. Your body relies on magic to survive. Without it . . . it will only be a matter of time before your body collapses."

Chloé froze. What did that mean? Was Asher telling her she only had a matter of time before her body gave out? She still wanted to do so much. She'd finally found a place for herself to truly be free. She needed to meet with Elliot and the others again. There was still so much world for her to explore, so many experiences to have.

"Is there nothing we can do?" Bunnie asked, her voice barely a whisper.

"I can transfer my magic to her, but without a proper home for it, my magic will eventually seep out of her body. That can slow down the deterioration, but . . ." Asher's voice trailed off.

It was clear what he was trying to say.

"How long?" Chloé asked, forcing the words out. "How long do I have?" She balled her hands into fists, her knuckles turning white.

Asher shook his head. "I do not know for certain. What I can tell you is no more than six months. And that is with my help."

Chloé pressed her lips together, trying to still the quivering that threatened to overwhelm her. "The others. I don't want the others to know," she said. "Please."

"Of course. This stays between us," Bunnie said, reaching out to Chloé again, giving her hand a squeeze. Chloé could feel the small tremble in Bunnie's hold.

"How often will I need to receive magic from you?" Chloé asked, trying to focus on how she could remain present rather than focusing on the fears of the certain end.

"As soon as you begin feeling the same kind of fatigue, please come to me. I will no longer be within the castle, so you will be able to find me easily."

"Your mission was a success, then?" Bunnie asked.

Chloé was grateful for the subject change.

"Yes. I wanted to report it, but I believe Chloé's situation was of more importance. I could see how worried you were for her. And I could sense how weak her body had gotten without magic."

"You will never cease to amaze me, Asher. Never failing a mission and always observant," Bunnie said. "Chloé, I have a new mission for you," she started.

"Yes?"

"Your duty is to supervise Princess Arielle and see that she takes part in Nighthawk training. Ensure that her identity is not revealed to the others and especially hidden from the royal family."

26
SENTINEL

It was a miracle that Owen and Luka were able to persuade the ship's captain to set sail to Oxing instead of their original route. Elliot was not sure how often Etheria residents ventured outside to other continents, but the captain's confidence suggested this wasn't his first time navigating unfamiliar waters. Throughout their journey, not once did the seasoned mariner display even a hint of uncertainty about their course.

Two weeks into their sea travel, Elliot caught the thinnest line on the horizon. As time passed, the thin line expanded into buildings, growing larger and larger with each passing hour. And soon, an increasing number of vessels began to join their route.

Some were cargo ships, like theirs, varying in sizes. Some were small, nimble fishing boats. And some had elegant wording on the side of the boat, carrying other travelers.

"We'll arrive by nightfall," Zarek, the captain, said, his rough voice breaking through the ocean winds. His skin was deeply tanned and rugged. He was shorter than most male humans, but that didn't stop him from having a firm presence. He kept his thick, dark gray hair in a shorter cut and had piercing, pale blue eyes. "You folk have an idea of where to stay?"

"Siren's Dwelling," Hiro answered, not missing a beat.

"Aye, that's a good place. Has the best soup in all of Astaria." Zarek took a deep inhale of his pipe, blowing out the smoke in one fluid exhale, his hand never leaving the helm. His eyes suddenly narrowed. He twisted the helm around, causing the ship to make a sharp left turn. Elliot reached for the edge of the boat, holding on to it for balance. The cold air whipped against his skin.

"What's going on?" Sage asked, dropping to a crouch. "Why are we turning away?"

Zarek didn't respond. He continued steering the ship, sailing it away from their destination. His lips were pressed together, brow furrowed as his eyes darted back and forth. "You're not normal folk, are ye?"

Elliot's blood ran cold. Had Ragnar detected their location? Was he trying to intercept them? But Luka had mentioned Ragnar's influence couldn't reach this far away from the kingdom. Surely they had already crossed the border between the two territories.

Pure-white ships materialized out of the sea mist, cutting through the waves with supernatural speed, sailing in their direction. With the speed they were going at, it didn't seem like they were concerned about colliding with them. In fact, it looked like that was what they were aiming for. Their speed didn't slow; rather, it increased as they approached.

"Those ships are Her Majesty's," Zarek said, his voice tense, yet it was void of any fear. "And they don't show themselves unless she's hunting ye. The tales of my fallen brethren are all I have of them now. And I'm not too keen on following them into the depths of the sea." Zarek huffed, his hands maneuvering the helm in an attempt to keep them off their trail. "But you lot do not have one ship on ye tail—ye have three of Her Majesty's ships. I don't even want to know what ye've done to trigger her to send out three of her sentinels on you."

Elliot's stomach sank. Was Zarek referring to the ruler of Astaria? The queen? But why would the queen be coming after them? The relief of it not being Ragnar quickly gave way to something even worse. He gripped the edge of the ship tighter as he watched the white vessels draw closer.

The ship jerked violently to the left as Zarek twisted the helm again, but it was clear that they could not escape, no matter what the captain did. "I doubt I'll be able to outsail them, but I won't die without trying. Near impossible doesn't mean impossible. Small chances are better than no chances at all."

Guilt gnawed at Elliot as he thought about how he'd caught Zarek up in this mess. The captain had offered them passage and was willing to deter from his original path to this. His kindness and time spent were being returned to him by putting his life in danger. Elliot couldn't let Zarek suffer because of them. There had to be something he could do to stop the ships. Some way to protect their ally.

The sight of his companions crushed Elliot's heart.

Behind their usual brave faces, he could see their fear. Mimi trembled ever so slightly as Sage pulled him close, the rush of the cold ocean air whipping their clothes into a frenzy. Luka and Owen, who were usually so composed, had gone pale with dread. Luka had his hand over the hilt of his sword, but Elliot could tell the ethereal was not sure if he could defend them. Hiro stood close to Elliot, his expression stern as he studied the approaching ships.

Elliot pressed a hand against his chest. What if he used his magic? He could create a barrier, protecting them from harm. But how long would he be able to hold out for? They were miles from nearby land, and he wasn't sure if Zarek had an idea of what to do if they did succeed in escaping. The energy required to maintain a shield against the three sentinel ships might drain him completely before they could reach safety.

Thick fog suddenly engulfed them, hindering their vision of the queen's ships. The air grew frigid, the bitter coldness biting into Elliot's skin. He staggered away from the edge as the ship's surface began frosting over.

"Aye!" Zarek shouted. "If ye want to freeze my ship over, ye goin' to have to take me with. I'm not leaving my dear Bella alone to sink into this ocean."

Calm and steady footsteps echoed through the mist. The clicking grew louder as it moved closer and closer. A silhouette crept through the fog before a tall, slender figure emerged. She placed her hand on her hip, her other occupying a slender, dark wooden wand. She used it to tap her shoulder. Her icy gaze scanned the group, her sharp features and pale complexion lacing with boredom.

She clicked her tongue. "You know, you don't have to run away whenever you see one of our ships." She brushed her long platinum braid over her shoulder, revealing her pointy ears.

She was an elf.

"Just because we're Her Majesty's sentinels doesn't mean you've done something wrong." Her piercing red eyes landed on Elliot. "Though I can see why you were worried. Our duty knows no mercy for those who deserve divine punishment." The silver plates of her armor clacked rhythmically against one another as she strode toward Elliot and stopped before him.

Elliot was frozen in place. He willed his muscles to move, but they remained still, falling silent to his will. He could only watch as his friends' eyes widened in desperation as they tried to run to him, but they, too, were frozen in some sort of spell.

Did the elf have the ability to use magic too? But how?

"You must be him." She placed her finger against Elliot's face, grazing her fingernail down his cheek. The touch was cold, sending shivers down his spine. "The oracle, no?"

Before Elliot could answer, the white-haired elf flicked her wand. His breath escaped his lungs, and his body lurched into the air. The last thing he saw was the concern

in his companions' eyes before the world around him
blurred into blinding white.

27
MOTHER

Elliot's vision distorted wildly as his body was torn in multiple directions, still in midair. The dizzying spell abruptly ceased as solid ground met the bottoms of his feet and the surrounding scenery solidified from the frenzy of a blur.

Elliot's steadying footsteps echoed through the vast chamber. The pure-white marble floors reflected whatever walked upon them, and the tall, pristine, white walls were decorated with large windows. The ceilings were arched with glass, allowing the natural glow from the moon to brighten the room. Between the windows, large burgundy drapes hung from golden rods, their rich color a stark contrast to everything else.

Dread filled Elliot's body as he watched the disguise spell Luka and Owen had placed on them disintegrate, revealing their faces and true race.

"I've brought them, my queen," the sentinel from earlier said. She knelt down, placing her wand across her chest. "I let the ship they were on go. Unharmed. He was not aware of their true identities. A simple sailor willed by coin."

Elliot let out a quiet sigh of relief. He was grateful that nothing ill had fallen upon Zarek, especially since the captain had done nothing to deserve it. But how long had these sentinels been watching them?

Ever since they'd arrived in the Snowy Hills?

Before that?

Ever since they'd departed for Astaria?

"Your services and loyalty are always appreciated, Flara." The queen's voice filled the chamber. "Liliana and Sophia."

"Yes, my queen?" two figures responded in unison from behind the group. They knelt, crossing their wands over their chests. They were adorned in the same silver armor as Flara and shared her distinctive white hair and piercing red eyes.

"See the other guests to their rooms. I want to speak to the oracle and the hero alone."

"At once."

With a single flick of Liliana's and Sophia's wands, they vanished in an instant, along with Mimi, Sage, Luka, and Owen.

Flara, Hiro, the queen, and Elliot remained.

Elliot's heart hammered painfully against his ribs, his breaths coming in shallow puffs. He and Hiro were in front of Astaria's ruler, in the heart of a potential new enemy in foreign territory. They were separated from everyone else, and Elliot didn't know what kind of magic the sentinel elves had. This was the first time he had witnessed other elves wield magic. What were the queen's intentions? If she ordered an attack, he needed to figure out a way to protect himself and Hiro.

Elliot clutched his chest, attempting to tap into his magic core.

His eyes widened. He couldn't feel it.

Elliot held his breath in cold dread. He looked at Hiro, panic threatening to seize his throat. There was nothing Elliot could do. He would have to rely solely on Hiro to get them out of here if they had any hope of escaping.

"I'm not going anywhere," Hiro whispered. "Don't worry. I won't let them hurt you."

The steadiness of Hiro's voice cut through the panic, calming Elliot's nerves. He let out a shuddering breath, finding the strength to breathe again.

The queen stood from her throne, her long golden dress cascading around her figure. Each step of her heels clicked quietly down the marble steps. Her fair skin seemed to glow against the moonlight. Light blond hair framed her slender face and ended at her waist. A golden crown adorned with rubies lay upon her head.

Her red eyes never left Elliot. Her piercing gaze locked on as she descended.

"Welcome to Sylvana, capital of the kingdom of Astaria," she said, her voice holding so much authority, Elliot felt small in such a grand presence. "You do not need to worry, Oracle. I did not bring you here to harm you." Her steps stopped once she reached the bottom. "Hiro, have you not mentioned me to them at all?" Her tone was laced with amusement. She waved a hand, shaking her head. "The oracle is terrified, like a cornered rabbit facing a hungry fox."

"Like a game of chess, the queen is free to move anywhere she pleases," Hiro said. "Queen Elyria, you made your move before I could make mine."

"Is that so? I clearly remember you telling me you were to return to the kingdom as soon as you found the oracle. Though your return seems to have been delayed. I only expedited it."

Elliot's head spun in a whirlwind of confusion. He was not surprised that Hiro had been to Astaria, but he had not expected him to know the queen. Hiro had been with the group for weeks, so why had he not mentioned Astaria or Elyria to them? It was only when Elliot had unlocked his memories that he'd learned of the new continent and Rainwell. Yet Hiro had had that knowledge with him the entire time, choosing to keep it a secret. Had Hiro been manipulating him from the start? Had he intentionally created a rift between Elliot and the others, wanting to isolate him? What was Hiro's motive?

"Young oracle, I do not wish to alarm you," Elyria said. "We are your allies."

"How can I trust you?" Elliot asked, his tone sharp. He glanced between Hiro and Elyria, waiting for an answer.

Elyria hummed. "You are here with plans to reach Rainwell, yes? That is the fate of the oracle and the warriors. I know of the prophecy, as I have lived a long time." A gentle smile graced her features. "I have lived even longer than Hiro here. While he is barely about to reach three hundred, I am nearing eight hundred. I have seen many things and have knowledge of many things. In all honesty, I requested that Hiro keep this place a secret until you regained your memories of the past. There is a reason for everything, young oracle. A path everyone must take. If Hiro had brought you and your companions here before you unlocked your memories, it would have served no purpose. You would not have had the drive or will to fulfill the prophecy that has been destined for you. So please, you may be at ease."

Elliot was at a loss for words. He was not expecting an honest answer. Rather, he was anticipating another wave of deception. "And the others? Where are they?"

"They are in their quarters. Warm baths were prepared for them," Elyria said. "I suspect they are relaxing at this moment." She paused, her demeanor shifting from soft to concerned. Her eyes studied Elliot and Hiro. "I had them taken away because I wanted to speak to you and Hiro alone. What we need to discuss is not for other ears." She nodded toward Flara. "You are dismissed."

"My queen." Flara bowed before flicking her wand, vanishing into thin air.

"Now, Oracle . . . Or would you prefer I call you Elliot?"

"How did you . . . ?"

Elyria pointed to her chest. "You can say we are connected, as we share the same magic. You cannot feel the magic flowing through you, correct?"

Elliot shook his head.

"That is because the magic flowing in you was originally mine. And I can choose where my magic goes and who I bless with it." Elyria stepped forward, stopping before Elliot and placing a hand against his chest.

A familiar sensation flowed from Elyria's palm into Elliot's body. His weariness began to dissipate, replaced by a sense of lightness and calm. The castle, formerly a daunting unknown place, now felt like home. The assembly hall no longer felt big and cold, but cozy and warm. He welcomed the tall ceilings and pure-white walls as a safe haven.

"I . . . I've been here before," Elliot said, his voice barely above a whisper.

"Yes," Elyria said softly, pulling her hand away. "Myru has been here before. I gave her sanctuary during her journey. As well as the others."

"But how is it that you were able to give me magic? I awoke to my powers back in Etheria."

Elyria cupped Elliot's cheek in her hand, stroking him with her thumb. "My child," she began, her voice quiet and gentle. "That is because I am the mother of elves."

28
MAGIC

"Mother of elves?" Elliot couldn't believe what he'd just heard. How could that be possible? From his teachings, he knew of Alder, Azar, Ara, and Aapo, deities who oversaw the four elements and the four races.

Alder oversaw the earth and elves.

Azar oversaw fire and humans.

Ara oversaw the sea and nixen.

Aapo oversaw air and ethereals.

And above them were Vylantra and Mykronos, gods of life and death. If there was a mother of elves, did that mean there was a mother for the others as well? Nixen? Humans? Ethereals?

"I understand your confusion," Elyria said. "And yes, to answer your question."

Elliot blinked. "You're able to read my mind?"

Elyria chuckled. "No, child. I can simply guess based on your reaction. Your expression is quite illustrative."

Warmth spread across Elliot's cheeks. He hadn't wanted to appear childish in front of Elyria.

"I wanted to tell you this because it comes at a cost," Elyria started. "As you know, elves were not meant to wield magic. It is not in their biology to do so. Wielding magic is unnatural for elves and, as such, can very well take a toll on the body. The magic you have in you, Elliot, is only a fraction of my power and only a fraction of what Myru had."

Elliot felt a hand on his shoulder. Hiro gave him a gentle squeeze. "This is where I come into play."

Elyria smiled. "Hiro has the ability to siphon magic from and to you. Something only he can do. A rare skill that was only possible due to the bond shared between him and Myru. Such bonds between elf and human are rare and usually unheard of because of the inability to procreate, but when it happens, they form a unique bridge, a connection that allows humans without magic cores to wield magic without the negative side effects."

"But," Elliot started, his brow furrowing, "Luka did something similar before. He pushed magic into me. But I don't recall feeling any kind of backlash or strain from it. No side effects at all."

Elyria shook her head. "Ethereals can share their magic with others, but their magic is different from what we have in our bodies. If you consider Alder as the deity of earth, think of the magic that flows within us as the earth element. Aapo oversees ethereals, thus giving their magic the wind element. Air is the wind as wind is the air, and while it is true that every living being needs air to survive, that is not the same as what can flow within us."

Elliot thought back to the time he and the others ran into a group of feral chimeras. He had overexerted his magic to the extent that Luka had to share some of his stamina. Without Luka's help, Elliot was sure he would have burned out. Or worse. "The time Luka shared some of his stamina with me was because I was using too much of my magic and felt my core straining to fulfill my demands."

"You don't need to worry, Elliot," Hiro said. "Luka sharing his magic with you is not enough to do any lasting damage."

"Elliot, if what you say is true, then what Hiro is saying is right. Because your core had nearly depleted its magic reservoir, it was more accepting of a foreign force. Over time, as you recovered your stamina, his disappeared." Elyria nodded. "As a matter of fact, it appears he placed a protective barrier around the heart of your core. I sensed dark magic there, though I have since destroyed it."

"Namir . . ." Elliot whispered. When he and Luka ran into her back in the chimeran village, Luka had mentioned sensing Namir's dark matter within his core. But he was distracted and had ignored the ethereal's words. Elliot's heart warmed as he thought of all the times the ethereal had been there for him.

Luka had been there when Elliot woke up from the horrendous torture he was going through while Oasis held him captive.

Luka had been there when he sensed Elliot's distress

during the feral chimera attack.

Luka had been there when he encountered Namir in the abandoned chimeran village.

And Luka had been there to warn him about the dark matter within him.

Elliot's mind had been scattered, and dark thoughts had found their way into his consciousness since encountering Namir. If Luka hadn't been there, would Elliot have gotten even more lost in the chaos of events? Would he have descended into madness?

Elliot had truly felt like he was alone and no one understood how he felt—to have his destiny predetermined without consideration of his own wants and needs. But it brought him relief to learn that those feelings were possibly because of Namir's dark hold on him. To learn that those were not Elliot's own thoughts and intentions. To learn that perhaps his and Minari's disagreements were because of Namir and not because of him.

But guilt quickly followed.

Elliot's chest tightened at the memories that flooded in. He was reminded of how terribly he had treated Minari. How awful it had been for him to doubt his closest and most trusted friend. He deeply wished he could turn back time and take everything back.

The memories of better days haunted Elliot. The endless afternoons spent trading stories and terrible jokes, the way Minari's eyes would light up just before he delivered a particularly awful punchline. The sound of his friend's laughter, bright and genuine, echoed in his mind. A delightful sound he would never hear again.

Elliot promised himself he would fulfill the prophecy and save the world. That was the least he could do for his fallen friend.

"The chimeran Oasis leader?" Hiro said, snapping Elliot's attention back. "I wish I could kill her myself, but she offed herself instead," he scoffed. "Good riddance to her, at least. I never liked her."

"This Namir . . . You mention she is a chimera?" Elyria asked. "I have only heard tales of a new race Etherians created. I assume two of your comrades are chimeras? They feel different."

Elliot hesitated. "Yes." He paused. He wasn't sure if it was safe for him to admit Mimi and Sage were chimeras, though it appeared Elyria already knew. "Mimi and Sage."

"Do not worry, Elliot. I mean no harm to them, regardless of their origins. Here, under my rule, all life is treated with equality and fairness. Your gains are your own, and your downfall is your own. This much would be true even if they weren't warriors. So, there will be no need to have the ethereals cast their disguise spell."

"Right, the spell," Elliot said.

"All magic that I do not grant permission to is not allowed to be cast inside my castle," Elyria said, her tone gentle yet firm. "That is why it evaporated and why you could not tap into your core. I wanted to explain the situation before anything got out of hand." She reached forward, taking Elliot's hands into her own. "I hope you understand."

Elyria's hold was warm, and it reminded Elliot of his mother, Estelle. The touch held the same nurturing energy and unconditional acceptance for who he was.

The tension in Elliot's body finally began to ease, and he let out a small sigh. "I understand."

29

IDENTITY

"Chloé, meet Princess Arielle. Princess, meet Chloé," Asher said, his voice seemingly louder than usual as it bounced off the stone walls. "Arielle, you will be under Chloé's care."

Chloé bowed, her heart hammering against her chest. "Pleasure meeting you, Princess." Despite all her years serving on the council, this was her first encounter with any member of the royal family. The only council member who had any direct communication with the Valentines was Ragnar, and any direct order from the royal family came from him.

The weight of such an important responsibility weighed heavily on Chloé's shoulders. Such an important task had been bestowed upon her. She had to do everything within her power to meet Bunnie's expectations. There could be no mistakes. No flaws. It had to be executed perfectly.

The three of them were in the underground meeting room, only accessible through Bunnie's office. It was an exclusive meeting place for Bunnie and her officers, those she trusted wholeheartedly. Bringing in an unfamiliar face was against protocol and unheard of for Bunnie, so she must have held great trust in Asher's judgement.

Chloé truly hoped the princess would keep this secret location to herself and uphold the trust Bunnie and Asher had in her.

"It is a pleasure meeting you as well," Arielle said, her voice regal, fitting of a princess. Though she wore the standard guild uniform like any other member, her appearance and the way she presented herself betrayed her role. Not only her demeanor, but Arielle's luscious blond hair was a dead giveaway she came from a prestigious background. The shine and silkiness could only be obtained with attention and care, something most common folk did not have the luxury or time for. "I hope we will get along." She tucked her hair behind her ear, exposing her diamond-shaped emerald earrings. "I have never been outside of the castle before, so . . . this is all new to me." Her eyes glanced around cautiously, and she tucked her arms close to her chest.

Not only was this Arielle's first time away from the castle, but it was also evident that she had never been in a such a dark and damp place and found it uncomfortable. The single torch that hung off a nearby wall made it difficult to see, though Chloé eyes had been trained to see even in situations darker than this.

Chloé hoped the princess's will to help their cause was stronger than her will to be comfortable.

Arielle cleared her throat. "Iris told me what you are planning. Going against Ragnar . . . going against my father. I want to be a part of it," she said as she fidgeted with the hem of her uniform.

Asher stepped forward, placing a hand on Arielle's shoulder. "It may not seem like it now, but she does have the resolve." His tone carried a weight of confidence, as if he was trying to send it to Arielle.

Immediately, Arielle nodded, her shoulders straightening, tilting her chin up as she stood taller. "I do not wish to be a simple puppet under my family's grasp, only playing the roles they want me to play. I want to make a difference. I want to be free from my family." The princess's voice was devoid of the uncertainty from earlier. Olive orbs met Chloé's gaze, filled with conviction and devotion.

"What is your name?" Chloé asked.

Arielle blinked, confusion written across her face. "Arielle."

"What is your name?" Chloé repeated, her voice firmer this time. She needed to know if the princess understood what it meant to be brought down here.

Arielle pressed her lips together, brow furrowing. Chloé could see the princess's internal struggle playing across her face as she attempted to comprehend why Chloé had asked the question twice.

"Kaia," Arielle finally said. "My name is Kaia. And you are?"

A smile formed on Chloé's face, pride warming her chest.

"I'm Chloé." She nodded toward Asher. "And he is Asher." Arielle may need to get used to calling Asher by his real name, but Chloé believed in her.

Arielle had determined something for herself, making a choice without needing permission or justification from others. Some might view this action as insignificant, but Chloé recognized it for what it was: the first step toward true independence.

In that moment, Arielle was no longer Princess Arielle of the kingdom of Etheria. She was Kaia, Nighthawk's newest member, who Chloé would take under her wing, ensuring she reached her full potential as she worked toward fulfilling her duty and promise to the cause.

"Well, what shall we do first?" Kaia asked.

"Here you are," Chloé said, holding a hand mirror in front of Kaia. "I can't say I have much experience in cutting hair, but I did what I could."

Chloé had taken Kaia into her chambers, and Asher had handed Chloé his bag of makeup, leaving them to have their fun.

Kaia stared intently at her reflection, taking in every detail. Gone were the long, flowy locks of blond hair that gracefully fell down her back. Now, her hair was in a short, boyish style, similar to what Deveran and Oliver had, and in a shade of rich burgundy. There were added layers to her hair, giving her volume and texture she'd never had before.

Kaia wore deep brown contacts to hide the beautiful eyes that she had inherited from the queen and darker makeup that altered the familiar complexion of her face.

"It's . . . strange," Kaia said, turning her head side to side, examining her new appearance. "I have spent years seeing myself as a complete mirror image of my mother. To be the perfect princess I was born to be. But now I do not even recognize myself." She delicately touched her cheeks, bringing the mirror closer. "This is the first time in my entire life that I feel like myself. Like I can truly express who I am."

"This is you now," Chloé affirmed. She understood that a change in physical appearance ran deeper than just skin. "This is you without the shackles of your lineage and family."

Kaia released a shuddering breath as she lowered the mirror onto her lap. "I would be lying if I said I am not nervous. I am not too sure how to act, in all honesty."

"You could try talking more casually," Chloé suggested.

"Casually? Ah, the way I talk is too . . ."

"Formal. Well educated. We will need to work on your accent as well." Chloé mentally took note of the changes still needed for Kaia's transformation.

Changing her appearance had been a complete success and would be something that had to be done on a daily basis.

Second would be changing how Kaia presented herself.

Kaia still walked with regal confidence, and her tone and the formal pattern of her speech were a clear indication she was someone of the royal family. It was distinct and could only be taught within the castle walls. It would take some time, but Chloé believed in Kaia and her conviction.

"Ready for your first lesson?"

30
LAVENDER

Each step Luka took against the marble floors brought back memories from long ago. The incredibly tall ceilings, large windows, and deep red tapestry were something he knew all too well. Something he'd never thought he would see again.

"My lords, your bath has been prepared," a maid announced, bowing deeply before him and Owen. The maid uniform had not changed since then. They still wore dark beige linen garb and a white apron. Simple, gray slip-ons covered their feet, protecting them from the cold floors, and their hair was tied back away from their face.

"Thank you," Luka said. "You are dismissed."

The maid bowed once more before departing, her footsteps light and quiet, ensuring her presence did not disrupt the quiet and peaceful atmosphere.

"Luka," Owen started. "I assume you know what is going on?"

"I do." Luka made his way to the bath, every stride bringing waves of recollection.

The oval-shaped bath remained grand as ever. Its vast expanse was surrounded by beautifully detailed trim that caught the natural light from the large, frosted windows. Three baskets stood near the edge of the water: one empty one and two that had a change of clothing for both Luka and Owen.

The air was warm, cozy with a strong scent of a lavender, something the ethereal had not realized he missed. It was nostalgic.

Luka slipped out of his robes, his fingers nimble as he loosened his sash and pushed his garment down his shoulders. He placed them in the nearby empty basket before dipping into the relaxing bath. The water rippled around him. The calming sound was like music to his ears. He closed his eyes and settled in, leaning against the wall. He heard Owen mimic his actions, joining him in the comforting bath.

They both sat in silence, enjoying how the heat seeped into their muscles, alleviating any lingering fatigue of their travels.

The lavender scent grew stronger as the steam engulfed his senses, the aroma bringing back memories he'd thought were all lost.

Allix methodically inspected the bedroom chamber, checking every nook and cranny he could stick his head into. He checked behind the dresser and the curtains and even under the large beds.

Kana watched him, amused that the other elf was so inclined to doubt the hospitality of the land's queen, though she understood where he was coming from. They'd been taught to be cautious and to always be prepared for betrayal, no matter how small or big.

Rain heavily drummed against the window. Its path ran down the long glass, blurring the scenery outside. If not for Queen Elyria's kindness, they would have been trapped outside, drenched in the storm. They'd barely made it inside Sylvana's walls before the rain started. The air was heavy with humidity, and the strong scent of rain was explosive. They were fortunate to have run into one of the kingdom's sentinels near the gates. He'd immediately recognized Myru and had led them into the castle walls. The urgency he had was suspicious at first, especially when he had informed them that Queen Elyria was expecting them. But it soon dissipated when they saw Alder waiting for them in the castle.

The deity of earth had been there when they left Rainwell, ensuring them he would help and guide them on their mission. They had been worried at first when Redd, Alder's familiar, had ceased communication.

They had learned it was to reserve Alder's energy, nothing more and nothing less.

"If you keep going on like that, you are going to wear a hole in the floor," Kana said. Allix was just about to start his third round of inspections. If he didn't find anything the first time, it was highly unlikely he was going to find something the third time. "You know Her Majesty means us well. She certainly didn't assign her sentinels to set traps or to attack us in the middle of the night."

Allix paused, side-eyeing Kana. "You know the rumors of the sentinels. The fact that Her Majesty sent one to fetch us could very well mean the death of us. No one who runs into one sees the light of day again." He huffed, continuing his inspection. "Myru is our responsibility, and we let her get assigned with Hiro. How can we rely on a human?" he mumbled.

Kana sighed. "Unfortunately, that wasn't for us to decide. I'd have it any other way too."

She understood where Allix was coming from and the nervousness he felt. She didn't like that they were separated. She couldn't allow herself to truly be at ease even in the presence of such luscious comfort simply because she wasn't with Myru. Any one of them would be uncomfortable leaving their precious oracle.

They were assigned two per bedroom chamber. Yumie and Noé were together, and Myru was with Hiro.

Kana was not sure if it was luck or not that Hiro was with Myru. She would have preferred someone else be with her.

Everything about Hiro was suspiciously kind, especially toward the female oracle. It had taken some time for Kana to determine if Hiro's feelings were genuine or pure curiosity. Interracial affection of any kind was unusual, and it was rare if it lasted a lifetime. It historically was marked with tragedy rather than triumph.

Kana did not want to see her friend get hurt over a human. Emotions could cause immeasurable pain, worse than any physical wound. If Kana could choose how her life ended, it would be dying from a stab to her heart rather than the pain and agony of heartbreak.

Though Hiro's infatuation had been due to curiosity at first, Kana saw how it grew. Both he and Myru had grown quite fond of each other, and it had bloomed into genuine love and affection.

Kana hoped Hiro would never betray Myru. That was all any of them could ask for.

"I understand you're worried," Kana said. "I am too. And Noé and Yumie as well, no doubt."

"Humans are unpredictable. Her Majesty's still hopeful that interracial relationships will somehow work out. I heard she wanted to alter the rules of the kingdom because of it."

"It would be difficult." Kana knew the races were weary of one another. It had always been like that.

"Exactly. So why bother? It's not like they could start a family."

"Perhaps there is something more that lies beyond that," Kana mused. "Pure love for each other knows no bounds. Knows no restrictions. They only need each other. I think . . ." Kana paused, thinking over how to word her thoughts. "I think sometimes we have to trust in possibilities we never would have expected. Hiro may be human, but his heart seems true enough."

Allix sighed, stopping his rounds. He turned to Kana,

giving her his full attention. "And what if we're wrong?"

"Then we will be there to pick up the pieces. To support Myru with our utmost ability. To be there for her. To ensure she survives the hurt of betrayal. Because we will never do that to her. That's what we have always done, is it not?"

31
REMNANTS

Valor's head throbbed with a dull pulsating ache. He groaned, eyes screwing shut, and his brow furrowed as he attempted to block out the annoyingly loud chirping that bled through the thick windows. The bright singing voice scorched itself into his skull.

Valor's body was incredibly heavy and sore and painfully hot. A searing heat coursed through his veins. His muscles screamed in protest as he attempted to will his body to move. He felt crushed, as though a particularly large animal had fallen on top of his body, relaxing the entirety of its weight onto his smaller frame. Valor winced at the thought, his head suddenly thrumming with such intensity and agony that he held his breath. A low and slow anguished hiss escaped his lips as he waited for the turmoil to pass.

As the remaining tendrils of pain left his body, a loud knock on the door jarred him into a fresh wave of torment.

"Excuse me," a maid said from the entrance. Her footsteps were accompanied by three others. From the weight and sound of their strides, Valor knew one of them was the princess and the other was another maid. The fourth was unknown to him, but he knew it was a male.

"Is he awake?" Arielle asked, her voice full of concern. "It has already been nine days."

"He is," the male said. "His fever is still prevalent though."

Nine days? Valor had been asleep for nine days? How was that even possible? He didn't believe this body would be so delicate as to succumb to an illness for that long.

Through the haze of the fever, he could hear the two maids walking around the bedroom chamber, and the smell of cleaning supplies assailed his nose. Valor groaned, cracking his eyes open. His vision was blurry, but he was able to make out the male who was standing by his bedside.

The man was tall with a slender build. His chestnut-brown hair was neatly combed. His navy clothes were adorned with gold trim, and he wore a red cloak over his shoulders.

"Good morning, Valor," he said. "Let me introduce myself. I am Dr. Vincent Laurent. I am the royal family's personal physician. Although I am fairly new here, as my father was assigned here before my time, I can promise you I will take good care of you." Vincent laid a brown, leather-bound book on his lap, opening it and flipping a few pages until he found the spot he was looking for. The spread was marked by a quill, and he took it into his hand, ready to write. "Princess Arielle reached out to me nine days ago when she found you unconscious outside her chambers. You were running an unusually high fever and have been asleep since. Can you tell me how you're feeling right now?"

"Like Xander trampled me." Valor hissed, a sharp stab coursing through his skull. The words he spoke were not his. They were Minari's.

Like Xeno trampled me.

There was a small twist in his memory. He'd responded using the name of his ovis rather than Elliot's.

Valor's chest tightened at the memory of Xander, a pain he couldn't quite explain. Even though the animal was not his, he could feel the heartbreak like he had experienced it himself. The image of Xander's lifeless body was engrained in his mind so vividly that he could feel the sinister malice from the one who had murdered the innocent animal. His heart pounded against his chest, and he swallowed hard, attempting to push the dark memory back. They were not his. He needed to remember that.

"Xander?" Arielle asked. "Who is Xander?"

"Your Highness, my lord," the maid started. "I sincerely apologize for interrupting. It is time that we change the sheets and his clothes."

"Ah, yes. Please do," Vincent said. "A fresh set will do him well in his recovery."

Arielle turned around, giving Valor privacy as one of the maids adjusted him so her peer could quickly pull out the used sheets and replace them with fresh ones. They worked together, quickly tucking in the corners. One of the maids worked her hands quickly across his body. She unbuttoned his top with ease, sliding the clinging fabric down his shoulders, and his trousers were replaced by the other maid before he could think about it.

"We will be taking our leave now. Excuse us," the maid said. They both left as quickly as they'd entered.

Arielle cleared her throat before turning back to Valor.

Vincent moved around the bed, checking Valor's pulse and breathing. "The willow-bark tea is helping, but he needs more rest. His body is still fairly frail."

"Is there anything else we can do to speed up his recovery?"

"I am afraid not, Your Highness. Unless Valor can stomach foods, the only thing we can do now is wait for his body to fight off whatever infection it has." Vincent looked through his book. "I have shared his symptoms with Father, and he, too, is bewildered by what he has. No members of the royal family have ever fallen this ill before. Please believe me when I say I am doing the best I can."

Arielle sighed. "I know. It's just that . . . I feel like this is partially my fault."

"Your Highness, it is his duty as your personal guard to stand watch over you. I know you have a kind heart and care for him, but please understand that he was fulfilling his duty to you. Whatever ailment befalls him is an honor, as it fell upon him rather than you."

"I understand . . ."

"He is improving," Vincent said, his tone light. "From the first time I saw him to now, I can confidently say he is only getting better. It's only a matter of time now."

"Do you think Father will dismiss him?"

"I cannot speak for what King Valentine has in store for Valor. I only know that he wishes the best for you." Vincent paused. "Though I believe Valor will not be replaced so easily. As someone who is strong enough to fight this illness, it would be unwise to let him go."

"Thank you. I needed to hear that."

"Of course, Your Highness."

As their voices blended into quiet murmurs, Valor's eyes began to close.

Nine days had been spent lying in bed. His body was weak, vulnerable. Anyone who'd wanted to kill him could have. His duty was to oversee Arielle and report every single detail of her activities to Ragnar. He was to silence the princess if Valor detected even the smallest bit of treason.

Yet here Valor lay, unable to move even his finger without assistance. Rather than him overseeing Arielle, Arielle was overseeing him. She was so concerned for his well-being that she had summoned the royal physician.

Valor's brain ached the more he tried to read into the princess's actions. Ragnar was suspicious of Arielle, so everything she did that could possibly be out of the ordinary had to be taken with caution.

As consciousness faded from Valor, his mind drifted to images of the large, brown animal. Minari's ovis had been his most trusted companion. Valor could feel how strong of a connection elves had with their ovis. The love and devotion lasted a lifetime. A promise of complete understanding.

The memories, thoughts, and feelings were weaving together, making it difficult for Valor to see which were his and which were Minari's.

What was his mission?

What was his purpose?

32
FATE

The night sky above Elliot was dark and empty, as if the stars were hiding themselves from curious eyes. The air was heavy with moisture. A thick fog swirled around him, making it difficult to make out his own hands, even if he placed them in front of his face. His feet crunched against the ice-laced grass as he continued to walk down the unknown path before him.

The chill of the night air seeped through his thin clothing, sending shivers up his arms. His ragged breathing sent small clouded puffs of air against his lips.

Where was he? He could have sworn he was in Sylvana's castle walls. He had settled in for the night after his discussion with the queen and ensuring the others were all right. Just when the clutches of rest were about to take him, he had been thrust into this unknown place.

Elliot looked around, attempting to make out any familiar landmarks in the empty void.

But there was nothing.

It was like this place was an endless abyss.

Elliot opened his mouth, attempting to yell for help, but his voice was caught in his throat. His cries were silent. He placed his hand against his neck. Why couldn't he talk? It was as if the strength he needed to let out his voice had been stripped away.

Elliot felt a surge of panic rise, a cold dread that tightened his chest. He needed to find the others. He needed to make sure the others were all right.

This must've been a trap set by the Necromancers. They must have found him in Sylvana. They knew Elliot was in Astaria, making his way to Rainwell, and this was their way of intercepting him. Separating him from the others was a sure way to stop him from fulfilling the prophecy.

Elliot ran. He ran with all his might. Adrenaline fueled his will, or else his legs would have given out from pure exhaustion and fear. But the more he moved, the quicker his body grew heavy, like weights that attached themselves around his ankles and wrists. His quick breaths were all he could hear as he kept moving, holding on to the hope that he would find someone.

Suddenly, the grass turned red. Elliot slowed to a stop, choking back a breath. The smell of iron flooded his nose.

Blood.

Sheer panic exploded in Elliot's chest.

No.

No.

No.

It couldn't be.

Elliot pushed the fatigue that threatened to pull him onto the ground aside. He continued, following the trail, his pace quickening with each step.

And then it stopped.

The trail had disappeared.

Elliot finally collapsed, his knees hitting the ground with a deafening thud. But he was numb to the pain, only feeling the ache in his heart, which was constricting with each passing second.

Elliot grew dizzy as dark thoughts flooded his mind. He could see their bodies, lifeless on the cold ground. Mimi. Sage. Chloé. Luka. Owen. Hiro. He balled his fists, clawing up the dirt into his palms. Why? Why had this happened? Was he not enough? Was he completely useless? What good was he if he couldn't even protect his friends?

Just when Elliot was about to lose himself to the endless tormenting thoughts, he felt a presence in front of him, their warmth seeping into his cold skin.

"Elliot."

Elliot's eyes widened, and he held his breath, afraid to move. He was scared to look up. Scared to learn that his mind was playing tricks on him. Scared to learn the presence in front of him wasn't real.

"Elliot," the voice called out again, radiating with the same compassion Elliot was so familiar with.

Elliot gasped as he allowed air to finally fill his lungs again. He clenched his eyes shut, still afraid that whoever was in front of him was going to disappear as soon he looked.

A gentle hand touched his shoulder, urging him to meet their gaze.

Elliot bit his lip, finally letting himself come face-to-face with his fear.

Minari.

Elliot sobbed, pushing himself up into Minari's embrace. He never thought he would see the familiar head of purple hair again. To see the familiar shade of amethyst and gray eyes. To see the familiar smile. The other elf was clad in his scout's attire, not a single drop of blood on him.

Relief washed over Elliot as he felt arms wrap around him. The cold and emptiness he felt from the abyss vanished instantly.

"I missed you," Minari said, stroking Elliot's back.

"I'm so sorry. I'm so sorry," Elliot said in between sobs. He couldn't believe it. Minari was here with him. He didn't care how or why. He was happy. And he held on to that feeling as if his life depended on it. "I'm so sorry!"

"Shh," Minari said. "It's okay, Elliot. It wasn't your fault. You have nothing to be sorry for."

Elliot shook his head, clutching Minari even tighter. He didn't want to lose him again. He didn't want to see Minari's lifeless body again. He desperately wanted Minari to be alive. To be here with him. For the warmth he felt to be true.

"If anything, I should be the one to apologize." Minari chuckled. "I'm your keeper. Your scribe. Yet here I am, six feet under. What kind of friend am I to leave you alone?"

Elliot scoffed, finally pushing himself away from Minari to meet his gaze. "What kind of friend am I to have doubted you? What kind of friend am I to have let you . . . die?"

A sad smile curled Minari's lips. "I was destined to. So, you have nothing to be regretful over."

"Regret?" Elliot bit his lip, his face twisting in anguish. He had so much regret it hurt. He had wished countless times he could take everything back. "I treated you so horribly . . . doubted you when I should have trusted you. Isolated you when I should have included you."

"It wasn't your fault," Minari said. "I don't blame you for anything. In fact, I wanted to apologize for keeping the secret of Mistfall from you. For keeping your family a secret." He paused. "I didn't want to worry you. You already had so much you had to do as the oracle. So much responsibility. I should've at least been there to help carry the burden." He chortled, eyes looking down. "I can't even do that for you anymore."

The two elves sat in silence, simply enjoying each other's presence.

Elliot had so much to say, but he couldn't form the words. His mind was a whirlwind of thoughts, making him dizzy as he tried to find anything to say.

"When you see me again in Rainwell, please kill me."

Elliot blinked.

What?

Elliot tried to form a response, but a combination of random sounds left his lips instead.

"You know when my father died?" Minari began. "On

that day, we ran into one of the Necromancers. Valor. My father was able to intercept Valor, striking a blow that killed him. But out of desperation, Valor was somehow able to force his soul into my body." He covered his left gray eye. "This is the cause of him doing so. He was watching our every move and every decision through my eye. I didn't know . . . I had no memory of this until Lily killed me. Then it all came rushing back." Minari frowned, pausing. "My memories and Valor's memories are beginning to mesh. It's becoming difficult to differentiate between mine and his. There are times where I can see what he's doing and hear his thoughts, but I cannot do anything. Valor has complete control over my body."

The truth of Minari's words slowly sank into Elliot. What he was afraid of was becoming evident.

This was not reality.

It was a dream.

When Elliot woke up, Minari wouldn't be with him.

"Take this." Minari reached into his coat. Taking Elliot's hand, he tucked something into his palm. "I meant to give this to you earlier. I guess better late than never, hmm?"

Hot tears welled up in Elliot's eyes, the salty sting burning his skin as they traced a path down his temple, each drop a fresh wave of anguish.

Elliot didn't want to open his eyes. He clung to the numbness of sleep, unwilling to wake up to a world where the sound of Minari's laughter was gone forever. The hollowness in his chest ached with a dull, throbbing pain, his heart twisting in ways he hadn't thought was possible.

Suddenly, Elliot became aware that something was in his hand. His breath caught in his throat, and he slowly brought it to his face and opened his eyes.

It was the wooden pendant Lily had made for him.

Tears flowed uncontrollably, his vision blurring. He clutched the pendant tightly against his chest, his body racked with silent sobs.

Even after everything they had been through, Minari had so much trust and love for Elliot.

A fierce resolve took hold of Elliot. He made a vow to himself, a promise to uphold and fulfill Minari's wish to him.

Elliot would make certain of it, even if it meant sacrificing everything.

It would be his final act.

33
TRUTH

"Elliot! Elliot, wake up!" Mimi yelled, pounding on the large wooden door. "Elliot!"

Mimi had woken up in the morning feeling an odd sense of dread, like something was off. The pit of his stomach was heavy as anxiety grew more intense with each passing second. There was a slight taste of iron in the air, and everything was still. Quiet. Not even a single bird's song could be heard.

Except for a scream.

The sound had pierced through the silent morning. Both Mimi and Sage had lurched from their beds, nerves on edge. The scream was the kind of scream when coming face-to-face with something so fearful, it was the only sound that could escape one's lips after being paralyzed by terror. Other thoughts were inconceivable.

"Mimi?" Elliot said, opening the door. His green hair, which was usually smooth, was disheveled, and his eyes were puffy, fresh tear stains on his cheeks. "What is it?"

Mimi wanted to ask Elliot what was wrong, but he knew that would have to come later. "Come quick. Luka and Owen, they're—" Mimi didn't have a chance to finish before Elliot bolted past him. He quickly followed after the elf, their hasty footsteps echoing through the castle's empty corridors.

The door to Luka and Owen's room was still open, though a few maids who had not been there before stood by the doorway, whispering amongst one another. No one dared enter unless permitted. Their faces were pale, hands clasped tightly together as they exchanged worried glances.

Luka was sitting on one of the bedroom chairs, completely leaning back with his hand covering his eyes. His usually smooth silver hair was in disarray, sticking up in places Mimi did not think was possible. His brow was furrowed, and his lips were pinched into a tight, thin line. His robes were soaked in blood, but there were no obvious wounds on the ethereal. His bed was also drenched in dried crimson, possibly from the same source. The metallic scent that had been in the air was overwhelming here. It made Mimi's stomach churn uncomfortably.

"Luka, what happened?" Elliot's voice was steady, but Mimi knew it took a great deal of self-restraint from the elf to not panic at the scene. Elliot's shoulders were tense as he made his way to Luka.

The ethereal shook his head, the motion slow and pained. He winced. "I am trying to understand myself . . .

My apologizes, Elliot. My head feels like it was split in two." His voice was barely above a whisper, each word strained.

"I asked the two maids here if they knew anything," Sage said, nodding at the two who remained in the room. They were the ones who had found Luka in this predicament. "They repeatedly said this was how they saw the room in the morning when they were making their rounds. Luka was alone, and Owen was gone." The ox chimera crossed his arms. "What's weird is that it doesn't even look like there was a struggle."

Besides the blood-soaked ethereal and bed, the room was immaculate. There was not a single thing out of place. The shelving and desks were where they should be, and even the curtains did not have a single wrinkle on them. It was like what had conspired in here had happened in a different dimension.

"What is this?" Sophia's sharp voice cut through the hallway, her swift footsteps growing louder and more urgent. The presence of one of the queen's trusted sentinels seemed to make the air even more tense. The maids shrank in her wake. "What conspired here? Speak now."

"Sentinel Sophia, we are not sure ourselves," one of the maids from outside said, keeping her head down. Her hands trembled as she spoke. "Apologizes, we will return to our duties." The maids quickly scattered, their soft steps fading into the distance.

Sophia frowned, striding into the room, her metal armor clacking with each movement. She glanced around, taking in every detail with sharp crimson eyes before standing in the middle and taking out her wand. She whispered a few words before pointing the wand downward.

Pale blue mist suddenly formed around her, spreading across the floor. It swirled and flowed, forming three figures that grew more distinct with each passing moment.

Luka.

Owen.

And Hiro.

But why was Hiro there?

The human was supposed to be with Elliot, so why had he been with Luka and Owen?

Mimi glanced over at Elliot, and what he saw made his heart sink to the bottom of his stomach.

Elliot was biting his lip, attempting to hide the anguish he felt. His eyes were full of pain and shock, wide with a mixture of horror and betrayal. Mimi desperately wanted to run over to Elliot and comfort him, but he knew it was not the time, so he turned his attention back to the misty figures.

There were no words that could be heard, but the smoky figures appeared to be in the middle of a discussion. Their lips were animated, expressions full of concern. Luka's and Owen's gazes met before Hiro moved.

Without warning, Hiro's hand glowed before he slapped his palm against Luka's chest. With his eyes and mouth wide, the ethereal fell back onto his bed, arms outstretched and limp. Blood gushed everywhere from the gaping wound, soaking the sheets and his robes.

Then in a motion so quick it was almost missed, Hiro

grabbed Owen's neck, and with a single twist, it snapped. The other ethereal's body hit the floor, unmoving, like a puppet with cut strings.

A feathered cloak morphed around Hiro, and he vanished, the blue mist going along with him. The fog dissipated, leaving behind only the heavy weight of pure betrayal in the air.

No one uttered a word. The maids who remained in the room quietly wept, unsure how to take in the gruesome event that had occurred in the very room they were in.

They were still missing information. The scene that was shown to them had shown how Hiro had betrayed them and murdered the two ethereals. So how was it that Luka was alive? And where was Owen? Where had his body disappeared to?

"You have some explaining to do," Sophia said, disappointment in her tone. She pointed her wand toward Luka. "I will not let this disgusting crime go unpunished within my queen's castle, especially after she put her trust in you. This is a sacred place, and I will not let it be defiled."

"As much as I wish to inform you of what conspired, I've been attempting to wrap my mind around it since it happened," Luka said. He removed his hand and leaned forward. There were dark shadows beneath his eyes, and his complexion was pale, even for him. His usual grace had disappeared, only to be replaced with exhaustion and confusion. "I think . . . this was all predicted. By my brother."

"Maxwell?" Elliot asked. "You and Owen were looking for him."

"Yes." Luka furrowed his brow. "Maxwell knew this was going to happen. He knew there was going to be an attempt on my life. And . . ." Luka took a breath, pausing. He leaned his elbows against his knees, lacing his hands together. "Both my brother and Ragnar predicted this. Knew my life was in danger. Knew the kind of power I had. And knew this was going to happen."

34
SHADOW

"You sense it as well, don't you, Ragnar?" Maxwell asked, his piercing gaze focusing beyond the frosted window. "Something is inside Luka. Something . . . ancient."

Ragnar joined Maxwell by the window, gazing into the same storm that had Maxwell entranced. A midwinter snowstorm was raging beyond the glass. The snow itself was white. Pure. Yet it brought destruction if anyone dared to tread its depths.

"I do," Ragnar said. "Though only recently. And whatever is dwelling inside him . . ." His voice trailed off. There had been a shift in Luka's magic, an otherworldly resonance that should not have existed within an ethereal, no matter how powerful.

"Luka will bring unwanted attention to himself," Maxwell finished, as if reading Ragnar's mind. He sighed.

"Do you think it has to do with the prophecy?"

"The one regarding the oracle?" Ragnar's mind raced through the ancient text and documentations he had read during his years serving the Yunmei family. The prophecy spoke of a savior who was chosen by the god of life, Vylantra. The savior, who was deemed the oracle, would defend the world against the uprising Necromancers. The oracle had five companions with them, and together, they would be able to put a stop to the Necromancers' plans.

Did Maxwell believe Luka was the savior? The oracle?

Maxwell nodded. "Though it does not pertain to us ethereals, I feel like the prophecy may find its reach to others."

"If that is the case, then Luka is—"

"Perhaps," Maxwell interrupted. "We will not know for sure, but we should take precautions."

Ragnar quickly ran through various scenarios and opportunities he could take to help Maxwell's younger brother. Both of them were like family to him, so Ragnar, too, wanted to protect the young ethereal.

Ragnar tried to pinpoint when he had begun feeling the change in Luka. He had always possessed extraordinary magical talent, but this was different. Something more than magic resided within him now, something ancient and powerful.

It could very likely be the oracle's soul.

"It grows stronger," Ragnar started. "Whatever is inside him, it is as if it's beginning to awaken. I fear if he has what we believe he does, then he will be targeted."

Suddenly, memories of a book flooded his mind, a dark

spell that he had come across within the Yunmei library years ago.

Shadow play.

Protection magic would be too predictable and easily outdone. A shield could easily be broken. But a shadow play would be difficult to detect. In fact, it would be nearly impossible.

It was dangerous and forbidden, but it might be their only option.

"I may know of something," Ragnar said. "Shadow play."

"You want to perform a shadow play?" Maxwell's eyes widened, and he shook his head. "You know that is forbidden."

"Yes, but what choice do we have? Maxwell, you know a protection spell can only go so far. If it is broken, Luka will be gone with it. But with this, they will not know he is still alive. That they have been outplayed." Ragnar knew his friend would disapprove, but that did not stop him from wanting to persuade Maxwell. He valued the other ethereal's thoughts and opinions.

"You know very well why this sort of magic is forbidden, Ragnar." Maxwell's voice was firm, his eyes narrowing. "You cannot be considering this."

Ragnar knew Maxwell spoke the truth. Shadow play was forbidden because of the materials required to perform one. They would need a vessel, a sacrifice. Something that was an empty shell, welcoming of Luka's soul. It would be tasked with duties that it couldn't defy. The perfect puppet.

A life for a life.

"Leave everything to me, Maxwell," Ragnar said. "I will protect Luka."

It had taken Ragnar a little over a month to make all the necessary arrangements for the shadow play spell. The elixir was difficult to create, requiring many rare herbs. Whoever consumed the elixir would cease to exist, their soul vanishing into the ether. Whoever consumed the elixir would become an empty shell, welcoming of a new soul.

And the new soul would be Luka's.

Ragnar had another mixture ready for Luka. Once he took it, he would experience temporary amnesia. He would forget the immediate events that had occurred prior to drinking the potion, though he would regain the memories of the play, plus the vessel's, if the shadow play spell activated.

Ragnar hoped that never happened.

Because he knew Luka would not forgive himself if he learned of Ragnar's sacrifice to the Yunmei family.

But Ragnar knew this had to be done. He had decided that he, himself, would be the sacrifice.

Unlike Maxwell and Luka, Ragnar did not come from a notable family. His heritage was . . . normal. Mundane. The Yunmeis, on the other hand, came from a line of ethereals with an incredible amount of magic. The Shoheiis's magical abilities were considered average at best. Their magic cores only achieved a maturity level that was a fraction of what those in the Yunmei family could achieve. And because of this, the Shoheii family and its members were servants. Generation after generation, the Shoheii family had served the Yunmeis.

But the tradition had been broken once Maxwell became head of the clan.

Maxwell had revoked the bindings of servitude from the Shoheii family, thus releasing Ragnar from his duties. But even after what Maxwell had done, even though Ragnar was free to do as he pleased, he still wanted to remain by Maxwell's side. They'd grown closer, and a new friendship had been born. Ragnar was able to study magic freely and expand his magical skills.

Being a vessel for Luka was the least he could do for Maxwell. To return his kindness. To return the gift of freedom to Ragnar. For their friendship.

For being family.

Ragnar glanced around his desk one last time. He studied the vials, ensuring they were the exact amount required for the spell. He had hidden all other ingredients that would show evidence of his plan. His eyes stopped at the bottom drawer of his desk. Locked away with a seal was his notebook illustrating the entirety of his plan. The seal would release once his life ended. Only then would Maxwell and Luka learn of Ragnar's deepest intentions.

A knock on the door broke Ragnar from his thoughts.

It was time.

"Ragnar?" Luka peeked in from the other side. "You called for me?"

The unknown entity within Luka was even stronger than Ragnar remembered. With how much energy was flowing within Luka, the oracle's soul must've been residing in him. There was no doubt about it.

"Luka, thank you for joining me in my study," Ragnar said, keeping his voice steady. "I wanted to test something with you."

Luka chuckled. "Another one? What did you make this time?"

"It is a secret." Ragnar smiled. Luka had always been eager to help Ragnar with his magical experiments. It pained him that this would be the last time. The betrayal of trust would be his final burden. "Here." Ragnar handed Luka a vial. The liquid shimmered a translucent blue. Luka received it without hesitation while Ragnar took his own vial in hand. His was the opposite of Luka's—deep purple, blocking out any sort of light.

Luka raised a brow. "Yours does not look appetizing."

"I suppose it does not." Ragnar managed a smirk. "But that does not matter. Are you ready?"

"As ready as I will ever be."

They lifted the vials, giving each other a single nod before tipping them back to drink.

But Ragnar's never reached his mouth.

Before the potion could reach his lips, the vial disappeared from his grasp.

Maxwell stood by the doorway, the vial that was meant for Ragnar now in his hands.

"Maxwell, no!" Ragnar reached out, but it was too late.

Maxwell smiled, a silent somber farewell etching his features. "Thank you, Ragnar. For everything." The contents disappeared into Maxwell's throat.

Luka clutched his chest, and the vial shattered as it

collided with the hard ground. He gasped for breath as he stumbled. Maxwell mimicked his brother's reaction to the potion.

All of the strength in Ragnar's legs disappeared. He wobbled backward, his work desk breaking his fall before he collided with the hard ground. Ingredients shuffled around, rolling off the surface of the desk.

The noise fell on deaf ears. The only thing Ragnar could hear was the rush of his own blood. What had he just done? Maxwell was gone. And it was all his fault. If he hadn't been so adamant about using shadow play, this never would have happened.

But if not Maxwell, it would have been Luka. Ragnar did not want to lose either of them.

Ragnar remained on the floor of his study, frozen in place by the remnants of his failed sacrifice. He had meant to protect both brothers, but in the end, he could only watch as one sacrificed himself for the other.

Ragnar struggled to breathe as the weight of his failure pressed down against him.

Maxwell would wake up as Owen Ko, the name Ragnar had crafted for the vessel, with no memory of his true identity. He would serve as Luka's butler, always by his side. Protecting him.

Even when Ragnar could not.

35

SHATTERED

Luka took a deep breath, letting it out through his teeth. That was the only memory he seemed to have absorbed when Owen's—no, Maxwell's—body had initiated the final act of shadow play. The sensation lingered uncomfortably in his head, slowly fading through his fingertips.

Luka's fragmented soul had finally healed, the piece of his soul that had been separated from him for eighty-five years. It was . . . strange. It was as if he was finally looking at himself in the mirror, truly seeing who he actually was. Removing a mask that had been forced upon his face. One that he hadn't even known had been thrust upon him until this very moment.

Even moving around in his body had a foreign sensation. He was alarmingly aware of how everything felt, like whatever had been used to cloud his senses had been removed, giving him full clarity. He was aware of how soft the chair was, how bright the room was even with the curtains drawn, how hard everyone held their breath as they took in the weight of everything.

The world seemed sharper, more vivid, as though he had spent the last eight decades viewing everything through a clouded window.

"Your brother . . . Maxwell. So, he wasn't missing at all? He was with you this entire time?" Elliot asked slowly, as if he was still trying to decipher the memories Luka had shared. "And the memory of the mansion attack? It was all fake?"

"Fabricated by Ragnar," Luka said, the name feeling both familiar and foreign to him. "I know his position now versus what he did for me in the past do not line up, and I am trying to understand that as well." Luka closed his eyes, attempting to tune out the overwhelming sensations as he treaded through his memories, attempting to dig up any clues as to what had happened to Ragnar. But each recollection of Ragnar felt like he was trying to catch a snowflake in a blizzard. The more he tried, the harder it was to follow.

The older ethereal had always been there, a constant presence, supportive of him and his brother. Ragnar knew of the prophecy, and if he truly believed Luka was the oracle, he would have done everything he could to protect him.

The shadow play spell had been used as the ultimate protection. A final resort to keep Luka safe from harm. Ragnar's wish to protect him was evident. So, why was it that Ragnar was now with King Valentine VI? Luka was not an elf, so he did not have to worry about facing the same elven prejudices as Elliot and Minari. There had to be more to it, some crucial piece of the puzzle he was missing.

What had happened to Ragnar?

Luka's head throbbed the more he tried to untangle the mystery. The notebook in Ragnar's study might hold the key to understanding the entire picture. But the study was surely gone, with the notebook likely in Ragnar's possession within the kingdom. Luka did not know how he would be able to obtain it.

But what he did know was that Hiro was a traitor.

And Hiro was a Necromancer. Two important details they should focus on.

He had been keeping an eye on everyone ever since they'd met.

Which meant he also knew of Chloé's whereabouts and her condition.

"The time for shadows is near, and yours will be cast upon the wall first."

Hiro's last words to him echoed in his mind.

Though Luka was certain Hiro was not aware of the shadow play spell, those words brought an eerie premonition.

Shadows meant eternal darkness. The darkness that would engulf the world if the Necromancers succeeded in summoning Mykronos from Kelemvor, the divine realm. A world without light. A world without hope.

Hot anger suddenly erupted in Luka's chest.

Hiro.

Elliot had trusted Hiro from the moment they'd met. The human was full of mystery, yet it did not matter to Elliot. His kind heart saw only trust and good. What connection did they have in the past life? The past oracle's soul within Elliot must have been the reason for his complete trust in Hiro. So why was it that Elliot was always the one who got hurt? His kindness seemed to always be returned with betrayal and sadness.

Luka detested it. It only caused his blood to boil.

"So, the culprit to this whole thing . . . is gone." Sophia lowered her wand. Her eyes landed on Luka, full of pity and wariness. "You, too, were a victim, and this spell is the only reason you're alive."

"Yes," Luka said.

Sophia tucked her wand away. "To believe there was a traitor within our walls . . ."

"Elliot," Mimi said, taking Elliot's hand into his. "How are you feeling?"

"I'm . . . managing, I guess," Elliot said. "We can't stop moving just because Hiro isn't here anymore. We need to keep moving."

"The queen must have known about this," Sage interjected, his voice sharp with suspicion. "Did she trick us?"

"Do not slander Queen Elyria's name," Sophia snapped. "She would do no such thing."

"So, you're saying she was tricked, then?" Sage raised a brow, challenging the sentinel.

"Blasphemy."

"There's a reason for everything," Elliot said. "No

matter what, what we know now is that Hiro is no longer with us." The elf's voice trembled as he uttered the human's name. "He will be in Rainwell."

"It all leads there, doesn't it?" Mimi said. "Rainwell."

"Rainwell," Sophia mumbled under her breath, her expression hardening. "If you plan on leaving, you will meet with Queen Elyria first. No one leaves without her permission."

The name of the small elven village hung in the air, a reminder that no matter what path they took, Rainwell would always call them back, like a thread of fate pulling them toward their destiny.

Luka deeply wished this would put an end to Elliot's suffering. But as he glanced at the oracle's face, he was surprised to find whatever sadness that had taken ahold of Elliot was no longer there. Now the elf's expression was filled with determination and a fire that Luka had not seen before.

Perhaps the realization of betrayal—being used and deceived by those closest to him—was all Elliot needed to fuel his path. To set it ablaze and create a new one for himself. To not fall into the traps of expectations others placed for him as they tried to break Elliot down.

Luka could not stop himself from smiling. This was different than when Elliot had lost Minari, and the ethereal welcomed his newfound strength.

36
CHANGE

The throne room felt colder and larger than Elliot remembered. It hadn't been that long since he was there, but the recent revelations made it seem more stark, more hostile. Tension hung in the air.

Queen Elyria sat upon her throne, her presence heavy with authority and rule. Her legs were crossed, cheek resting against her hand as she gave her attention to Luka as he spoke. Her eyes blinked slowly as she took in the details.

"And that is what happened, Queen Elyria," Luka said, head bowed low. "We did not anticipate this would happen."

Elyria merely hummed. The lack of shock in her response made Elliot's skin crawl with unease. Had she expected this to happen? Had she known Hiro was a

Necromancer?

Elyria drummed her fingers against the armrest of her throne. "So it may be."

"My queen, we should go after him," Sophia said, stepping forward. "We cannot let this disgusting being go without judgement. He needs to be punished."

Elyria shook her head. "It was predetermined."

Predetermined?

The word hit Elliot like a blow to his gut. His stomach felt as if it were twisting in on itself, and his chest tightened. His breath was caught in his throat as he tried to remember to breathe.

"So, you knew this would happen?" Sophia asked.

Elyria nodded, and Elliot grew dizzy. The queen knew. She knew this was going to happen. Memories of meeting Hiro, their interactions, his support, and every genuine smile he'd given the elf—they were all lies. An act. But why had he done it? Why had he gone through the trouble of traveling with them? Why had he let them live?

"My queen, why—" Sophia began, but she was cut off when Elyria waved her hand.

"There are things even I cannot meddle with. Even as the mother of elves, I am merely a piece that plays a part in a much grander story. I cannot change how it was written."

The words spun around Elliot's head. He thought about all the choices and events that had brought him here. He recalled Minari's words to him in his dream, telling him that Minari was destined to die. Destined to return as a Necromancer.

"You think everything we're doing has been

predetermined?” Elliot asked, his voice barely above a whisper.

“Indeed, young oracle. Everything.” The queen’s red eyes met Elliot’s, full of understanding, yet sad at the same time. Like she knew what it was like to feel powerless. “Though I knew of Hiro’s betrayal, I knew not when it would happen.”

“You knew he was a Necromancer and didn’t tell us?” Sage yelled, balling his hands into fists.

“Do not raise your voice against the queen,” Sophia snapped.

“I do not mind, Sophia. In fact, it would have been odd if they had not felt this way,” Elyria said. She closed her eyes, pausing momentarily before continuing. “Unfortunately, it was not my place. Vylantra and Mykronos determine what can and cannot be done in this world. It was by their will that Hiro’s identity was revealed this way.”

Something suddenly snapped within Elliot. An itch of defiance. An itch to go against all that had been predetermined for him. “Then what about you?” Elliot challenged. “Was deceiving us by their will also?”

When Elyria’s eyes met Elliot’s again, they were somber and full of regret. A slight frown lay upon her lips. “If I could tell you everything I know, I would. But what I discussed with you two prior was all true. That, at least, I wanted to tell you in case you needed it.”

The warning Elyria had given Elliot earlier replayed in his mind—Hiro’s ability to siphon magic from Elliot to himself and from himself to Elliot.

Elliot knew that when he came face-to-face with Hiro again in Rainwell, he would need to protect himself, to guard himself from Hiro's skill. Elliot could not let Hiro take his magic.

"What did she tell you?" Sage asked.

Elliot glanced at Elyria, seeking permission to share what had been private counsel. The queen only nodded, her expression completely neutral, allowing Elliot to make the decision for himself. She would play no part in it.

"Luka, do you remember when you pushed your stamina into my magic core?"

"I do," Luka said.

"It seems Hiro can do it too. Except he can pull from me as well."

"Elliot, that is not good," Mimi said. "He can pull magic from your core? Wouldn't that leave you vulnerable?"

"We need a strategy," Luka said. "We cannot let Hiro come into contact with Elliot when we reach Rainwell."

"Stay close to us," Mimi said.

Elliot shook his head. "You know during battle, whatever happens happens. I need to be able to defend myself regardless." The elf knew full well he could not completely rely on his friends' protection. They needed to focus on their battles. And he needed to focus on his.

"Plan even for the worst-case scenario," Sage said. He slammed his fist into his palm. "Once I see that sleazy human again, I will plow his face into the gravel. I'll make sure of it."

Elliot had never been a vengeful person. Even now,

after Hiro had attempted to assassinate Luka and Owen and had left without a trace, Elliot couldn't shake the memory of comfort and warmth Hiro offered when the elf needed it.

Elliot did not want to harm Hiro.

There had to be more to the story. A reason for his actions. Something they weren't aware of. He refused to let the darkness invade his mind and heart again. He would find truth.

"I suspect you plan on leaving as soon as possible," Elyria said, breaking Elliot's train of thought.

"Yes. They'll be waiting for us," Elliot responded.

Elyria raised her hand, giving a slight wave. "Vale."

A small whirlwind formed at the base of the stairs. Another sentinel appeared through the wind, though he was one they had not seen before.

He was tall, with broad shoulders, completely clad in the same silver armor. His pointy elf ears stuck out from his long, white braid. And his eyes were crimson.

"You called, my queen?"

"Vale, you will assist the oracle and his companions to Rainwell."

"As you wish."

"Vale is the general of the sentinels. He is strong and can communicate with me and the other sentinels directly through the magic weave we have created. If you need anything from me, please do not hesitate to ask."

"I thought you were just going to sit back and watch everything happen," Sage said, raising a brow.

Elyria smiled. "Your oracle has persuaded me

otherwise. Perhaps even the smallest things we do can have an impact."

The words settled over Elliot, offering comfort against the pain of betrayal and uncertainty. Maybe their fates weren't as set in stone as Elyria had initially claimed. Perhaps there was still hope for all of them.

Even for Hiro.

Even for Minari.

37

COMPANION

Chloé focused on the sloshing of hot water entering the teacup. The sound of the jar opening and the extraction of flowers. The crackling of the firewood and the smell of burning warmth. From the window, she could hear the gentle breeze, the rustling leaves tapping against the glass. Asher's private quarters were quiet and peaceful. Gentle.

The sensation of stamina returned to her body, tingling with a sense of renewed vitality. Chloé felt refreshed, the fatigue fading like a distant memory. Her muscles, which had felt thick with unmovable weight, now responded to her will with ease. She flexed her fingers, pleased at how little effort it took to move them.

"All right, Chloé, we are done for today," Asher said, letting go of Chloé's hand. She already missed the sensation. There was something in his touch that brought her comfort. His hands were always warm and reassuring. She opened her eyes, her vision clear once again.

Chloé had been seeing Asher on a weekly basis ever since she had learned that she needed him to share his magic with her. Usually by the fifth day, she felt tired, and by the end of the sixth, she found it difficult to focus. Waking up on the seventh day, it was difficult for her to even get out of bed. The dependency gnawed at her. She did not want to burden the ethereal, but she had to learn to accept her condition.

It was who Chloé was now.

It had been embarrassing for Chloé when Kaia found her still tucked away under her sheets, too weak to move the first time it happened. She had been late for their practice, something Chloé hated. She took pride in being punctual, never wanting to waste even a single minute. So succumbing to an ailment as this made her wish she could hide away and disappear forever. This was something she didn't want anyone, especially someone of the royal family, to witness. What if the princess thought everyone in the guild was as weak as Chloé? What if she had second thoughts on helping their cause? She had crucial knowledge, and spilling it to the wrong people would be detrimental to everyone.

"Here," Kaia said, pushing a cup to Chloé and taking a seat next to her. The steam of the tea rose in spirals from the porcelain. "I heard your favorite tea was chamomile. Of course, I added a splash of lemon in there too."

"Thank you," Chloé said. "You know me well, huh?" She wrapped her palms against the cup, enjoying the warmth it sent up her arms.

"Well, my teacher instructed me to be observant of my surroundings, both the environment and the people." Kaia smiled. "What kind of student would I be if I didn't know how my teacher liked her tea?"

Chloé was so proud of Kaia and how quickly she'd adapted. It was as if she was never meant to be part of royalty. The way she easily tossed aside her old identity and embraced the ways of the norm made Chloé think this was perhaps what Kaia's soul was yearning for. Freedom of expression. Freedom to choose. Freedom to be who she wanted to be. The nix wondered what the princess would do once everything was over. Would she return to the castle and her heritage? Or would she remain with the guild?

There was no telling what Bunnie had in store for Stryx once everything was over. There would be no reason to remain under the guise of Stryx, so returning to their old identity as Nighthawk was probably the next step. What happened afterward was unknown.

Chloé herself did not know what she wanted to do.

At least, not with the time she had left.

"It has only been three weeks," Chloé said as she watched Kaia pull her pistol from her holster, "and you're already acting like one of us. Are you sure you were who you said you were?"

"Whatever do you mean, Chloé?" Kaia said innocently. She twirled the pistol around her finger before tucking it away. Chloé had learned the gesture was something Kaia enjoyed doing, like a new trick that one would want to show off. "I've been Kaia my whole life! I was moved when I learned what Stryx was doing. I just had to be a part of the cause."

"And what is our cause?" Chloé tested the princess.

"Well, right now, it's to hinder the recruitment of the knights. The royal decree issued by the king calls upon recruitment of anyone willing to join the knights. The kingdom of Etheria has announced war against the elves, and we, being on the elven side, want to stop them," Kaia responded casually and matter-of-factly, as if she'd not recited or memorized the cause but rather knew this like the back of her hand. "I was assigned to you because the captain believes you're the best fit for the job!"

Asher chuckled, covering his mouth with the back of his hand. "Kaia, your enthusiasm is contagious. Now I feel like perhaps I can take on the knights of Etheria myself and put a stop to this."

Kaia covered her cheeks with her hands, shying away. "Don't embarrass me—not in front of Chloé!"

"How am I embarrassing you?" Asher said, amused and enjoying the princess's reaction. "I am merely making a statement based on observation." He leaned against the table, lacing his fingers together and resting his chin against them. His eyes studied Kaia. "I have never seen you this bright. The way your eyes sparkle tells me you are genuinely happy. This is the first time I have ever seen this side of you, and honestly . . . I am glad."

Kaia's mouth opened and closed, a spew of sounds leaving her lips. She looked at Asher before glancing back down to her lap, her hands fidgeting with the hem of her tunic. "Thank you, Iri—ahem, Asher."

Chloé placed a hand on Kaia's shoulder, giving the princess a light squeeze. "I'm proud of you." She smirked. "Even if you occasionally mispronounce Asher's name. I do wonder where you get the name Iris from."

"Ah, maybe in a dream?" A blush crept up Kaia's neck and into her cheeks, visible even beneath her carefully applied makeup. She gave Chloé a shy smile. "Thank you . . . to the both of you. It really means a lot to me. I can finally be myself, and I'm glad I have the support and care from you two."

"Well, what kind of friends would we be if we didn't support you?" Chloé asked.

Kaia's eyes widened as her mouth dropped. She stared at Chloé before staring at Asher. "Friends?"

"What is that reaction for?" Asher laughed. "Of course! Friends. Family. That's who we are to one another here in Stryx."

Chloé nodded. She hadn't expected the word to have an effect on Kaia. An idea suddenly popped into her head. "Kai, you are one of us now."

Kaia simply grinned, and her eyes glistened as tears began to well. The nickname seemed to have a positive effect. The nix could tell Kaia was feeling a wave of emotions and was not sure how to process it. Here was a princess who had everything she could possibly wish for yet had been given nothing and was finally finding her place in the world.

"Thank you, Clo," Kaia said. Her voice shook with emotion. "You can count on me."

Chloé mimicked the grin Kaia had just a few moments ago. It was such a simple gesture, but it had so much meaning behind it. "Likewise, Kai."

38
PUSH

Valor opened his eyes, his body feeling completely refreshed. Yet his chest tightened with anguish. There was an unexplained heaviness. The feeling brought tears to his eyes, and they threatened to spill down his cheeks. He blinked them back, not understanding why he felt this way. The Necromancer couldn't recall anything that had happened between when he fell ill and when he woke up. The last memory he could recall was when Arielle and Vincent were here checking in on him. At the time, only nine days had passed. So, how much time had passed since then?

The air in the room shifted, causing the hair on the back of Valor's neck to stand up. He suddenly became aware of two other presences in the room. He bolted up, muscles tensing as he looked for the intruders. He did not see anyone, but his body was on edge, still sensing movement within the shadows. Whoever was here . . . he could not decipher if it was friend or foe.

The single small window was the only source of light Valor had, though the years of training this body had proved he did not need it. He held his breath and closed his eyes, homing in on the location of the intruders.

There were not many places to hide. Knight quarters were small in comparison to the royal family's quarters. They did not have a need for extravagant furnishings or baths. Knight quarters were quaint, only housing necessities: a bed, a desk, a weapon rack, and a small wardrobe.

Valor looked straight ahead where he sensed the presence. A swirl of black feathers appeared by the front of the bed. "Rhea."

"Valor," Rhea said, emerging from the portal.

"Who is with you?" Valor's voice was rough from disuse.

Rhea tilted her head, her red hair catching the small bit of moonlight. "What do you mean? It's just me here." She crossed her arms, shifting her hips slightly. "When I couldn't contact you, I was worried. The others couldn't reach you either."

"Ah . . ." Valor had forgotten that Necromancers were able to communicate through telepathy. The ability had once seemed natural to Valor, but for some reason, it now seemed slightly foreign. "What's today?"

"The first month, twenty-first day. Approximately five hours from sunrise."

Valor's eyes widened, and his stomach dropped. He'd been asleep for another twelve days? He had been unconscious for twenty-one days in total. What was happening to him? There was no way fatigue could have taken him out for so long—especially not for a Necromancer who did not even need to sleep.

Valor clicked his tongue in frustration. He couldn't remember anything. The only memory he could bring up was the garden, but even that memory was starting to fade. He could barely make out what the place had looked like. It was like trying to grab smoke.

"I asked Father where you were," Rhea began, interrupting his thoughts. "To find out you were here all along . . . What's happening?" Her eyes softened. "This isn't like you, Valor. You're usually so diligent when Father assigns you tasks."

"I don't know myself." Valor hated that he had to admit it.

Rhea frowned, her white orbs narrowing. "Well, what did Father ask you to do? Have you completed it yet?"

"He asked me to supervise the princess," Valor started. "And to kill her if I suspect her of treason." He grunted, tossing the sheets aside and getting off the bed. He welcomed the sharp bite of the cold as his bare feet touched the floor.

Valor couldn't be a failure to Ragnar anymore. He had already failed him in the past. To be asleep for so long when a Necromancer didn't need it . . . It made sense why Ragnar had sent Rhea to check in on Valor. He needed to return to his duties. He needed to prove his worth.

Valor tapped into his core, willing the sleeping garments away, turning them into his usual black attire.

Rhea grabbed Valor's wrist. "You can't be thinking of going now."

"Why would I remain here?"

Rhea's hold tightened. "Valor," she whispered, "I know you're not yourself."

"What are you getting at?"

"The host's soul . . . Minari. You feel him, don't you?" Her voice was rushed and quiet, as if she was afraid someone would overhear.

Valor froze. How did Rhea know about this? Was she in a similar situation?

"Me too," Rhea said, as if she'd read Valor's mind. "Sometimes . . . there are moments where I black out. When I come to, I'm somewhere else, and I don't know how I got there." Rhea bit her lip. "I can only assume it's Lily's doing."

"And what happens after that? Do you feel anything?"

"Oftentimes, I feel sad for no reason. Or fatigued." Rhea huffed, running her hand through her hair in frustration. "I hate it. Why doesn't this happen to the others also?"

"Raven and Aiden are not affected by the wills of their hosts?"

Rhea shook her head. "When I asked the two of them about it, they said we must be weak. Seeing as we are the only two elves, they immediately jumped to that conclusion." She scoffed. "Ignorant assholes . . ."

"I suspect it must be because they don't have a close

bond with the oracle, like we do," Valor said, the pieces finally falling into place. It all made sense. When he looked back at Minari's memories, he could see the close ties they had with Elliot.

The friendship.

The loyalty.

The love.

It was very likely their souls, even in a deep slumber, were trying to reach for that connection. The deep desire they had to protect not just the oracle but their friend as well was giving them strength to pull Valor and Rhea from consciousness.

Valor and Rhea needed to find a solution to completely block Minari and Lily. And they needed to do it quickly. If the two hosts could pull themselves out from their slumber at any moment, they would be putting the final mission at risk. If they woke up during the battle, everything could fail. And they could not afford for that to happen—not when they were so close to achieving what they deserved.

"The presence I felt earlier. I said there were two." Valor paused. "The other must be Lily."

Rhea's eyes widened. "You think she'll come out?"

"I can feel her, though she's weak. Maybe she's trying. Do you feel anything?"

Rhea shook her head. "No, I don't." Her voice was full of anger and fear. "Dammit! If I can't tell when Lily is trying to come out, how will I be of any use to Father? You and I are a risk to the mission!"

"I know," Valor said, his mind racing through possibilities. What could they do? Was there even anything they could do? If what they thought was true, the oracle had the upper hand in the fight. Once his and Rhea's bodies saw him, he was certain they would react.

Wait.

All they needed to do was not see him.

Or perhaps they just needed to forget about him entirely.

"Raven," Valor started. "We can ask Raven to control us. If he takes control of our minds and memories, Minari and Lily won't be aware of what's going on around us."

"So, before the final battle, we just get Raven to control us?" Doubt was evident in Rhea's voice. "It's bad enough that we can't control when our hosts' souls come out, and you want Raven to control us?"

"To an extent." Valor frowned. "I don't like the idea of being controlled either, and I hate how neither of us can detect when we'll be pushed out because our hosts can't keep quiet, but Raven is our best bet. We need to still be able to control our powers, so he'll just need to control what we see, what we hear, and what we know."

"You want him to block our senses and memories so our original bodies won't know we'll be going against the oracle." Rhea rested her hand beneath her chin. She pondered for a bit before continuing. "You think they're listening to our conversation now? You mentioned you could feel Lily." Rhea's voice dropped to barely above a whisper.

"It's a gamble we will have to take."

Even if Minari knew of Valor's plan, he would make sure the elf couldn't do anything about it.

39
UNKNOWN

Bunnie quickly wrote down what Wren was telling her, her quill scratching against the pale yellow parchment with urgency. The small candle flickered with each quick stroke. They needed to move fast if they wanted to have the upper hand. There was no telling when the kingdom would find out what Stryx was up to.

"Unfortunately, he was missing this morning. When I went to check in on him with the doctor, his bed was empty," Wren said, finishing up. The guild member wore a black cloak, hiding what she wore underneath. Her colored blond hair was tied up in a messy bun, stray hairs resting against her cheeks, hiding a bit of her freckles. Her eyes were her usual cinnamon, since she was not wearing contacts.

Wren was assigned as Arielle's double while the real

princess was here. Wren was one of their best actresses and had studied the art of disguise closely under Asher. Her demeanor was a perfect reflection of Arielle's, from the slight tilt of her head when listening to others to the precise way she held her teacup during occasions. Her voice, tone, and word choice all indicated she was who she appeared to be. And the fact that none of the royal family or maids had even taken notice of the swap meant that Wren's performance was flawless.

Bunnie tapped her quill, creating a splotch of ink on the corner of the page. "His symptoms were improving though?"

Wren nodded. "They were, though whenever he gained consciousness, his eyes were fogged over, and he would mumble incoherent things. Dr. Laurent could not find the source of his condition or figure out what caused it. But . . ." She paused. "I can sometimes make out names."

"Can you recall what names?"

Wren stood there for a moment, silent as she tried to recall. "Elliot and Lily."

Bunnie was not surprised. Those two were Minari's closest friends. "And this began at the start of this month . . ." She placed her quill down and massaged her temples, leaning back in her chair. She had kept it a secret from Chloé that Minari was alive and working in the castle. If the nix knew, she would've barged through the castle gates and demanded answers from the elf. Bunnie was trying to understand why Minari was working under Ragnar. She had thought he had amnesia, but based on Wren's report just now, she ruled that out. Unless he could only say those names when he was in a certain state—when his muscles remembered but his mind did not.

It was also concerning that Bunnie had received detailed reports stating Minari had died by the hands of Lily back in a chimeran territory.

But who exactly had brought his body back?

And why had she killed him?

The chimeran village and Valquent weren't exactly close together, so carrying an unconscious elf would have been difficult.

Was it a trader, then? They usually carried wagons with them, and it wouldn't be surprising if they had passed through the village. But if it was a trader, her men would have reported back. She had eyes on all the major trade routes. Someone would've noticed the elf being transported.

It was like Minari had just appeared out of thin air.

Just like magic.

To make matters worse, Hiro had stopped sending her reports after they had left for Astaria. There were no members outside of Etheria, so she relied on Hiro to make frequent reports. Each day that passed without receiving word from him was another weight added to her shoulders. More unknowns to maneuver around.

Bunnie just hoped nothing had happened to them.

But hope was a luxury she could not rely on. She needed concrete facts. She needed contingency plans.

But the constant waiting was putting Bunnie on edge. With no word from Hiro, and Minari suddenly vanishing, her gut was telling her to prepare for the worst possible outcome.

The leader did not know if they were going to survive after everything was done. The thought of failure loomed over her like a shadow, but she pushed it aside. She couldn't afford to be paralyzed by fear—not when so many people were counting on her.

Bunnie knew she needed to send Chloé to the Snowy Hills. She needed to reunite with the others. But in order for her to make the journey, Asher would need to accompany her. Bunnie would lose two of her trusted officers when she needed them the most.

Bunnie needed to consider who could temporarily take their positions. Otherwise, Vivian, Deveran, and Oliver would be the only three she had. Not impossible, but not ideal either.

"Is there anything you would like me to do?" Wren asked, breaking Bunnie's internal planning.

Bunnie shook her head. "If you do anything differently, it might make you appear suspicious. For now, just do what you think is best and how you think the princess would react." She paused before adding, "But keep your eyes and ears open, as always. The smallest details could change the outcome and fate of what's to come."

Wren bowed. "Of course. I shall take my leave now."

As the door closed behind Wren, Bunnie pulled out a fresh sheet of parchment. She rewrote key events that had happened thus far.

Chloé's separation from the group.

The group reaching the Snowy Hills.

Elliot regaining part of Myru's memories.

The group departing for the kingdom of Astaria.

Minari appearing within the castle and being appointed as Arielle's personal knight.

Minari falling to an unknown illness.

Minari disappearing from the castle.

Hiro's silence.

There were too many pieces in motion, too many variables.

Bunnie couldn't seem to shake the feeling that they were all being maneuvered into position by an unseen hand.

40
PUPPETS

Arielle's orbs rolled back as the light in her eyes faded. Valor took deep gulps as he tried to clear his vision. His heart raced, thudding painfully against his chest. He dropped the fake princess's body, and it landed on the hard ground with a loud thud, the noise echoing off the walls of her bedroom chambers. The princess's blood pooled around her body, seeping into the intricate patterns of the stone floor.

Valor could not believe he had let this fake play him for so long. Ragnar was right to be suspicious of her. The moment he had seen Arielle slip something inside the sleeve of her dress, he knew the person he had been watching over wasn't the real princess—there was no reason for her to send messages as discreetly as she had done. If she was the princess, then there shouldn't have been anything for her to hide.

Valor looked at what Arielle had tried to hide. It was a small piece of parchment, folded multiple times to be as small as her fingernail. Furrowing his brow, he unfolded it, eyes scanning the contents. The handwriting was elegant but hurried, as if it had been written in haste.

The haze has returned.

Valor crumpled the parchment before tossing it over Arielle's body. The pale yellow quickly turned red as it soaked in her blood.

Who was she reporting to? And what did she mean by the haze?

The questions repeated in Valor's mind as he tried to recall who Arielle had interacted with.

Valor quickly moved through Arielle's chambers, his footsteps silent. He searched for anything he could use as a clue to reveal her true identity.

Valor went through every possible hiding place. He opened every drawer. Threw the sheets off the bed. Checked behind the dresser. Tore through her wardrobe.

Unfortunately, his efforts were made in vain.

Everything was clean. Immaculate. A clear indicator that the maids had done a diligent job at keeping the princess's chambers clean. But on the other hand, it was void of any personality. It was as if Arielle had been here just to be here and had no intention of actually living here.

After the fifth round, the Necromancer failed to find a single spare parchment Arielle would've used for future messages. Had she anticipated this, ensuring nothing was left behind? Or was this letter from someone else? If it was, then who was it? Who was working with her?

Movement out of the corner of his eye caught Valor's attention. He peered out the window. Arielle had a clear view of the courtyard where the recruited knights held their training. The afternoon cast shadows across the practice yard where the knights moved through their drills.

Had one of the knights been working with her? Valor cursed under his breath. He didn't have time to weave through the numbers. There were already well over four hundred volunteers, each one a potential conspirator. He needed to find the traitor now.

"What do you think you are doing, Valor?" Ragnar's cool voice dripped annoyance.

Valor blinked, the fog in his mind suddenly receding, making him very aware he was standing in the middle of what could only be described as a complete massacre.

The Necromancer recognized the bodies that lay around him. They were the knight recruits from team three, their training armor now punctured and stained crimson. Their bodies flooded the courtyard, the once-cream stone ground now drenched in pure red. Faces frozen in expressions of shock and betrayal stared up at the darkening sky.

What disturbed Valor the most was not the bodies or why Ragnar was here.

What disturbed Valor the most was that he had no recollection of what had just happened.

Why was he in the middle of the courtyard? Why did

he reek of metallic iron? Why were his clothes heavy with blood? Why were his hands stained?

Why couldn't he remember anything?

The gap in his memory and his failure to report a good reason for his current situation to Ragnar hurt him the most.

Ragnar's sharp gray eyes narrowed at Valor, his frown deepening with each breath he took. His presence made the outside night air itself grow colder. "You have killed seventy-two knights." His voice was steady, but Valor knew Ragnar was angry. The careful control in his tone reflected his suppressed rage. "I ordered you to silence the princess if you expected her of treason, which—"Ragnar's eyes flashed toward the window of Arielle's room before returning to Valor"—you have."

"She received a secret message," Valor said slowly as he attempted to recall what had happened before he'd found himself here. "The haze has returned," he recited.

"And this?" Ragnar gestured around them, at the bodies of the fallen knights. "What is your reason for this?"

"I . . ." Valor did not know what to say. He had no excuse—especially since he did not even remember why he was in the courtyard in the first place.

Did the other royal family members know Valor had just assassinated the princess? What would happen to Ragnar if they found out? He was a prominent figure in the royal court. Surely nothing would happen to him.

At least, Valor hoped not.

"You've tested me for the last time," Ragnar seethed, his hand suddenly around Valor's neck. His grip was tight, only allowing Valor small, quick breaths. Ragnar's fingers dug into Valor's neck like icicles.

"Even in this lifetime, I do not have complete control over you, hmm?" Ragnar said. "Perhaps I ought to be rid of you before you cause any more harm."

"Father."

Rhea.

Valor moved his eyes in the direction of her voice. A black whirlwind of feathers appeared as Rhea stepped from the portal.

Ragnar released Valor, standing up straight. "Rhea."

Valor staggered backward before collapsing to his knees. He pressed his hand against his neck, feeling the frozen indents where Ragnar had held him. He bit back a wince as pain shot through his body. He quickly pulled his hand back.

"Father, could you please excuse Valor?" Rhea asked.

Ragnar was silent, merely staring at the other elf as if he was weighing the options of her plea. The tension in the air increased with each second of silence.

"Please," Rhea begged. "We still have plenty of knights as our disposal."

"Fail me again, and I will erase your soul from this very existence."

Ragnar's words were not a threat. They were a promise.

"We will begin the plan earlier than expected," Ragnar started. "This minor incident took us off track, but destiny will always find a way. Rhea, I trust you to begin."

Rhea bowed. "Yes, Father. I will not fail you."

"No, you will not." And with those last words, Ragnar disappeared in a tornado of black feathers.

Rhea quickly rushed to Valor's side, helping him up. "Valor, what were you thinking?"

"I don't remember . . ." Valor shook his head, wincing at the movement. The chilled nerves on his neck were still there even after Ragnar's departure. It may be a while until the spell vanished.

Rhea cursed under her breath. "Well, that can't be helped. I was hoping we'd have more time to gather resources. But I guess this will have to do."

"What do you mean?"

"The knights here were supposed to be used as cannon fodder. Throwaway bodies for the battle. I was tasked to turn them into imps when the time came. The reason Father didn't share the plan with you is because he does not trust you—not after what you did in the past. And from the looks of it, he probably barely trusts you even now."

Valor bit the inside of his cheek, tasting blood. Ragnar had every right to not trust him. He was the reason they were here in the first place. The reason why they were attempting to raise Mykronos from Kelemvor once again.

They were so close, but Valor had let his righteousness get in the way of loyalty.

And now, standing in a courtyard full of dead knights with no memory of how or why he had done what he did, Valor wondered if history was about to repeat itself.

41
TIME

Errol stared up at the night sky. Each star sparkled as if it were trying to talk to him, attempting to send him a message. He closed his eyes, listening to the soft, gentle sound of the running river. The soothing noise never failed to calm him down. Tonight, his nerves were on edge, and he couldn't figure out why. He had hoped sitting by the river would clear his mind and stop the growing sense of unease.

Three months had already passed since their arrival in Rainwell. Errol would remain forever grateful for Azriel's hospitality. The Mistfall elves had fully settled into their new homes, meshing well with the natives.

That was all Errol could ask for.

Small crunching of the grass alerted Errol. Based on the speed, he knew who it was.

"Azriel," Errol said.

"Errol," Azriel started. "I have yet to succeed at sneaking up behind you."

"Do that and you may find a dagger between your eyes."

Azriel chortled, taking a seat next to Errol. "I think I could make do without that, thank you."

"And I can make do without someone sneaking up behind me." Errol smirked. Even after giving up his scout duties, the years of training would be hard to get rid of. The elf found himself reacting on instinct as he would back home. Unfortunately, he had frightened local elves that way. It was something he was still working on improving.

"I want to show you something," Azriel said, finally breaking the comforting silence between them.

"What is it?"

"You'll know once you see. Follow me."

"You feel it too, don't you?" Azriel asked as they treaded down the dark spiral stairwell.

Errol felt the tingling in his skin and the hair on the back of his neck prickle. He wished he did not feel it, but the air, the space, and the aura around the village had begun shifting.

"They can sense the time is near," Azriel said. "Their bodies are calling for their souls to return to them. I've kept this catacomb hidden away for so long. No one else here knows of this location."

Errol understood the heavy burden of secrecy. He was

no stranger to it. He'd spent his entire life keeping Elliot's identity from him. In the end, he wondered what good it had done.

The entrance of the underground catacombs had been discreetly located deep in the forest away from Rainwell. The path to it was blocked by a thick layer of trees, making it difficult for the average person to trek through. Azriel's knowledge of its location and Errol's nimble footwork made it possible for the two. The stairwell was narrow, allowing only a single person to pass. Errol had to tilt his shoulders slightly as he descended. Azriel experienced the same tightness. A single torch lit the way for the both of them, and Azriel held it in front of him.

Luckily, the farther they went, the wider the stairwell became, making it easier for them to walk. A long tunnel greeted them at the bottom, wide enough for Errol and Azriel to stand side by side.

The air was damp and dense. The sensation Errol had felt earlier was stronger here, his body alerting him that there was danger.

The two elves' footsteps did not make a single noise as they proceeded down the corridor. The stone ground and walls felt like they had eyes and were watching their every move. The path led them to a dead end. A stone wall blocked them from proceeding. A crescent moon was etched in the center with thorny vines wrapped around it. The edges had symbols all around, likely an ancient language that Errol did not recognize.

Azriel placed his hand against the stone and mumbled a few words under his breath.

A low rumbling reverberated around them, and the stone wall that was blocking their way slowly moved downward.

Azriel and Errol entered the circular chamber. Frozen in midair were four bodies—two male and two female humans—encapsulated in vines, thorns, and flowers. It was as if time itself stood still. The bodies appeared as if they were merely sleeping, their expressions devoid of any emotion.

"These are the four," Azriel whispered. "The four that we, the Rainwell leaders, have been watching over for centuries. These are the four that nearly brought the god of death into our world."

"Do you know their names?" Errol asked. The more he looked at the bodies, the more he felt unnerved. It was eerie how peaceful they looked, unaware of their presence.

"Mason, Hazel, Rhea, and Valor," Azriel said, turning his head from left to right.

Mason had a warm, sun-kissed complexion with bright blond hair. In contrast, Hazel's skin was pale, her short curly red hair framing her delicate face. Rhea and Valor had a similar complexion to Hazel's, but a little deeper. Rhea's hair was long and a rich chestnut brown, while Valor's hair was brown with hints of ash gray.

"It is like they are just sleeping," Errol mused.

"In a way, they are." Azriel paused. "Once the Necromancers return here, these bodies will wake. The spell Myru cast will be lifted, and with that, the protection these vines provided will be dissolved."

"Do they know their bodies are down here?"

"They don't need to. They simply will feel their presence here. Once they call for their bodies here . . ." Azriel shook his head. "We will need to plan an evacuation."

Errol couldn't agree more. The longer they stayed within the chamber, the thicker the air grew, making it difficult for him to breathe.

42
SACRIFICE

Vale's red eyes turned white as the sentinel surveyed the surrounding area, his gaze remaining unfocused before his eyes returned to their usual sharp crimson appearance. The forest around them had grown quiet save for the occasional rustling of leaves due to the evening breeze. The sky was a blend of orange and purple.

"This area is secure. It will suffice enough for setting camp," Vale declared firmly. His voice held his usual authoritative tone, but Elliot caught a hint of weariness. "We may be near Rainwell, but we must not exhaust ourselves. We will need to assess our condition and ensure we are in the best possible shape for a higher chance of success."

Without skipping a beat, Vale took his wand and began to weave a pattern in the air before him. And with a swift final flick, the ground beneath them burst into a flash of light. Elliot squinted, stepping back. The light expanded outward into a large circle until moving upward into a dome shape.

The barrier Vale had created was a shimmering translucent wall with a soft ethereal glimmer, encompassing the group in its protective embrace. Everything within its walls seemed gentle, the dark silhouettes that threatened to engulf them receding.

A fire burst into existence in the center, its warmth immediately pushing back the evening chill in the air.

"It's been, what, eleven days since leaving the castle?" Sage asked, taking a seat by the fire. It cast flickering shadows against the chimera's face.

"This will be our twelfth night since departing Sylvana," Vale corrected. He remained standing as the others gathered around the fire. The sentinel stood between them and the edge of the barrier. Even though it was meant to protect them, the general never failed to keep watch.

"It's strange. Even though we've been traveling for this long, it doesn't feel like I've exhausted myself," Sage said.

"That is because the barrier I have been conjuring possesses healing properties. As long as you are within my protection, I am able to restore your energy and nourish your body as you rest."

"What about you?" Elliot asked, studying Vale closely. Though faint, he could see a red outline beginning to form around Vale's eyes. Had the other elf been skipping rest himself? "How are you feeling?" Elliot added.

"Oracle, my strength comes from my queen. I do not tire as long as she is well." Vale's voice was tense, as if he was trying to avoid confessing crucial information. Years of hearing Minari attempting to hide something of importance from Elliot had trained him to catch cues such as this.

"I am curious," Luka said. "How are you able to cast magic? I have noticed all the sentinels have a similar appearance: white hair and red eyes."

"Those who wish to serve Queen Elyria with utmost loyalty are given a piece of her magic. This, in turn, strips us of our natural elven appearance."

"Can she do that for anyone?" Sage asked.

Vale shook his head. "The queen's magic affects only those of elven blood, and only those who carry it can claim her power. Moreover, she possesses the insight and ability to look into one's soul, discerning true loyalty from false intent. To be chosen by her is no simple matter. It requires more than mere desire, ambition, or curiosity."

Elliot recalled Elyria's warning of foreign magic entering one's body. The repercussions were dire if it was a constant inward flow. "Is there anything else you lose?" Elliot asked carefully. "Other than your elven appearance."

Vale did not respond right away, the pause heavy with unspoken weight. His gaze fixed into the distance for a while before he returned his attention to Elliot. "My life."

"You already said you were giving her loyalty. Doesn't that imply your life?" Sage asked.

"My life is in her hands. She could end it at any moment if she willed it. And how long I survive is determined by how long my body can withstand the queen's magic." Vale paused, sighing. "I do not know how much longer I have left."

"How long have you been a sentinel?" Luka asked, his tone soft.

"Perhaps forty years or more. I have lost count. Each day I wonder if it will be my last. But perhaps guarding the oracle was meant to be the final mission the queen wished me to have."

"You feel weak?" Elliot whispered. His stomach dropped at the thought of Vale wearing himself down just for them. Another soul sacrificed to fulfill the prophecy.

"Each day," Valor responded. "But I promise you, I will not fail my mission to protect you and your comrades as we reach our destination. The others have already made it to Rainwell and will do their best to protect the villagers there."

"Good," Elliot said. "I would hate to have any more sacrifices than there already are."

As the night progressed, sleep soon took over, the group entering a restful dream.

Elliot lay on his back, staring at the stars. Their journey was almost over. Come nightfall tomorrow, they would be in Rainwell. His chest tightened at the thought of reuniting with Minari. He was not sure how he was going to react once he saw his friend again. Would Minari be happy to see him? Would Minari forgive him? Elliot had so much to say to the other elf, but he knew he wouldn't have the chance. Whatever battle was thrown at them in Rainwell, he knew there wouldn't be an opportunity for the two to exchange words.

At the very least, Elliot knew he would do his best to fulfill Minari's wish.

Minari would die by Elliot's hand.

43

AMBUSH

The door to Asher's office slammed open. Deveran rushed in, gasping. His skin was clammy, sweat glistening off his brow. He held cloaks bundled in his arms.

Chloé's heart skipped a beat as she saw what kind of cloaks Deveran held. They were stealth cloaks, reserved only for desperate times. The material was specially woven to be reflective, subtly mirroring the surrounding landscape and allowing its wearer to blend seamlessly into their surroundings, becoming nearly invisible in the process.

"We need to leave. Now. They've found us. They know what we're up to." He stole a glance at Kaia, who looked equally as shocked. "I trust this wasn't your doing. Everyone believes it. Don't worry."

"Kaia, do you remember the evacuation route?" Chloé asked, pulling away from Asher. The sudden tear from the flow of magic made her dizzy, but she forced herself to stand. She quickly took a cloak from Deveran, wrapping it around her shoulders and fastening the hook securely in front of her.

"I . . ." Kaia was still frozen from the sudden outburst. She stood still, unable to move.

"We do not have time," Asher said. After he secured his cloak, he wrapped Kaia in hers and took ahold of her arm. "Come, Kaia. Follow me and Chloé."

"Boss, Oliver, and Vivian are attempting to delay the knights. We need to move. Each second we stay here, the higher the risk they'll find us."

"We're counting on you," Chloé said, giving Deveran a small nod.

Chloé, Asher, and Kaia rushed out of the room. Bunnie had given them special instructions if they ever had to evacuate due to a raid, though it had changed slightly after discovering Chloé needed Asher.

Originally, the ethereal would stay behind, ensuring anything related to Nighthawk was destroyed. He would use his magic to burn parchments and destroy evidence.

But since Asher needed to stay with Chloé, Deveran would be in charge of that task. Unfortunately, that meant the whole place would be burned down. Chloé's throat tightened at the thought. Memories of her time spent within the walls played through her mind like a record, and it hurt to think she would no longer see their base again. But she knew this had to be done. She knew if this place stayed, the entire guild would be in jeopardy. If anyone was caught, there was no telling what sort of punishment they would be subjected to.

Chloé's heart hammered against her chest as she followed Asher. The nix held on to Kaia's hand, making sure the princess kept up. Kaia's grip was tight. She held on to Chloé as if her life depended on it.

In a way, it did.

Chloé had no doubt that there would be bloodshed if any one of them was captured. She could imagine the knights having a field day. If a prisoner or two were killed before they could be questioned, it wouldn't mean anything to them.

Asher ripped open the door to the cellar, and they barged through. Their hard breathing was all Chloé could hear as they made their way down the stairwell. The air was thick with moisture and had a strong scent of wood.

Asher slowed to a stop before he lifted a hand. A dim outline formed around a wooden crate. It moved to the side, revealing a trapdoor. Asher lifted it.

"Go, I will join you two after. I just need to seal this entryway," Asher whispered hurriedly.

"Come on, Kaia," Chloé said. "You first. I'll be right behind you."

Kaia nodded, her expression still petrified. She slipped inside the small entrance, her movements stiff, as if she were going through a nightmare.

Distant shouting reached Chloé's ears, and her body went cold, dread filling her every nerve. She glanced at Asher, who only gave her a nod.

They were running out of time.

Chloé slipped inside, and not a moment later, Asher

followed. With a wave of his hand, everything fell back into place. The door glowed once more before flashing.

They were engulfed in complete darkness before a small orb formed above Asher's palm. The glow around it was soft, casting shadows against their features, but bright enough for them to see ahead.

"We need to move quickly," he whispered. "This passage will take us beyond the city walls."

Chloé nodded, trying to push away the thoughts of everyone else above. She could only hope everyone made it out safely. Her worries threatened to choke her, but she forced herself to focus on the matter at hand.

44
DEPART

Chloé, Asher, and Kaia had been traveling by foot for what felt like weeks, ever since the raid on Lonin's Nighthawk base. They had yet to receive word from Bunnie or any other officer or member of the guild.

They had been forced to camp outside, traveling during the day, avoiding every major road, and hiding deep in the forest at night. When they reached smaller villages, Asher would become Iris, entering the villages and returning with food and water. It was not much, but it was enough for them to get by as they continued on.

Bunnie had instructed Chloé to reach Solime in case a raid ever happened. The Solime base was small, hopefully small enough to pass under the kingdom's radar. But it was going to be at least a two-month journey to reach Solime.

Luck was not on their side as it began to pour during

the peak time of their travels. Chloé's clothes stuck to her skin uncomfortably, and she shivered as the wind blew.

She stopped at the sound of a thud behind her.

Kaia was on the ground, panting, struggling to breathe. Her complexion was deathly pale, with a flush across her cheeks.

"Kaia?"

Chloé's eyes widened as she quickly jogged back. She mentally cursed at herself. When had they gotten so far apart from each other? She placed a hand against Kaia's forehead. Pulling back, she bit her lip. "She has a fever."

"We need to slow down," Asher said, his voice barely audible through the rain, which seemed to pour down even harder. "She must not be used to this sort of travel."

Chloé chewed the inside of her cheek. How had she not noticed how sick Kaia was getting? Of course the princess wouldn't be used to hiding low and traveling during the night. Even if she had spent weeks training with them inside Lonin, that did not mean she would be ready for this kind of hardship.

"Do not be too hard on yourself," Asher said, as if reading Chloé's mind. "I haven't been thinking either . . . Just going through the motions." The ethereal glanced around, trying to find a spot they could hide out. A fire would be nearly impossible to start in this weather, but if they didn't get Kaia out of her wet clothing and warmed up . . . Chloé did not want to think about the consequences.

Asher knelt down, taking Kaia into his arms. "We do not have that many options," he started. "I will leave the decision to you."

"What do you mean?"

"We are near Trox. If we hurry, we can reach there in a little over an hour. I am sure you are aware of the risks."

Chloé nodded. As per protocol, if the base in Lonin ever got raided, no member was to enter any city but the one they were assigned to. This would help mitigate the risk of being found. Trox was not their destination, and Chloé did not know which members were assigned there.

"The other option is we find camp here." Asher paused. "But you know the risk with that as well."

Asher didn't want to say out loud what Chloé was afraid of. Kaia's fever was dangerously high, and camping out in the pouring rain would only prove to worsen her condition.

"We head to Trox," Chloé said. She would not risk Kaia. If they were caught in Trox, she would not go down without a fight.

"D-don't worry . . . about me," Kaia said weakly. She opened her eyes, her gaze foggy as she glanced at Chloé. "I will . . . be—" Kaia coughed, interrupting herself.

"Save your strength," Chloé said. "My decision is final. We will head to Trox. Find an inn."

Asher nodded. "I will hold on to Kaia. Let us hurry."

Chloé placed a cool, wet towel on top of Kaia's forehead. Her temperature was still high, but at least they were in shelter. The chance she would make it through the night was just a bit more.

Asher had cast a disguise spell on her and Kaia before

they'd entered Trox. Chloé and Kaia were given human male appearances, their cloaks folded away and hidden. There was no telling what sort of information was floating around the kingdom. Whatever they had that could hint they were members of Nighthawk had to be kept out of the public eye.

There was a soft knock on the door before it squeaked open.

Asher entered, tray in hand. "The kitchen was already closing, so this was all I could bring." He placed the tray down on the nightstand.

It was a single serving of soup and a loaf of bread. The bread oddly reminded her of the first meal she had shared with Elliot and Minari when they had arrived in Venin. It felt like it had happened so long ago. Her heart twisted as she recalled how weary and cruel she had been to them. It was unfair and she regretted it, but she was thankful for everything that had happened—it made her who she was today. And she was proud of who she was now: no longer blinded by false truths, her opinions were now based on what she'd seen and learned rather than speculation.

"I don't need to eat," Asher said before Chloé could think about offering it to the ethereal. He had already exerted much of his energy, from carrying Kaia to using a disguise spell to get them into Trox before dispelling it once they were safe inside a room. It was not too long ago he had also shared his stamina with Chloé.

"You need it more than I do," Chloé said. "Take the bread. I will save the soup for Kaia when she wakes."

"You and I both know she probably will not wake

tonight. If she wakes, it will be in the morning. Eat."

Chloé sighed. "Half?"

"Chloé, I do—"

"You take half," Chloé said, her voice stern. "I will not argue."

Asher and Chloé stared at each other for a while, until Asher caved. "All right. I will take the bread. Chloé, please have the soup."

"Deal."

<h1 style="text-align:center">45</h1>

<h1 style="text-align:center">PROTECT</h1>

"Her Majesty should have notified you of our arrival."

"Aye, she has," Azriel said. "You all have arrived earlier than I expected."

Five elves stood at the entrance of Rainwell, clad in silver armor. Their stoic demeanor made Errol feel like a child, small and needing protection. He was taken aback by their appearance. Their hair was devoid of any color, and all had piercing red eyes. The way they surveyed the village made Errol feel exposed. It was as if none of Rainwell's secrets or entries were hidden from them. They knew everything. Saw everything.

"The Necromancers' bodies are calling out for their souls," one of the elves said. "The ringing in the air is hard to ignore."

"It is deafening," another said.

"It will not go away until this battle is over."

"And this is why we are here."

"Please," Azriel said. "Let us discuss this in my home. My daughter is with her friends, and I don't want to worry any curious eyes."

Flara. Liliana. Sophia. Xarath. Lloyd.

Those were the names of the five elves Queen Elyria had sent out to protect Rainwell. They were her sentinels, chosen ones who were like an extension of the queen herself, bestowed with her magic.

"General Vale is with the oracle as we speak. They should arrive within the week," Xarath said.

"Their journey was more or less uneventful. A good thing," Lloyd said.

"Why are they not with you?" Errol asked. It didn't make sense to him why they'd traveled alone and made Elliot and the others travel by themselves.

"We are here to prepare Rainwell," Flara said. "It seems you are aware of the Necromancer bodies below this village, or else Azriel would not permit you to be here."

Errol nodded.

"The queen wants us to protect this village from calamity," Xarath said. "At the least, begin our plan to protect the villagers."

"We will send the villagers to a safe place and then cast a barrier with our magic. No one will be able to touch them without going through us first," Sophia said.

Errol recalled the spell Mayleen had cast before the fall

of Mistfall.

The ensnaring trap.

It was meant to destroy everything inside. Nothing was meant to survive the spell. They were left alone when Lily attacked the village, sending imps to destroy their home. Anger boiled up inside Errol as he compared Rainwell's strategic preparation to Mistfall's pathetic vulnerability. Their village wouldn't know loss and suffering, as his people did.

No.

Errol should not think this way. It was improper of a leader. Mayleen wouldn't want him to be spiteful toward others, especially those who did not deserve it. Rainwell was their home now, and he should do everything within his power to protect it.

Errol's jaw tightened as he pushed away the bitter thoughts. He'd learned from Mistfall's fall—both from their successes and their failures.

This time would be different.

This time, he wouldn't let his people down.

"I want to help," Errol said.

Azriel looked at Errol with wide eyes. "You do not have to. The sentinels are more than enough for us."

Xarath raised a brow. "Why do you wish to help? You are a simple elf. No magic flows in your body."

Errol frowned. Magic? He had survived this long without the use of it. He had spent countless hours, days, and nights training with the other scouts. There was no need for magic.

"I do not need magic to defend myself," Errol said,

standing tall. "I have trained my whole life in combat. I know how to fight."

In an instant, Errol felt a hard blow to his chest, and his body flew across the room, colliding with the wooden wall. He fell forward, instinctively using his hands and knees to break his fall. He gasped for breath, completely winded.

What was that?

Errol hadn't seen the other elf move. The attack had come without warning, faster than anything he'd encountered before.

"How do you expect to defend this place if you cannot even defend yourself against me?" Xarath asked, his voice steady.

Errol staggered up, using the wall behind him as support. His eyes met Xarath's stone-cold ones. The elf held no emotion in his expression, merely observing Errol.

This was a warning. If Errol did not have what it took to defend against Xarath, how could the sentinels trust him to defend Rainwell by their side? He would be a hindrance. A risk.

"I defended my home . . . up until its demise," Errol started, his voice rough from the ache in his chest, making it difficult to breathe. "Rainwell is my home now." He winced, taking a shallow breath. "And I will not stand idly by when I know an attack is coming."

The silence that followed was heavy with unspoken assessment. Errol remained standing despite the protest of his muscles. As much as he wanted to collapse on the ground, he kept himself up. He'd learned long ago that sometimes leadership meant enduring pain with dignity, showing strength not through dominance but through resilience.

"You speak of defense, yet you show no fear after being struck down. Why?" Xarath asked.

"Because fear doesn't protect anyone," Errol replied. Memories of Mistfall's attack flowed through his mind: the sheer fear on the villagers' faces as they relied on the scouts to defend them. How some scouts' lives ended from hesitation.

How Estelle's life ended from hesitation.

"I have learned that the hard way. Fear makes you hesitate when you should act, makes you run when you should stand." Errol straightened fully now, ignoring the pain that threatened to overtake his entire body. "I watched my own home burn. I will not watch another fall—not while I can still fight."

Lloyd stepped forward. "You understand that what you will be facing is beyond what you have faced before? You experienced one Necromancer. Here, you will be up against five."

Five? But Errol had only seen four bodies down in the catacombs.

"There is another Necromancer. His body was not sealed like the others," Flara said, answering Errol's bewildered expression. She nodded to her fellow sentinels. "I like his spirit."

"I agree," Liliana said, finally breaking her own silence. "Where our magic falls short, perhaps his strategy will prove useful." She chortled. "Not saying our magic will fall short."

"Are you sure about this?" Azriel asked, moving toward Errol. He placed a supporting hand on Errol's shoulder. "The sentinels would be more than enough to defend Rainwell and all the people here."

"I am certain," Errol said, his voice firm. "I may lack magic, but I have something else that gives me strength." He paused, reflecting on past experiences. "The memory of what failure costs. And the determination to never pay that price again."

The atmosphere in the room shifted. The initial tension and skepticism disappeared, replaced by empathy and compassion.

"Very well," Xarath said. "But before we will permit you to fight alongside us, you will train with us. Up until the Necromancers arrive. We will test you to your limits."

"I understand." Errol smirked. "And I will test yours."

46
NECRO

The inside of Ragnar's study was dark. The drawn curtains did little to light up the surroundings. Day and night had already begun to mesh together, making it difficult to discern what time of day it was. The skies remained overcast, and the sun was buried away.

Their time was drawing near. The time to act was now.

Valor, Rhea, Raven, and Aiden all stood beside Ragnar's large desk, their hands tucked behind them, their feathered black cloaks draped across their shoulders.

"Father, the preparations are complete," Raven said, his eyes emitting a soft red glow before it disappeared. "We can depart at a moment's notice."

"Very well," Ragnar replied as he rose from his desk. "As you all can feel, your bodies are calling out to you. The time trap they were stuck in has finally reached its last bit of strength. Now is the time to reclaim what you lost hundreds of years ago. Each of you knows what you must do. I have assigned you all special tasks."

The four nodded in unison. Valor kept his attention straight, playing Ragnar's absolute commands in his mind.

The plan was divided into five phases. Each one had been determined based on each of their strengths.

The first phase was to reach Rainwell through Kelemvor. They would need to move quickly, as the plane was not meant for beings like them to traverse. Though they were Necromancers, there were still limitations to their powers and where they could tread. As Mykronos's host, Ragnar would create a corridor, but it would be limited by time and space, as he did not have the full strength of the death god.

The second phase would start once they exited Kelemvor. The gate would have them at the outskirts of Rainwell. From there, they would locate their bodies. At close proximity, finding them would be simple. Valor had already begun to feel the pull his body was emitting, longing to be reunited with its soul. Weak, but there.

The third phase would be the ambush. Ragnar was certain there would be resistance, likely from the oracle and his companions.

Rhea was to advance upon the northern and eastern borders of Rainwell. Raven's preparation within the village had gone well. He had deployed the recruited knights, ensuring Rhea would have an abundance of imps to aid her when she turned them.

Aiden was to advance upon the western and southern borders. With the help of the imps, he was to ensure their pathway to the catacombs was secured.

Raven was to guarantee Rhea and Valor did not stray from their task, using his mind-control abilities to keep their original souls at bay. He was to stay in the core of Rainwell once the path was clear, so he was within proximity of the two Necromancers. In addition, Raven would also alter the perception of reality of anyone who got too close to the catacombs.

Valor would summon a shadow beast capable of burrowing through the ground, creating an underground tunnel to their original bodies. He had already decided to use the centipede.

It had proven useful during the attack on the chimeran village.

Phase four would be when they reunited with their bodies, a moment Valor knew each Necromancer anticipated. Their itch had grown each night. Their powers were only a fraction of what they could be. Reuniting with their bodies would be like finally drinking from a fountain after being parched for years.

And phase five would mark their triumph. With their original bodies and powers unleashed, they would summon Mykronos, Ragnar serving as the host and vessel. But before this could happen, the oracle and his companions would need to perish.

The plan was sound. Perfect. If executed flawlessly, it would bring them a victory they had been denied for so long. The Necromancers would finally claim what they deserved.

A revenge that was long overdue.

What would follow would be more than mere victory.

It would be rebirth.

A new beginning under the rule of one who understood the true meaning of power and balance. Their god understood that sometimes death was necessary for life to flourish, that strength required sacrifice, that true rule demanded both wisdom and ruthlessness. Mykronos would never have let the disease, Death's Kiss, take root, ravaging the land.

Under their god's guidance, there would be order.

There would be strength.

There would be rule.

This time, they would not fail.

47
ALIVE

Elliot winced as a sudden sharp pain pierced his skull. He pressed his hand against the side of his head, hoping the pressure would ease the aching resonance.

"Elliot?" Mimi asked. "Are you all right?"

"Yeah . . . Just my head."

"Are you experiencing discomfort?" Vale asked. "We are nearly at Rainwell. About another two days' journey."

The random jerks of pain Elliot felt seemed to have become more frequent the closer they got to Rainwell.

Elliot stumbled as a ringing blared in his ears, disorientating him. He could barely sense the others as they knelt before him, trying to see if he was all right. He could barely see their moving lips, his vision blurring with each passing second.

Elliot shut his eyes, his swimming vision only

increasing his pain.

"H-Hiro . . . ?" Myru's eyes slowly opened. Her vision was cloudy as she searched for her beloved.

"Myru," Hiro said, grabbing her hand. "I'm here. Save your strength."

Myru lay in Hiro's arms, her energy completely gone. She could hardly find the strength to keep herself breathing. Her eyes threatened to close, her body urging her to fall into a slumber.

"It is done . . ." Myru said, her voice barely above a whisper. Why was it so hard to stay awake? She had so much she wanted to say to Hiro. Now that everything was over, she could finally tell him how she really felt.

The Necromancers were finally dealt with. The sacrifices Noé, Yumie, Allix, and Kana had made had stopped the rise of Mykronos. The world had been saved. She had fulfilled the divine task Vylantra had bestowed upon her.

Myru just had one wish. One selfish wish.

The elven oracle shivered as a wave of cold coursed through her veins.

"Hiro," Myru whispered.

"Don't speak. Please, Myru . . ." Hiro's voice shook as his bottom lip quivered. Tears began welling in his eyes. The hold he had on Myru's hand tightened as he pressed her body close to his.

Ah. Myru must be fading. She felt her senses

disappearing. She could barely make out the warmth of Hiro's hand, could barely smell the comforting notes of his skin, could barely hear his trembling breath as he held back tears.

Myru knew the risk she had taken when she used the spell. The others knew it as well. But even through it all, they'd supported her. Supported her decision. Myru could not bring herself to banish the Necromancers' souls. They did not deserve the punishment. They were hurt, and hurt should not be returned with punishment as severe as this.

Myru had defied Vylantra's order of banishing the Necromancers' souls. Instead, she'd bound their bodies, keeping them frozen in time. There would be another chance for them to wake, though she knew not went. She could only hope when the time came, they could forget their rage and hurt. She hoped they would open their hearts and heal from their wounds. She hoped there would be someone stronger than her who could achieve what she could not.

"Hiro," Myru said, forcing herself to stay awake. "Would you ever . . . forgive me?"

"Myru, please. You did nothing wrong."

Myru shook her head. "I was selfish. Acting out."

"No. No, Myru. You are nowhere near selfish."

Myru weakly chuckled. "I was not supposed to freeze them, Hiro." She tried to lighten the mood. She did not want to see Hiro cry, especially since she did not deserve his tears. "I was supposed to banish them. Their souls were not supposed to remain."

"You did the right thing," Hiro said. "You did nothing

wrong."

Myru's vision was beginning to fade. Black crept in from the corners of her eyes, and Hiro's face began to blur.

It was now or never.

"I love you," Myru said. "I love you so much."

"I love you too. Now and forever. Even through death, my love will never fade," Hiro said, tears flowing freely from his eyes. A few drops fell onto Myru's cheeks, but she could not feel them. He bent down, pressing his lips against Myru's in a deep kiss.

Myru closed her eyes, focusing her remaining energy into feeling the love Hiro poured into her.

48
DOUBLE

Upon entering Kelemvor, the Necromancers' eyes shifted in color; the whites turned black, and their pupils turned red. Valor blinked a few times, adjusting to the deep scarlet aura that glazed over his eyes. A boody hue enveloped his vision, shifting everything into crimson shadows.

It was Valor's first time entering Kelemvor. Even in his past life, neither he nor the others had had a reason to enter the divine realm. It was like a dark abyss. A thick fog was cast over the group, and the air felt still. There was an invisible pressure that seemed to push against Valor's shoulders as they walked down the dark path, following Ragnar.

"You've made it," a voice in the distance said. The figure was a silhouette, his appearance blurred by fog.

Valor recognized the voice from Minari's memory:

Hiro.

"I see you have made it," Ragnar said, countering Hiro's earlier statement. "I trust preparations are complete?"

They stopped once Hiro was in full view. His appearance was different than what Valor had seen in Minari's memories.

Hiro's brown eyes were replaced with deep bloodred orbs. The whites of his eyes were black, mirroring those of the other Necromancers. A feathered black cloak was draped over his shoulders.

So, Hiro was Rurik, the last Necromancer.

Valor almost felt sorry for the oracle. They must have played right into Hiro's trap.

"I created an exit, as you requested. It will lead us to the outskirts of Rainwell, close enough for us to ambush them."

"And they suspect nothing?"

Hiro shook his head. "No. The preparations that were set years ago are still in place."

"Good." Ragnar peered behind him, making eye contact with Valor before returning his attention to Hiro. "I want you to watch over him."

Hiro frowned. "Is he causing issues?"

"It seems it is not just him. Rather . . . they."

"I understand," Hiro said immediately. He gave Ragnar a small bow before making his way toward Valor. "Hello, Minari. I suspect you remember me."

"I do," Valor said. "I must say, my host was not too fond of you. At least, based on his memories," he mused.

Hiro chortled. "He never trusted me."

"It seems he was in the right."

"Yes, but it doesn't matter now."

"No. It doesn't." Valor would be lying to himself if he said he was not disappointed in Ragnar's decision to have Hiro keep watch over him. Valor had done his best to rebuild his trust, but it seemed like it wasn't enough.

Time did not pass at the same time as the mortal realm, and neither did distance. Time moved slower in Kelemvor, and the distance between places was shorter. What would be a month's travel to Rainwell would only take a few moments of walking through the divine realm.

"Do not get in my way," Hiro warned, his voice loud enough only for Valor's ears. "I know what you and Lily are going through. But it seems you are having more trouble controlling yourself."

Valor tried to hide his surprise. He hadn't expected anyone else other than Rhea and Ragnar to know what he was experiencing. Minari's consciousness was coming out more often than he liked.

"Raven can only hold you back for so long," Hiro added. "Do not depend on him."

"I know," Valor snapped. "You don't need to tell me."

"I'm just keeping my promise. Whatever you do, just don't get in my way."

Valor blinked. Promise? What promise?

Light suddenly exploded around them, their surroundings now filled with tall trees.

"The time is now," Ragnar said. "The hunt begins."

49
REUNION

Elliot cracked open his eyes, the splitting headache he last remembered completely gone. He blinked a few times, attempting to take in what he was seeing and feeling.

A wooden ceiling. A window. A soft bed. And cozy covers.

The familiar scent of wood reached his nose.

"Ah, you're awake," a male voice said. He moved a plate of freshly cut apples from his lap to the nightstand next to Elliot.

Elliot's breath hitched. The man was an elf. His pointy ears poked through his long, blond braid.

Was he in Rainwell?

"Let me call for your father," he said, standing up.

Elliot's throat tightened. His . . . father? He was here? His face heated up as he tried to remember the last time he'd seen Errol, the last time he'd spoken to him.

"Elliot."

Elliot leaned up, staring straight at Errol. His lips quivered as he searched for the strength to call out to his father, but his voice was stuck. He had so much to say. His mouth opened and closed, but nothing came out. Tears quickly formed in his eyes before falling down his cheeks. He didn't even care why his father was in Rainwell.

Errol rushed over to Elliot, tightly embracing him. Elliot could only press himself against his father, the rush of emotions taking over. He couldn't stop the tears from falling, couldn't stop his body from shaking.

Elliot prayed this wasn't a dream. He hoped that it was actually Errol holding him. He didn't want to let go, fearing that if he did, he would wake up and find himself without the warmth of his family.

Errol pulled away, and Elliot reluctantly let go. The bed sank where Errol took a seat beside Elliot.

"I missed you," Errol said. He gave the top of Elliot's head a gentle pat. "Look at you . . . all grown up."

"D-Dad . . ." Elliot sniffled.

"Your mother and grandmother would've been so proud." Errol smiled, yet sadness filled his eyes. "You grew into a fine young elf."

Elliot's heart tore; he'd nearly forgotten both Estelle's and Lyla's deaths. Upon recalling the memory of how he'd found out, a fresh wave of tears fell.

Lily was the one who'd told him. The same night she'd murdered Minari.

Elliot suddenly felt alone. Those he'd grown up with—

his family—they were gone. He only had his father left.

Xeno.

If Errol was here, did that mean Xeno was here as well? Elliot ached to see his ovis. He missed him dearly.

"I'm sure I have a lot of explaining to do," Errol said. "But you must be tired from your travel."

Elliot shook his head. "I'm all right." He chuckled. "I've been through worse." Elliot had so many questions, but he did not even know where to start. All he could think about was how he didn't want this moment to end. His father's warmth felt so real. Elliot was sure that he was not dreaming, that this was reality and Errol was here with him.

"How much do you know?" Errol asked.

Elliot hesitated, unsure how to answer. "Lily . . ."

"Ah." Errol took a deep breath, his gaze downcast. He leaned forward, resting his elbows against his knees and clasping his hands together. "So you know . . . she is a Necromancer."

Elliot nodded. "Yes."

"And you know she . . ." Errol tightened his grip, his knuckles turning white. "She—"

"Yes," Elliot interrupted, not wanting the older elf to relive the memories. Elliot knew all too well how painful it was. "I know." His voice was barely above a whisper.

The two sat in silence, enjoying the comfort they brought each other. It almost felt like Elliot was home. The familiar elven craftsmanship of the room he was in reminded him of the ones in Mistfall.

"Where is Minari?" Errol asked, finally breaking the silence. "I didn't see him when you arrived with the others."

Elliot froze. He bit his lip, taking a single swallow that barely quenched his dry throat. "Lily . . . She killed him."

"I am so sorry, Elliot," Errol said. "I wish things could have turned out differently."

"It is not your fault, Dad. It was mine." Elliot's mind had relived his and Minari's last moments together, and each time brought him pain. No matter how hard he searched for any happy moments they'd shared the night Minari had been murdered, Elliot could not find any.

"I will be here to help, at least."

"What?" Elliot looked at Errol, eyes wide. "What do you mean?"

"The battle. I will be here to help."

"You can't! It's dangerous!"

Errol smirked. "Elliot, did you forget I am the captain of the scouts? They had the advantage of surprise last time, but this time, we will be prepared."

The look Errol gave Elliot was one of a set mind. There was nothing Elliot could say or do to change that.

The only thing Elliot could do was trust him. Trust everyone would make it out alive.

"Okay," Elliot said, taking a deep breath and letting it out slowly through his pursed lips. "Let's make it home. Together."

50
PORT

"Chloé, wake up."

Chloé groaned, feeling a gentle shake on her shoulder. Her body protested the movement; it was stiff and sore from sitting on the floor, leaning against the side of the bed, and using Kaia's bed as a pillow. The nix did not remember when she had fallen asleep. Her last memory was of watching Kaia's chest rise and fall in the candlelight, waiting until the princess's fever finally broke in the early hours of morning.

"Chloé," Kaia called out once again, her voice clear.

This time, Chloé's eyes snapped open. She looked up, Kaia's smiling face greeting her. Kaia's complexion was still ashen from the illness, but she looked remarkably better than the night before. Her hair was a tousled mess, and pieces clung to her face from sweat, yet there was life in her eyes again.

"Where are we?" Kaia asked. She shifted, pushing herself up to rest against the headboard.

"Trox," Chloé replied, chewing the inside of her cheek, her gaze drifting to the window. The morning sun cast a soft glow around the drawn curtains. Hopefully nothing had happened during the night. Asher had volunteered to remain on watch, ensuring they received no speculating stares. Since Asher hadn't returned, Chloé assumed everything was all right.

"Trox? We are a ways away from Solime." Kaia frowned. "This is all my fault."

Chloé shook her head. "No. You did nothing wrong, Kai. Things like this can happen, and we just need to adapt."

"But the plan—"

"We always prepare for the unexpected. Plans can be created, yes, but if they fall through, it's up to us to navigate the chaos." Chloé smiled. "What's a little adventure, anyway? This is more exciting!"

Kaia chuckled, the sound warming Chloé's heart. She was trying to lighten up the mood, and it seemed like it had worked. But a cough from Kaia turned the warmth to worry. She hunched over, covering her mouth as her shoulders shook.

"Are you okay?" Chloé asked, standing up and placing the back of her hand against Kaia's forehead. It was warm, but nothing like the scorching heat from the night prior.

"I'm all right," Kaia responded, letting out a few more coughs before taking a breath. "Just an itch."

"How do you feel overall?" Chloé studied Kaia's features, hoping not to find any signs of the fever returning.

"Truthfully, a little tired, but I can move. We should not stay here."

"Right," Chloé said. She was uncertain if it was wise to move Kaia. The princess may be feeling better, but there was a risk of her succumbing to the illness again, especially since she had not fully recovered.

Ideally, they should stay another day or two.

It was risky, and the longer they stayed, the higher the chance they'd be found. Weighing their options, Chloé felt like it would be better for them to remain in Trox until Kaia was back at full strength. If they remained inside the inn, Asher would not need to use magic to disguise them. And the ethereal would have time to recover as well. It had been about three days since Chloé had last received stamina from Asher, so she had some time before it became critical for her to have another session. But if they left, that meant Asher would need to use his magic on Chloé and disguise them on the way out. It was a big ask for Asher, and knowing him, he would not mind it at all. In fact, he would probably insist upon it.

"Let's go," Kaia said. She started to pull the covers off her lap, but Chloé stopped her.

"We should stay another night or two," Chloé said, echoing her earlier thoughts. "It would be better for all of us. I'm pretty tired," she added, not leaving room for Kaia to retort. The excuse wasn't entirely false. She did feel tired; her muscles were aching from sleeping in an awkward position, and their journey had made it so she couldn't allow herself to fall into a deep slumber. She teetered between being awake and being asleep.

A soft knock against the door alerted Chloé and Kaia. Dread filled her chest until she heard Asher's soft voice from the other side.

"Can I come in?"

"You may," Chloé said, relaxing slightly.

Asher swiftly entered, his movements fluid and quiet despite his obvious exhaustion. The door clicking shut barely made a sound. He had shadows underneath his purple eyes, and his skin was dull.

"Kaia." Asher blinked. "You are awake. How are you feeling?"

"Better now, thank you. I suppose I needed rest."

Asher chuckled. "You can say that again." He took a seat at the small, round, wooden table in the center of the room. "I surveyed the town. There were no other members."

"Really?" Chloé asked. How could that be? Surely there ought to have been at least one other member here by now. Had they been traveling faster than the others? That couldn't be it. That seemed unlikely given their detour and Kaia's illness.

"Who was supposed to be here?" Kaia asked.

"We do not know," Asher said, running a hand through his silver hair. "We were given specific towns or cities by Bunnie herself. No one knows where the others are going unless they were grouped together."

"Ah, I see . . . This makes it so we would be harder to

track," Kaia said.

"Precisely. Though it is concerning that I couldn't find any other member." Asher sighed, rubbing his temples.

"Asher, I want to stay another night or two," Chloé said. She held her breath, wondering how the other would respond.

"I had a feeling you were going to request that," Asher said, a small smile curling his lips. "I have already requested an extended stay with the innkeeper. We will leave in two nights."

"Thank you," Chloé said, relief washing over her as they shared the same unspoken agreement.

Despite the risks of staying, the nix knew they had made the right choice. She knew the importance of regaining their strength. They would be more prepared for any dangers that came their way.

Chloé just hoped their stay was going to be a peaceful one.

51

RAIN

The departure from Trox and the arrival in Solime went smoother than Chloé had imaged. Not a single event had occurred while they were recovering in Trox, and their entry into the port city had passed without incident. Traders were moving about their day as normal, their carts and wagons full of merchandise.

The one thing Chloé noticed was how the sun hid behind the clouds. It made day and night appear almost similar. The usual bustle of the port city seemed muted under the heavy sky.

Chloé knew it did not bode well.

Something within her stirred, a sense of reminiscence. She knew she had seen this sort of scenery before, where day and night meshed together, making it difficult to discern if it was midnight or morning. The memory danced around, refusing to let her recall the moment she had experienced this weather before.

Chloé had to meet up with Elliot and the others. But how could she bring it up with Asher and Kaia? There was no way Asher would leave Chloé, and leaving Kaia alone was out of the question, especially after her recent illness.

Chloé tapped on the wooden table, peering out the tavern window. Her internal clock was telling her it was a few hours past sunrise, yet the thick clouds blocked any sort of light the sun would have provided. The townsfolk and traders seemed to have adapted to the change in weather, bringing lanterns and keeping the streetlamps ablaze. It was like it didn't bother them in the slightest, but the nix couldn't shake the feeling of oddity.

The group had decided to split their efforts. Asher and Kaia had left to patrol the town, listening for potential news around the capital and to seek a captain who was willing to sail them to the Snowy Hills. She wasn't sure if Elliot and the others were still there, but hopefully she would be able to find clues of their whereabouts.

Chloé waited inside a tavern, where drunken travelers and tradespeople would gossip amongst themselves. But so far, nothing useful had come from them.

A figure suddenly took a seat across from Chloé.

"The owl speaks," he said, his tone low.

Chloé froze. A Nighthawk member. But she didn't recognize his voice. She kept her gaze locked outside, deliberately avoiding eye contact. She didn't want to bring any attention to them, especially since she was still under Asher's disguise spell.

"Gray skies," Chloé responded in code.

Blue skies meant they were in the clear to proceed with the discussion.

Gray skies meant they were to proceed with the discussion in a specified location.

"It looks as if it's about to rain," Chloé added.

Describing the weather was an indicator of where to meet.

If it was sunny, they were to meet in the Nighthawk base.

If it was cloudy, they were to meet in an inn.

If it was rainy, they would meet outside town.

"I will be sure to bring an umbrella. It does look like it's about to rain," the figure said before standing up and leaving. His soft footsteps were barely audible against the wooden floor as he departed.

Chloé let out a breath she hadn't known she was holding, her heart hammering against her chest. Should she wait for the others to return before telling them she'd met with another member? But the message he'd said meant he had something urgent to tell her. Each minute she spent waiting for Asher and Kaia to return was a minute wasted. There wasn't time for her to dawdle on her decision. Time was not a resource they had.

Chloé left the tavern, the voices of the patrons falling mute to her ears.

Chloé found the hooded figure a bit away from the city. He kept himself hidden within the trees, but Chloé's training had made it easy for her to spot him.

Detecting her presence, the figure turned, removing his hood. He had black hair and brown eyes. A human. But Chloé did not recognize him.

"I'm relieved to see you. I didn't think I would find you in time."

Chloé raised a brow, keeping her distance. "What do you mean?"

His voice was genuine, but she was wary of his presence. Could he be the one who had singled them out and caused the ambush on the guild? Was he the double agent?

"Ah, apologies. You probably don't recognize me." He reached into his coat, pulling out a bronze coin, but the flash of the man's outfit made Chloé's blood run cold.

He was a first officer. Which meant he was a double agent.

"Before you jump to conclusions, no, I was not the one," he added quickly, likely noticing Chloé's tension. "Who it was is still unknown." He tucked the coin away. "The only member who knows of my existence is Bunnie herself, so it makes sense why you do not recognize me."

"Then who are you?" Chloé's patience was running thin.

"My name is Hiro, and I have a message for you, Chloé."

"How did you—"

"I can use magic and see who you really are," Hiro said. "Unfortunately, as much as I would love to exchange pleasantries, I have an urgent message. Elliot and the others are nearing Rainwell, and you will need to reunite with them."

Rainwell? Chloé blinked. The name sounded familiar. It resonated within her. It was a place she had been before, though she couldn't quite grasp when.

"I can help you get there." Hiro extended his hand. "The others are waiting for you as we speak."

"But—"

"If you are worried about Asher and Kaia, I will notify them. Please do not worry," he said gently, though with a sense of urgency.

Chloé hesitated, unsure if she should trust Hiro. There was no way for a human to be able to use magic, yet everything he'd said made sense. It sounded like he was aware of the prophecy and aware that Chloé was a warrior.

A gentle smile graced Hiro's features. "Yumie."

Chloé's eyes widened. A familiar and comforting warmth filled her chest.

All doubt disappeared instantly as he said her name.

Hiro knew her. Knew who she was. Knew of her mission.

"Hiro," Chloé said instinctively. "You better not do anything to hurt Myru."

Hiro smirked, the expression painfully familiar to Chloé. "You know me." He held out his hand.

And Chloé didn't hesitate to reach for it.

52
MOVE

Errol led Elliot into the living space of the house they were in, and Elliot rubbed his eyes, not believing what he was seeing.

Silas.

Stella.

Mimi.

Sage.

Luka.

And Chloé.

Elliot's heartbeat quickened as his eyes darted from one familiar face to another, struggling to process just how long it had been since he had seen them. The faces he'd dreamed of seeing again for so long were now before him.

Chloé looked . . . different. Her hair was short, and she did not wear her usual pink, but that did not stop Elliot from knowing who the nix was. But he didn't see Bunnie. Had Chloé traveled to Rainwell without her? And how had she gotten here in the first place?

A small twist formed in Elliot's gut as realization hit him. It must have been Hiro's doing. Elliot just knew it. The thought of Hiro aiding their journey only caused confusion within Elliot. He knew he could not trust him, not after everything he had done to betray him and the group. But deep down . . . Elliot wanted to trust Hiro wholeheartedly. That there were good intentions in Hiro's actions.

"Finally decided to show yourself?" Chloé asked, placing a hand on her hip. "I was wondering how long you were going to keep us waiting."

Elliot's mouth opened and closed; he was unsure of what to say. He felt rooted to the spot, unsure if he should give in to the urge to run into everyone and embrace them or ask them how any one of them had even gotten to Rainwell.

"Cat got your tongue?" Sage asked. "Our reaction was the same when we found out how she got here."

"Apparently, Hiro aided her," Luka said. "He used magic to transport her here."

So it was true: Hiro helped them.

"But he was gone the moment Chloé found herself in Rainwell," Mimi added. "The sentinels found her outside the village."

"They recognized me immediately as one of the warriors," Chloé said. She placed a hand over her chest. "Even though I cannot use magic anymore." She chuckled, her eyes reflecting sadness even when her lips were in a smile. "I don't really know how much help I will be without it."

"That doesn't matter," Elliot said, his voice finally breaking through the knot in his throat. "You're here now. And that is what's important." He reached over, taking ahold of Chloé's hand. The familiarity that filled Elliot's heart was the same. Chloé had not changed, and that brought a curl to Elliot's lips. "I've missed you, Yumie," he whispered.

Chloé's hands twitched. "I've missed you too, Myru."

Elliot released Chloé, giving her a smile. "It's good to have you back."

"As touching as the reunion is, we need to discuss how we plan on intercepting the Necromancers," Flara interjected. "As you can see from the skies, their powers are growing, and they are drawing near. They want their bodies back."

"We formulated a plan while you were resting," Vale said, stepping forward. To Elliot's surprise, he did not look as fatigued as when they were traveling. The shadows under his eyes had disappeared, and his gaze was more alert. "We will split into five different groups. Four will defend the northern, eastern, southern, and western borders of the village. And the last group will defend the underground catacombs."

"We've already decided who will go where," Sophia said. She unraveled the scroll she was holding, laying it across the round table. "Luka and I will take the northern border. Flara and Mimi will take the western border. Lloyd and Sage will take the southern border. Liliana and Chloé will take the eastern border. Vale and Elliot will be inside the catacombs."

"Xarath, Silas, the other scouts, and I will help aboveground," Errol said. "We won't be stationed anywhere specific. We will survey the area and provide backup where we see fit."

"It's good to see you again, Elliot," Silas said. "You've grown."

Stella nodded, smiling. "You are much more handsome now."

Elliot's cheeks warmed, and he rubbed the back of his neck. "You're as beautiful as ever." He wished this moment could last forever, but he knew it would be impossible.

Stella playfully slapped Elliot's shoulder. "We have much to catch up on. I will see you after the battle."

Elliot dearly wanted that statement to be a promise. He simply nodded, not wanting to think of any other possible ending.

The gentle patter of rain started hitting the window, and something within Elliot stirred. It was a strange tingling sensation crawling up his spine. He walked over to the window, peering through the glass.

Elliot's heart nearly stopped. The darkness that had quickly loomed into the village was not natural. There was a fog that followed, thick and devouring everything in its path.

"The time is nearing," Liliana said, extending her hand to Stella. "Stella, please take my hand. I will bring you to the others where it's safe."

Stella's fingers trembled slightly as she reached out. "Good luck, everyone. I believe in you." The words had barely left her lips before she and Liliana vanished.

"Let's move," Vale said.

53
ORIGINAL

Elliot picked at the skin around the crescent-moon scar on his wrist, his breathing labored. He stood in the middle of the underground catacombs with Vale standing not too far from him. The air was clammy, and the temperature was warm. His eyes darted between the Necromancers' bodies. They were unmoving, but he could hear them. He could hear them crying, speaking, yelling, yet he could not make out anything.

It disturbed him to his core.

"Elliot," Vale said, his voice barely audible through the noise. "Everything will be all right."

Elliot shook his head, the voices growing louder with each passing moment. He could feel them coming. The Necromancers were drawing near, their presence a crushing weight of pure rage and hatred that threatened to swallow him whole. His picking turned to clawing, fingernails scraping against his skin as he desperately tried to ground himself against the rising tide of anguish.

Vale grabbed Elliot's shoulder, giving him a hard shake. "Elliot, stop." His tone was authoritative. Demanding.

"They're coming." Elliot bit his lower lip until he tasted iron. "They're already here . . . I can feel them."

A mixture of dread and anxiety filled Elliot's chest until he could barely breathe. He desperately wanted to know what was happening aboveground, to run up and help the others. Yet he knew he had to stay here. He had to stand here, guarding the Necromancers' bodies. It was part of the plan, and he knew better than to act independently.

But Elliot was not sure if his abilities were going to be enough. Compared to the warriors and sentinels, he was woefully unskilled. He did not know how to fight. He only knew how to defend. Would that be enough? He had no doubt Vale was strong, but something deep in Elliot was telling him he shouldn't be in the catacombs. It was dangerous, and he needed to leave.

Suddenly, there was a tremor, a small vibration before a low rumbling echoed off the walls. The noise was coming from everywhere all at once.

Vale held his wand out, ready for the undeniable incoming danger.

They were here.

The rumbling grew louder. And louder. And louder. And louder.

Until it just stopped.

Complete silence.

The screaming in Elliot's head had also stopped, as if it had never occurred in the first place.

The two elves stood frozen in the center of the catacombs.

Footsteps.

Elliot's eyes darted to the stone wall, his heart hammering so hard his chest ached.

A dark light glowed around it. The stone door shook, vibrating before it descended into the ground.

Ragnar.

Hiro.

Minari.

"When you see me again in Rainwell, please kill me."

The words replayed in Elliot's mind as soon as he saw his once-alive friend.

Minari merely stared back at him, void of all emotion and familiarity they'd once had. He looked back at him with coldness that Elliot had never imaged he would see in Minari.

"Min—"

"I expected as much," Ragnar said, cutting Elliot off. He raised his hand, and before Elliot could raise a shield, his vision succumbed to complete darkness.

Elliot's body felt like it was floating yet falling at the same time, stuck in a state of uncertainty until his back collided with something solid, pushing the wind out of his lungs. He gasped for breath, the impact sending waves of pain down his body.

Elliot slowly gathered his bearings, forcing himself up. Where was he? He barely made out the tall trees surrounding him through the thick fog. The frigid air made his skin chill.

"Vale?" Elliot called out, yet he was met with silence, his voice disappearing into the darkness. "Minari? Hiro?" he called out again, taking frantic steps forward, denying his mind, which told him to stand still.

Wait.

The place around him was eerie, yet it was hauntingly familiar.

This was where Elliot had met with Minari in his dream. A place where Minari had requested Elliot to end him. But where exactly was this place? It was teetering between real and unreal, like a memory that didn't have a physical form.

Elliot's feet came to a halt as he saw an outline of a figure. His heart hammered against his chest. Could it be . . . Minari?

"Minari?" Elliot called out, hoping whoever it was heard him.

The silhouette moved, its body turning to face Elliot. It paused for a moment before beginning to make its way toward the elf.

Elliot clenched his hands as he tried to control his breathing. It was starting to come out in anxious puffs.

But Elliot's dread disappeared as soon as he saw who he was looking at.

She looked . . . almost like he did, yet noticeably more feminine. Her pale green hair was braided back out of her face save for a few shorter strands that framed her cheeks and chin. Her soft white tunic was tucked into her brown skirt, and she wore brown boots that went up to her knees. Her bright blue eyes glowed as she smiled at Elliot.

"Hello," she said. She placed a hand against her chest, giving Elliot a small bow. "If things have gone how they were intended, you are the new oracle."

"I . . ." Elliot was lost for words. "New?"

The girl chuckled. "Yes, as I am the original you. I'm Myru."

54

UNMASKED

The original . . . ? The way Myru had suggested Elliot was a fake compared to her made him sick to his stomach. He was his own person, not a copy of someone else.

"I apologize," Myru said. "It appears I have offended you." She tucked her hair behind her ear. "Come, let us walk together."

Errol rolled, tucking in his arms as he propelled across the ground. His side collided against a tree, and he bit back a cry. Sharp pain radiated through his ribs as he took deep, slow breaths before pushing himself back to his feet. Smoke and fire filled the village and surrounding area. It reminded him of Mistfall's final moments. The chaos. The destruction. The helplessness.

But it was different this time. This time, not only were the villagers safe from harm, but there were other companions with him. The scouts. The sentinels. The warriors. They were all here, united, sharing the same purpose and goal.

To protect and prevent the rise of the Necromancers and Mykronos.

"Captain!" Silas called out. From above the branches, he landed next to Errol. "We need a new plan," he said frantically. "The Rainfall elves. They were actually undead!"

A chill ran down Errol's spine as he registered what Silas had just reported to him. If they were undead, that only meant one thing. And Errol dearly hoped he was wrong. "How do you know?"

"I met up with Liliana. She sensed something wrong with the barrier the sentinels had set up. Nothing was supposed to get in, but there were things leaving." Silas chewed his bottom lip. "The elves of Rainwell. They transformed into imps."

Errol's stomach dropped, and his blood ran cold. The thing he had feared had come true. The noises around him muted as he thought of everyone who had retreated within the sentinels' protection.

All of Mistfall's villagers. Men. Women. Children. And their trusted ovis. Gone. Slaughtered at the hands of Lily.

Errol's mind drifted to Azriel and his daughter, how their entire relationship had been built on peaceful moments. They'd shared meals, had quiet conversations, and shared genuine laughter. And just like that, they were mere memories now. They had been undead the entire time, yet he had felt their warmth and kindness. They'd been full of life. How was this possible? What sick game had the Necromancers been playing, turning the dead into puppets that could so perfectly mimic life and emotion?

Errol's mind went blank as it tunneled into a specific thought: the decision to leave Mistfall, hoping to start anew, only to have led them to their ends. Had they remained in their own desolate village, they would still be here. Still be alive.

What was the point of anything?

All the strength in Errol's legs disappeared, and he staggered. Silas quickly caught him, preventing the captain's face from meeting the ground. His grip was firm.

"Captain! Get it together! This isn't the time to mope."

Mope? When had Errol ever allowed himself that luxury? Even when despair threatened to consume him, he pushed forward. Being a leader meant carrying others' hopes and fears, their lives and deaths. Wallowing in his own pain felt like a surrender, like betraying their trust.

Was it truly so selfish for him to want just a single moment to himself?

"So, this is where you two were hiding."

That voice.

Lily.

"I was wondering where I would find you two."

Through the smoke, Errol could make out something in her left hand. She held it casually, allowing it to dangle in the air.

"Captain, go somewhere safe. I'll handle her," Silas said, stepping forward with his dagger drawn.

"He will be going nowhere," Lily said.

The hair on the back of Errol's neck suddenly stood. They were instantly surrounded. Imps gathered around them, materializing through the smoke, staring at them with hungry eyes, waiting for their leader to give them the command. Their fingers twitched, arms swaying in front of them as deep, gurgling noises came from their throats.

Errol couldn't breathe. He could make out the familiar faces behind the imps. They were those he had sworn to protect.

"A gift for you," Lily said, tossing whatever she was holding at Errol and Silas. It rolled against the ground with a sickening thud, stopping at their feet.

Stella's lifeless, bloodshot, sapphire eyes stared up at them, her face frozen in an expression of terror and betrayal.

Errol saw red.

Rage exploded through the elf, burning away any rational thought and reason he had left. A scream tore from his throat before he darted straight for Lily, his dagger raised high.

She would pay.

She would not make it out alive.

A promise Errol intended to keep.

55
DECEPTION

Mimi swung his rapiers, slicing off the imp's head. He quickly moved through the crowd of grotesque beings, nicking off whatever he could. There was no end to the horde. Whenever he decapitated one, two more took its place.

Mimi did not know how much longer he could keep going. Mimi and Flara had been separated a while back, and he did not know how the sentinel was faring. The adrenaline from earlier was beginning to wane. No one had expected such a large number of foes to appear.

The swarm seemed to have died down, giving Mimi some time to rest. He ducked behind a boulder, leaning his elbow against the hard surface. His lungs burned with each ragged breath he took, the smoke not doing him any favors. His muscles ached, and his body desperately wanted to collapse. Hours of constant combat had pushed him well over his limits. He was surprised he had lasted this long. His thoughts briefly went to Sage and how he was doing.

Until he heard crunching of leaves close by.

"I know you're here. Come out, come out, wherever you are!"

Aiden.

Aiden was a Necromancer. There was no other possible reason the human would be here. Alive.

Renewed energy surged through Mimi as he pushed himself off the stone, his grip tightening around his weapons.

Mimi stood face-to-face with Aiden. The burning forest did little to hide the smirk on the human's lips as he waved his sword around like it weighed nothing.

"Ah, there you are," Aiden said, his crimson eyes glowing through the darkness. "Glad I could find you. I came to do you a favor." His voice was full of mockery, attempting to provoke Mimi.

Mimi frowned, not giving in to Aiden's taunts. He crouched, getting ready to lunge at his next prey.

"So eager to meet your lover? I see the similarities between you two."

What? Mimi furrowed his brow. He refused to listen to Aiden. There was no way Sage would have fallen to the likes of him.

"The way he desperately begged me to leave you alone after I tore his limbs from his body. Ah . . . His cries were music to my ears."

Mimi's fingers trembled as he tightened his grip around

the rapier handles. "Shut up," he breathed. "Shut up."

"I wonder what kind of expression you'll make when I rip the organs from your body," Aiden mocked. His smile suddenly dropped. "But no matter what I do to you, nothing will bring my beloved Charlotte back. Killing both of you is the least I could do to honor her. Her beautiful soul was so much more sacred than your disgusting existence."

Aiden shoved his blade into the body of a nearby fallen imp. He slowly raised the sword, bringing it above his head. The black liquid ran down the silver blade, dripping from the tip. "Do entertain me for a bit." With a single swing, Aiden slashed his sword midair.

Mimi almost missed it, but he could barely make out the blood that had once been on Aiden's sword, pulsing through the air like a torpedo. He jumped to the side, the bloody projectile slashing his calf.

"That's more like it!" Aiden grinned. "Dying from a single swing like that would've been oh so boring." He repeated the same movements, dipping his sword into the dead imp before slashing it into the air. The blood flew at rapid speeds, but Mimi managed to dodge it again.

The deadly dance continued. Every time Mimi tried to put some distance between them, Aiden only moved forward, using the endless supply of dead imps around him. Each swing of his sword sent multiple projectiles hurling through the air, forcing Mimi to stay on his toes. He had been nicked a few times on his arms, legs, and face. The wounds burned with each movement he made.

If Mimi did not think of something fast, it would only

be a matter of time before Aiden's sword used Mimi's blood as ammo.

The chimera's eyes widened in realization. The projectiles only traveled in a straight line. They were fast, but predictable. If he could time it right, Mimi would be able to close the distance between them. Close enough for him to strike.

This time, instead of jumping back, Mimi lunged forward, but only enough so Aiden hopefully wouldn't notice his plan. He moved his body in a way that appeared as if he were still dodging and creating distance. Aiden still took steps forward, oblivious to the encroaching chimera.

"Your footwork is impressive," Aiden sneered, drawing more blood. "But how long can you keep dancing like this? Why not call it quits?"

Mimi ignored the human's remarks, remaining focused on his plan.

Just a bit more.

There!

As Aiden prepared to dip his blade into another imp, Mimi pounced forward. Aiden would have to either move away from the imp or meet Mimi's attack.

Aiden's eyes widened; he was seemingly now aware of his mistake. But Mimi did not miss the flash of a smirk across his face.

Mimi's rapier sank into Aiden, his blood spraying into the air.

Aiden dropped his sword, his hands grabbing Mimi's arms in a vise grip. "Playtime's over." Aiden's sword began to glow, an eerie red outline radiating from the edges. It hurled itself into the air before plunging itself through Aiden and then into Mimi's chest.

Time seemed to slow as Mimi struggled to process what had just happened.

First came the pressure.

Then the cold.

Then pain.

Unbearable pain.

A scream caught in his throat. The only sound he could emit was a gargle from the blood rushing into his mouth. His legs buckled, but Aiden's grip held him in place. The strength in Mimi's arms disappeared, his rapiers falling to the ground.

Mimi's thoughts drifted to Sage. Had he truly fallen at the hands of Aiden? Had he felt the same pain he was now? The same frightening cold that was spreading from his chest to his limbs? Tears began to well in Mimi's eyes—not from the pain or fear of dying, but at the thought of Sage dying alone.

The two chimeras had once vowed that if they were to perish, they were to do it together. In each other's embrace.

Maybe it was a foolish wish, something so specific that it would not be plausible.

Yet Mimi deeply wished it were true.

I'm sorry.

The edges of Mimi's vision began to darken, but he forced himself to focus on Aiden's face. He refused to give the human the satisfaction of his pain and anguish. He summoned every ounce of energy he could muster, curling the corners of his lips.

Mimi closed his eyes, welcoming the cold darkness.

56
FREEZE

Luka leapt through the trees, barely placing weight on each branch before jumping to another. With a single swing of his sword, he sliced the wings off every imp, while below, Sophia was blowing the heads off imps with each flick of her wand.

The way the imps flocked to them was disorganized, making it easy for the two to maneuver around the foes.

Luka found it difficult to believe that the Necromancers would do something so haphazardly. Why send the enemies out in disarray?

"Luka!" Sophia called out, while sending another imp's head into explosion, its limp body thudding against the ground. "We cannot keep doing this!"

Luka knew what the sentinel meant. They'd been going for hours now, and it was only a matter of time before their energy was depleted. He was already beginning to feel drained, but he continued to move, his actions automatic to distract from the creeping fatigue.

They needed to buy themselves time. Any amount of time would do as long as it gave them a moment to catch their breath. He leapt down, landing beside Sophia. He moved in unison with her, and they went through the foes as if it were a practiced performance. "How are you faring?"

"If you're asking how much longer I can last—" With a flick of her wand, blood splattered across her face, hair, and chest. She grimaced but kept moving. "Not much longer. The queen's magic is beginning to wane between the six of us."

Luka's eyes scanned their surroundings. He could see smoke in the distance. A fire must have started, though he had not reached them yet.

An idea suddenly struck the ethereal.

The original plan was to guard the catacombs and protect the village. But since the entire village had become imps, it made sense to abandon the village and guard the underground catacombs, where Elliot was stationed. Standing guard in one area would be a more efficient way to use their energy.

"We need to retreat," Luka started. "Regroup near the catacombs. There is no reason for us to guard the village— not when all its inhabitants are here."

Sophia was silent at first, as if considering Luka's plan. Perhaps retreating was something she and the other sentinels did not prefer. But the situation called for it. The ethereal hoped she understood that.

"You are right," Sophia said. "There's no point staying here until we're dead. I'll inform the others. Let's make our way back now."

Luka had just finished his rounds for the eighth time, and worry was bleeding into his chest. No one had retreated to the entrance of the catacombs even after Sophia had ensured she had sent the message to the others. Roughly two hours had already passed. That was more than enough time to retreat.

Unless something had happened, preventing them from retreating.

"Nothing," Sophia said, also returning from her rounds. "No one is within the nearby area, and I don't sense any changes." She furrowed her brow. "I can still feel the connection we share with one another, so I know nothing ill happened."

Luka nodded in agreement. He, too, could still feel the connection he shared with the other warriors. He tapped into the connection again, searching for any signs of distress.

Luka's eyes widened, his throat catching his breath. Why hadn't he realized it sooner? The reason he could not feel anything was because the connection felt as if it was stagnant. Throughout the journey with the others, he had more or less been able to feel how they were faring, and the flow had been in constant movement. But the feeling now was as if it was still. Frozen.

"Sophia, are you sure you can feel them?" Luka asked. "Focus and tune out everything else."

Sophia raised a brow. "What are you—"

"Just do it," Luka interrupted.

Sophia frowned before closing her eyes and placing her hand against her chest. After a moment, she dropped her hand, eyes wide. "Nothing," she breathed. "I can feel them, but it's like they're not there. I can feel their presence, but I cannot feel them at the same time."

"It's the same for the warriors," Luka said. "Each warrior is paired with a sentinel, so your signal meant they knew to retreat with them. But we have been here for two hours now with no sign of anyone else."

"Something's happened. There has to be a reason why there are no imps here. You'd think this is where they would be swarming, especially since we left the north border."

Luka peered at the entrance to the catacombs, the darkness almost beckoning him to enter. The ethereal and sentinel had yet to run into a Necromancer. It was odd.

Just what were they planning?

"Should we enter?" Luka asked, his gaze still lingering on the entrance.

"That is not part of the plan," Sophia said, her voice stern. "We've already deviated enough as is. We should not deviate any further."

"Sitting here is not going to give us answers. We need to figure out where the others are. We need to figure out where the Necromancers are."

"Are you thinking they're inside?"

"Possibly. Something is blocking our connection with the others."

"And you think whatever it is, we'll find it in there," Sophia plainly stated. "No."

Luka snapped his attention to Sophia. "No?"

"No. We cannot. We should remain out here regardless of what you think. The Necromancers all have skills and magic that even we do not know the extent of. It's better to play it safe."

Luka clenched his jaw as he looked back at the catacombs. Sophia was not wrong, and that frustrated him. The stagnant connection pulled against his heart, his senses and instincts urging him to act, to tend to the feeling. Luka could almost feel their presence somewhere in the darkness down below.

Luka placed a hand against the hilt of his sword. "You are right," he said. His voice was quiet. "It would be foolish to enter without knowing what we are facing."

"I'm glad you agree."

"Which is why I am going alone."

Before Sophia could react, Luka sprinted toward the entrance. He heard the female sentinel's voice call out for him, but he ignored it. If there was even the smallest chance the others were in danger, he could not wait any longer.

57

MINE

The more Elliot and Myru proceeded forward, the more confused and impatient Elliot became. The two of them had not shared a single word with each other ever since the female elf had suggested a walk. The scenery around them had morphed from foggy darkness into a vivid and luscious forest. A small village slowly came into view, but Myru did not slow. She simply continued down the path.

Elliot held his breath as he tried to bite down the emotions that were storming in his chest. The village . . . was Mistfall. It was Mistfall as he remembered it.

Myru then stopped. They were in the village square. The evening sky was a brilliant orange, a soft purple slowly creeping through the clouds.

"So, this is where you're from," Myru said. "The place is beautiful."

"Yes . . ." Elliot took a breath, his eyes wandering to the bench he had sat on during his last birthday celebration with Minari and Lily. The strawberry bread Minari had baked was delicious. His lips formed into a frown as he realized he would never be able to taste the sweet dessert again. Elliot fought back the wave of sadness in his chest.

"You wanted to protect this place," Myru said. It was a statement, not a question. "I had a place I wanted to protect as well." She looked up into the sky. "But that changed. Rather than a place I wanted to protect, it was the people. I wanted to protect the people I loved."

Elliot pondered Myru's words. Had he originally accepted his destiny to fulfill the prophecy because he had people to protect? Or had he done it to protect his home? It had never occurred to him to separate the two.

Elliot pressed his lips into a thin line, realizing how complacent he had been. He hadn't questioned anything when he had learned of his true identity—he had merely accepted it. He had believed it was out of his control. By following Vylantra's wish, he had sacrificed everything: his family, his friends, his home.

"I want to apologize to you first," Myru started. "I was too weak to fulfill the task Vylantra gave me. I could not banish the Necromancers' souls. The result of my actions is the reason you are here. I let my emotions get the better of me, ignoring the words of everyone else, and now the suffering has repeated."

Elliot remained silent, listening to what she had to say. He could hear the pain and regret in her voice. Had she been wandering here alone, unable to express her thoughts?

"Hiro . . ." Myru whispered. "Is he alive?"

"He is." Elliot paused, hesitating to tell her the truth. It would surely pain her to learn he was a Necromancer. But at the same time, it was her right to know. "He betrayed me."

Myru blinked, tilting her head. "What do you mean?"

"He's a Necromancer."

Myru simply stared at Elliot. She did not appear to be shocked, or sad, or angry. It was as if she had expected Elliot to say that. "I see." She sighed, her shoulders dropping. "I wish this had never happened. All of this happened because I was weak."

"Myru," Elliot started, wanting to understand why he was here and Myru's intentions. "Where is this place?"

"Kelemvor. The divine realm. You were here when Vylantra first talked to you. Do you remember?"

"I do . . . but it was nothing like this."

The scenery around him when he'd met the god of life had been tranquil. They had been above the clouds, and it was bright—the complete opposite of what he saw when he first found himself here.

"That was likely because you were in the presence of Vylantra. What I have noticed during my time here is that it will morph into your strongest memories. There were many times this place turned into my home." Myru frowned. "Though it was truly never my home. It was empty. Lifeless."

"How long have you been here?"

Myru chuckled. "I don't know. One moment I was

with Hiro, and the next thing I knew, I was here. The only difference was . . . I knew why I was here and why I was brought back." She paused. "My final wish . . . Vylantra promised to grant it to me."

"What was it?" Elliot asked.

"I am not sure if you know this, but when elves pass, their souls return to Alder. Every time an elf is born, Alder grants it a soul. Since I had met my end, my soul returned to Alder. But I deeply wished to be with Hiro, even through death. So, Vylantra brought my soul here, to the only place I could exist without a physical body."

Before Elliot could process her words, Myru's hand shot out to grab his. Elliot hissed. Her touch was like ice against his skin, and his scar began to burn. He tried to pull away, but Myru's hold on him was tight.

"You are to be my host, so I can reunite with Hiro," Myru said.

The cold from Myru's hand dug deep into Elliot's skin, entering his veins and quickly spreading across his body. The heat from the oracle mark caused his vision to blur as the contradicting sensations raced through his body, finding their way to his core. His eyes rolled to the back of his head, his mind reeling from consciousness as the pain around his core grew stronger.

Elliot tried to resist, but the feeling of being pulled away from his body only grew stronger.

I'm sorry.

A loud ringing in Elliot's ears was the last thing he remembered before all that was left was nothing.

58
WEB

Chloé slowly inhaled and exhaled through gritted teeth. Hot pain pulsated from a large gash on her side. Warm blood seeped through her fingers as she desperately applied pressure. Cold sweat beaded down her forehead, and she fought to focus on anything else except the gaping wound. She leaned against the cold, stone wall, relaxing her head against it.

Chloé clicked her tongue. If only had she been more focused, this would not have happened. The only reason an imp had gotten to her was because Liliana had told them to retreat into the underground catacombs. She hadn't expected such a sudden shift to the plan, and that was enough to divert her attention away from the incoming attack. The monster had managed to dig its disgusting claws into Chloé before she blew its head off with a single shot of her pistol.

Retreating had been difficult in her condition, but she'd pushed through. The two of them had separated when they reached the entrance. Liliana told Chloé to wait inside while she kept watch outside for the others and any imps.

Chloé did not know how much time had passed since then. Her body shifted between feeling warm and feeling cold—a bad sign for her. The wound was giving her more problems than she would've liked. If only she still had her magic core, such a thing would not have happened.

"Chloé?"

Chloé's head snapped up at the sound of Luka's voice.

The ethereal rushed toward her. "What happened?" Luka asked as he knelt down. He frowned as he saw Chloé's blood-ridden hand.

"Just a scratch," Chloé breathed.

"It's much more than just a scratch, Chloé." Luka removed Chloé's hand, placing his own delicately over the wound.

A soft blue light emitted from Luka's palm, and a warm, comforting sensation circulated around the gash, the pain beginning to recede.

"Thank you," Chloé said as Luka pulled away.

"Have you seen the others?" Luka asked.

Chloé shook her head. "Once Liliana received word to retreat, we came here. Except she stayed outside. I have been here since."

"How long ago would you say that was?"

"Maybe . . . a little over an hour?"

Luka frowned at the response.

"Why? Do you know what's going on?"

"Sophia and I were waiting at the entrance for two hours. We did not see you enter, nor did we see anyone else."

Chloé blinked. "We did not see anyone either."

"Tell me, Chloé, can you feel my presence?"

Chloé closed her eyes, not questioning Luka's intention. He must have had a good reason to ask.

The nix focused on the invisible string that connected her to the other warriors and Elliot. There was usually movement, as if it swayed gently side to side, gracefully floating into existence.

But this time, the string was still. Stagnant. Quiet. The one she knew connected to Luka was still, even though he was here with her.

Chloé opened her eyes. "I can, but . . . there's something strange."

"Like the connection is frozen?" Luka asked.

"Yes. That is a good way to put it."

A chill suddenly ran down Chloé's spine. She pushed herself to her feet, using the wall as support. The wound was healed, yet when she moved, she still felt the sharp, stabbing agony, as if it were still open.

Something was not right.

Chloé's eyes scanned the surrounding catacombs, taking in the details of the hallway. "Luka," she breathed, hoping her hunch was not correct. "What did the entrance look like for you?"

"The entrance to the catacombs looked like a dark

entryway for me. The stairwell was wide enough for two or three people to descend."

Chloé swallowed, her throat becoming uncomfortably dry. "Wide? When I entered the catacombs, it was narrow. I was barely able to fit."

Luka frowned. "That was not what I experienced. You would have no issues going through."

"We need to get out of here," Chloé said, her voice clipped. She made her way toward the entrance. "This place. Something isn't right."

"Chloé, wait." Luka grabbed the nix's arm. "Where are you going?"

"The exit."

"The exit . . . is not that way."

Chloé paused, slowly turning back to Luka. She looked past him, but what she saw was the pathway that would have led deeper into the catacombs. She turned back to the direction she was originally headed, and she could see the narrow stairwell that had brought her to where they were at now.

"This . . ." Chloé said, her voice barely above a whisper. "This is a trap."

59
LOVE

Myru's eyes fluttered open. The damp catacombs brought back memories of her last breath. Cold stone pressed against her—no, his—back.

Elliot's back.

Myru pushed herself up, moving quicker than she had expected. She bit back a wave of dizziness. Elliot's body felt heavier than her own, and his limbs were longer and stronger, yet ungraceful.

Myru would need to get used to it.

The catacombs were just how she remembered. The Necromancers' bodies were suspended in air by vines and flowers, frozen in time by her and her friends' spell, though she could feel how weak the hold had become throughout the years. It was only a matter of time before it completely became undone and their souls reunited with their bodies.

But all of that did not seem to matter now. Myru had only one thing on her mind. And it was to be together with her love.

Myru had hoped Hiro would be here when she took possession of Elliot, but she was alone. She was positive Elliot would not have been able to enter Kelemvor without the help of Hiro, so where was he?

Myru walked over to one of the Necromancers—Valor, she recalled. Even after hundreds of years, not a single day seemed to have passed. She looked at Elliot's hands. His body was young, likely around the same age as she had been when she passed away. What would she have looked like if she'd grown old? What other experiences she could have had if she'd lived to an old age?

Was this spite?

Did she hate how her life had been taken away from her because of the task she had been given but had ultimately failed to fulfill?

Myru wondered if she could bring herself to blame the Necromancers who hovered in front of her for her failure, blame them for the ultimate end of her life. She had so much she had wanted to do, but it had been cut short because of them.

Just like how Elliot's life had been cut short.

Myru had taken over Elliot's body. It was no longer his.

It was unfortunate for him, but Myru could finally restart her life, living how she wanted.

"W-why . . . ?" Lily's eyes rolled into her skull, the light disappearing from the crimson orbs entirely.

Hiro withdrew his sword, quickly sheathing it without a second glance. Lily's body lay lifelessly against the ground, blood quickly pooling around her body. Hiro's eyes flickered toward the two elves, their eyes wide in disbelief.

One of the elves had just recently accepted Queen Elyria's blessing. His hair was white, yet it still had a tint of green to it, and only one of his eyes had turned red, the other still its original brown. From his features, Hiro could see the resemblance Elliot had with him.

"What did you just do?" Elliot's father asked.

Without answering, Hiro tapped into his dark core, transporting himself to the next location.

"I didn't expect you to be here. Didn't Father want you somewhere else?" Aiden asked. He was leaning against a tree, nursing a gaping wound in his chest.

Hiro looked at the dead snake chimera next to Aiden, his internal organs hanging haphazardly on the dirt next to him.

Disgusting.

Without a single word, Hiro unleashed his sword—a single slash, and Aiden's head rolled on the ground.

"Hiro?" Raven said, not sparing a glance at Hiro. Raven stood still, looking straight up. His eyes were completely white, his mind control still in place. "What are you doin—"

Hiro impaled his sword into Raven's chest, twisting it before retracting. The Necromancer's body fell with a thud.

Myru perked up at the sound of approaching footsteps. She hoped Hiro wouldn't be bothered by her new appearance.

"Myru."

Myru's heart fluttered. Hiro's soft, gentle voice was just as she remembered. It sent butterflies into her stomach, making her nervous and shy.

Hiro was still as handsome as ever, even if his chocolate eyes were now red. It was true, then . . . He was a Necromancer.

"Hiro." Myru smiled. She ran toward him, arms outstretched. Her body completely melted into his. Hiro's strong arms wrapped around Myru.

She felt like she was home.

After centuries of wandering Kelemvor, she was finally where she was meant to be.

Here, in Hiro's embrace.

They could finally start their life together, finally start something that had been stolen from them.

"I missed you," Myru said.

"I missed you as well," Hiro said.

The two pulled away, and Hiro caressed Myru's hair. His eyes were filled with love and longing. Myru's heart felt so full.

"Where were you? I thought you would be here when I woke up." Myru pouted, pursing her lower lip.

Hiro gave Myru a gentle smile. "I was finishing up some business."

"Oh? Like what? What could be more important than me?" she joked.

"Something I should have done years ago."

Before Myru could ask what Hiro meant, pain exploded in her chest. She couldn't breathe, blood quickly traveling up her throat.

Shaky eyes peered down. Hiro's sword dug through her chest, the blade pulsating with dark light. With all the strength she could muster, she pushed away from Hiro.

He let her go, his red gaze never leaving her.

Why did he look so sad?

Myru didn't have time to think. She took hold of the hilt, gripping it with all her strength before pulling the blade out. She tapped into her core, trying to heal the wound.

Myru's eyes widened. Why couldn't she use her magic? She could feel herself growing cold and weak. Why wasn't her magic responding to her will? She staggered, strength leaving her legs.

Hiro closed the gap between them, his hold breaking Myru's fall.

Hiro held Myru in his arms, the scenery painfully familiar to her.

"Why . . . ?" Myru asked.

"So we can be together."

Myru weakly shook her head. She did not understand Hiro's intentions. What did he mean?

Hiro cupped Myru's cheek, his warmth a stark contrast to her freezing body.

"I love you. And I always will." Hiro leaned down, placing his lips over Myru's. The kiss was deep, and Myru could feel the despair. The anguish. The conflict. And the hope.

Darkness spread from the corner of Myru's vision. Even through it all, Myru could not bring herself to despise Hiro.

60
ACCEPT

315 years ago . . .

Hiro waited patiently for Queen Elyria's response, though he couldn't prevent his fingers from twitching with anxiety. His heart felt as if it wanted to burst out of his chest, and uncomfortable knots twisted in his stomach.

He had just laid out his soul to her, confessing all of his attempts to end his life to finding ways to bring everyone back to life in the past five years. The desperate measures he had taken to find ways to bring everyone back now seemed like the actions of a madman. Perhaps he was going insane, given the thoughts that plagued him and the violent impulses that sometimes seized him. He could barely recognize himself anymore, and that terrified him more than the experiences of being close to death ever had.

"I see," Elyria said, her expression still. She remained stoic, legs crossed as she rested her cheek against her hand. There was no empathy or concern in her tone.

"That's all you have to say?" Hiro asked, his voice rising. He could not believe he'd wasted his time traveling to Sylvana. If he had known the queen had no desire to help him, he would have stayed in his self-imposed isolation. Or attempted to find another way out of this endless cycle of living death.

Elyria shook her head. "Please accept my apologies. I honestly did not expect you to return, much less to return in the state that you are in now." Her sharp red gaze pierced through Hiro, as if she was analyzing him carefully, ensuring what he had said was the truth. "You are undead. This is why you cannot die. Strictly speaking, your existence . . . should not be. I sense Mykronos in you. And another. Perhaps a Necromancer."

"What?" Hiro breathed in disbelief.

The death god? The others had stopped him from rising, so how had Mykronos entered his body? Memories of the final battle flashed through his mind. The others had sacrificed themselves to seal the Necromancers' souls, preventing the rise of the death god. And how would a Necromancer manage to find their way into him?

"That's impossible. The gate was never opened."

"I know not what happened when you faced the Necromancers," Elyria started, "but I can see the death god and another dark soul within you. Your presence is heavy, and it took much persuading for my sentinels to allow you within my castle walls. Though because you are here, I am able to suppress the dark powers to a certain extent."

Hiro raced through his memories of the final battle. Had they missed something crucial? Had the gates to Kelemvor opened without their knowledge, allowing Mykronos to slip through? But that wouldn't explain why he possessed a Necromancer soul either.

"What do you seek?" Elyria asked, breaking Hiro's spiraling thoughts. "You come here, telling me your woes, yet you have not stated what you are hoping to obtain from me."

"I . . ." Words caught in Hiro's throat. He'd come to the queen hoping she could help him end his life as the mother of elves. But if Mykronos was part of him, how could he make that possible?

Elyria remained silent, patiently waiting for Hiro to answer.

There was one thing Hiro truly wanted.

"I want to be with Myru," he finally said.

Elyria blinked slowly, lips pressed into a thin line. "She is no longer."

"I know," Hiro said through clenched teeth, balling his fists. "I know."

"Her soul has returned to Alder," Elyria continued.

"I know." Hiro's voice was barely above a whisper.

"But perhaps . . ." Elyria started. She paused, as if considering the option. "There is a way to bring you two together."

Hiro's eyes widened, hope bubbling in his chest. "Really?" he breathed. He could not believe what Elyria was saying. He deeply wished it were true.

"Alder can sense Myru's soul. He can sense the deep desire she has to be with you. If you two could not be together in life, she wished to be together through death. Though you know, it would be impossible for your two souls to meet. All elven souls are returned to Alder once they perish. As for yours, Azar takes control of your soul. There is a careful balance in the world that should not be meddled with."

Hiro's stomach dropped, his hope crumbling as fast as it had appeared. Of course. It was impossible to be together. Why did he bother wishing it?

"Would you like a gamble?" Elyria smiled.

"Gamble?"

"I can request that Alder bring Myru's soul back, but it requires a reason. A cause. We will be playing with the strings of fate. The balance of the world would depend on your actions."

"What else?" Hiro did not care for balance or rules. What had following the rules gotten him except endless suffering? The gods had failed to maintain their own order, so why should he bear the burden of their incompetence?

Hiro owed them nothing.

"I cannot say what circumstances Alder will request of Vylantra to bring Myru's soul back, though a mother cannot deny the suffering words of their children for long. Myru deeply wishes to be with you, and as a mother, I will grant it. Alder will accept my proposal and bring it up to Vylantra."

"And the cause?"

"That is up to the god of life herself. The strings of fate

will start to move once this request is made, and what you do after will determine the outcome of the world." Elyria outstretched her hand, offering it to Hiro. "Well, do you accept?"

Hiro pondered the risks he was making in agreeing with Queen Elyria. Did he truly care about the world? Did he truly care about its precious balance? Did he truly care about the repercussions he would be causing because of his selfishness?

No.

The world had shown no care for him, for Myru, or for any of their companions, who had sacrificed everything. Life had continued forward, with people living their peaceful lives, never knowing the price that had been paid for their tranquility. They took these sacrifices for granted, living in ignorant bliss while he suffered alone in this endless abyss.

The world did not deserve such peace and luxury.

Hiro took the queen's offered hand, determined to take control of his own destiny. His touch was cold against her warmth, a reminder of what he had become.

"I accept."

61

FAREWELL

Hiro gently laid the male elf's lifeless body against the stone ground. His eyes were closed, his expression at peace with a small smile on his lips. Even after everything, Myru still had a good heart. She still believed in him. She had truly believed after possessing Elliot's body, they could finally begin their life together.

That was what Hiro had intended at first.

But as time progressed, Hiro realized the mistake of his choices. The prophecy Vylantra had issued had repeated itself.

Every one hundred years, Hiro witnessed the rise and fall of the same elven souls, though they only had memories of their original lives. They never remembered their life during the actual attempt at fulfilling the prophecy.

Hiro had decided the third one was going to be the last

one.

He would bring a stop to the endless loop.

Hiro picked up his sword, the once-silver blade now completely black. When Ragnar pushed Elliot into Kelemvor, that was Hiro's chance to begin his plan. He had plunged his blade into Ragnar before digging the same blade into Minari. Both were shocked and surprised by the sudden attack.

Ragnar was a sacrifice Hiro had chosen to make, a new scapegoat in his mission. He'd had Raven brainwash him into believing he was destined to be Mykronos's host. He needed the ethereal to play a part in bringing all the Necromancers together while Hiro played his part and reunited with the warriors.

Afterward, he had slain the other Necromancers, absorbing their souls into the blade. And now Myru's soul rested inside. The metal sang, the ringing resonating with Hiro's core.

And with Rurik's core.

Hiro had learned that Rurik had intended to use himself as a vessel for Mykronos all those years ago. An interesting coincidence that they both resided inside him now.

A bitter smile crossed Hiro's lips. He was never meant to grow into his own person. He was a puppet, created by Mykronos, insurance if the Necromancers failed. He was supposed to house the god in his body when the time was right, but he had somehow formed his own thoughts, his own feelings. He eventually had forgotten the reason he was created in the first place. Myru had done that to him.

The purity of her soul had reached out to him and made him who he was.

"I was never meant to be the savior or the hero who defended the world," Hiro said. The sword pulsated, responding to Hiro's voice.

The Necromancers had tried to bring Mykronos into this realm, but they had failed each time, not knowing that Hiro was Mykronos himself. That was why he could not die, why he watched the same souls play out their tragedy century after century.

Hiro's immortality was not a gift.

It was a curse.

And if Hiro could not die, he would bring all the souls that had suffered through all of this with him. No longer would innocent lives be lost at the hands of reincarnation and destiny. He would be the one to cut the strings.

There would be no Necromancers; their souls would be banished alongside his and Myru's souls.

Without the Necromancers, there would be no prophecy. Without Myru, the other warriors would finally be able to rest, and their original elven souls could finally be within Alder and perhaps be reborn anew without the weight of their previous duties.

He and Myru would finally be together—perhaps not in the way she had hoped, but Hiro knew this was for the best. Their souls had to be erased, their existence gone. Only then would the cycle end.

Hiro turned the blade, pointing the tip against his chest.

"This is farewell."

With a swift and decisive motion, Hiro drove the blade home.

62
REQUIEM

Elliot stared at his reflection in the mirror, brushing his fingers through his hair, attempting to rid the knots that had formed while he was sleeping. The morning light filtered through his window, casting a soft glow across his face, highlighting the subtle changes six months had brought. His skin was not as soft as it had once been, and there were strands of his hair that did not have the same vibrant green as they'd once had. Each small change in his appearance marked the steady progression of days he hadn't fully noticed. He could not believe it was already Minari's birthday. How had time passed by so quickly?

"Elliot, are you ready?" Errol asked, his voice coming from the closed door. "The sun's already out."

"Almost!" Elliot's hair was not as smooth as he would've liked, but it would do. His hair had never returned to its once silky texture, and over time, he had learned not just to accept it but to also appreciate his new appearance. It reflected his growth—a physical reminder of new beginnings he'd embraced as he learned to navigate the world with himself, rather than others' expectations, as his sole goal.

Elliot grabbed the necklace Lily had made him off the table, tying it behind his neck. His fingers lingered on the crafted wooden pendant as he remembered how her eyes had lit up when she presented it to him for his sixteenth birthday. He quickly pulled on his boots and met with his father outside.

"Took you long enough, sleepyhead," Errol said.

"We still have time." Elliot frowned.

"I know. I know. Old habits," Errol said. "Sometimes I imagine we're back home with how things once were." He chuckled. "Only in our dreams, huh?"

Elliot knew what his father meant. Even after six months had passed, he still could not get used to his father's new appearance. Errol's hair was pure white, eyes now a deep red. Elliot did not know what exactly had happened, but he understood his father likely had not had a choice in the matter. Sacrificing his life to Queen Elyria meant he had strength he never would have imagined, but at the same time, his life was completely in her hands. If the queen decided to cease feeding him magic, his father's life would end. It was a bargain made in desperation, one that had saved them at a cost neither of them spoke about.

The two elves walked through the forest of Rainwell, neither saying a single word. They found solace in listening to nature's morning songs. Birds sang to one another in the branches above, and in the distance, a stream bubbled over rocks. The familiar paths they walked were starting to show signs of wear from their frequent travels, though that did not stop new growth along the edges.

"Looks like the others are already here," Errol said as they approached the clearing.

"Nice of you two to finally join us," Sage said. He wore a patch over his left eye, a wound he'd received during the final battle. His chimeran attire had been replaced with a black tunic, black pants, and boots, marking him an official member of Nighthawk.

"Good morning, Elliot," Luka said. His long silver hair, which had once freely cascaded down his back, was now styled in a braid and tied with a pink ribbon Elliot recognized as one of Chloé's.

"This is all of us, then?" Errol asked, even though they all knew the answer.

Luka nodded. "Bunnie sends us her best wishes. She could not pull away from her duties, unfortunately. The reconstruction efforts within the kingdom require her constant attention."

"Strange how the Nighthawk guild became the official council. They axed everyone else," Sage said. "Someone had to take charge, I guess."

"Chloé would have been proud," Elliot said, his voice soft but steady. "This was probably what she wanted. To see everyone united under one banner, working together instead of against one another."

"I am sorry, Elliot," Luka started. "If only I—"

"I don't blame you," Elliot interrupted. "I mean . . . I wasn't much help either." He placed a hand on his chest. A scar had formed where Hiro had stabbed him. He did not understand the details fully, but he knew there was probably a good reason. The memory of the moment was still hazy, but the elf made no efforts to remember the specifics.

One moment he was in Kelemvor with Myru, and the next he was waking up in a desolate Rainwell with only Errol, Luka, and Sage by his side. The wound on his chest had closed, leaving a large scar. The mark of the oracle had disappeared from his wrist.

Elliot chose to ignore learning the truth of what had happened that day. He only wanted to move forward, to keep on living. The ties that bound him to his destiny were gone. Elliot knew that much, and it was enough. The gap between those moments remained a mystery, one he chose not to solve.

The prophecies that had once guided and haunted his steps were silent now, leaving him free to forge his own path.

With the sentinels' help, they'd returned to Sylvana, where Queen Elyria had aided in their recovery. Not much had been shared between them, and Elliot appreciated it. Some truths were better left in the past, buried with those they had lost.

Elliot stepped into the opening. A memorial had been built for all the fallen who had bravely lost their lives during the battle. The morning dew still clung to the stone markers, making them glisten in the early light.

Elliot knelt, placing a hand against Minari's tombstone, feeling the cool, rough surface beneath his palm. "Happy birthday," Elliot said, biting back tears. "I would ask what you wanted, but knowing you, you'd probably just say nothing." A sad chuckle escaped Elliot's lips. "You were always like that, insisting you didn't need anything from me."

Elliot's fingertips traced the letters of Minari's name before his gaze drifted to the tombstone beside it. Lily's name was etched in elegant Elven script, mirroring Minari's. The gentle curves and delicate lines burned Elliot's eyes with a painful longing. He recalled every moment he'd spent chiseling his two precious friends' names into the hard surface, taking special care not to make any mistakes. "Remember how you two made fun of me on my birthday? I really miss those days . . ." He closed his eyes and rested his forehead against the stone. The memory of their laughter, their shared jokes, and the way they'd work together to surprise him despite his protests brought both warmth and pain to his heart. "I'm . . . not okay. I know you would worry about me even if I told you I was. There isn't a day that passes that I don't miss you two. Sometimes, I get nightmares where I don't understand what's happening. But I know I'm safe. In the end . . . there isn't anything for me to be afraid of."

The others remained behind Elliot, keeping a distance between them as they silently sent their words to the fallen in their own way. It reminded the elf that even though there were those who were gone, he was not alone. He still had loved ones here with him.

Elliot opened his eyes and stood. He gazed upon the memorial, the rising sun casting a warm glow against the flowers and stones. A gentle breeze caressed the greenery and colors. The scenery was peaceful. Beautiful. It seemed almost wrong that nature could be so serene in a place marked by such loss, yet perhaps that was part of its healing power.

Minari.

Lily.

Stella.

Mimi.

Chloé.

Owen.

Myru.

Hiro.

The elves of Rainwell.

Everyone from Mistfall.

"Thank you."

The End

AFTERWORD

Wow. It's finally over.

First and foremost, I want to thank each and every one of you who have made it this far. This journey wasn't an easy one. The Oracle Series was my first for everything—my first published book, my first series, the first dream I pushed myself to turn into reality. A debut that has only ever existed in my wildest imagination, had finally come true.

Throughout the process, I struggled with self-doubt, constantly worried if my writing was good enough. I watched countless videos on writing tips and pitfalls to avoid as a new author. I read numerous books to understand how to approach this incredibly large project I had set for myself. I didn't let those doubts stop me, knowing full well that writing is a creative craft—one at which I will constantly improve. A deep thank you to all my editors who worked with me throughout this incredible adventure, guiding me and offering words of encouragement.

To all my wonderful readers, who eventually became my fans! —Thank you so much from the bottom of my heart. I wanted to become a writer because there is just something truly magical about a beautifully crafted story. How it makes you feel, how you connect with the characters, and a sense of wonder it creates. I wanted to share that enchantment. To those I've inspired to write your own stories—I hope you've reached your dreams (or are working toward them)!

Thank you for accompanying Elliot on his journey to fulfill the prophecy. Though this may be the end of the Oracle Series, there is still more to come. After all, there are many tales awaiting to be told in the world of Etheria!

Aim for the stars and beyond—

With love,
jaemi lee